"IT'S REALLY

"JUS

"It doesn't look like it ... , Vincent replied. "Do you feel dizzy? Lightheaded?"

Yes, but not from the head wound. From having him touch her here in this private cavern. It felt like a sanctuary. The faint light spilling through the darkness created shards of colors like a rainbow across the gray walls.

She pressed her hand to his cheek, need spiraling through her. If—*when*—they left they had to face the world again, fight the demon.

His throat worked as he swallowed. "Try to relax. I'll go ahead and hunt for a way out."

"Not yet," she whispered. "It's safe here, free from the demons."

She parted her lips on a sigh, then pressed a kiss to his lips. He was so handsome and virile, so protective and strong, that her body ached for him.

"Clarissa, don't," he growled. "I told you my rules."

"We might not make it out of here alive," she said softly. "And if or when we do, we might not survive this demon." She wet her lips, traced a hand down his chest, and began to unbutton his shirt. "I don't want to die without having you one more time."

INSATIABLE DESIRE

RITA HERRON

FOREVER

NEW YORK   BOSTON

Copyright © 2008 by Rita Herron
All rights reserved. Except as permitted under the U.S. Copyright Act of 1976, no part of this publication may be reproduced, distributed, or transmitted in any form or by any means, or stored in a database or retrieval system, without the prior written permission of the publisher.

Cover illustration by Alan Ayers
Book design by Giorgetta Bell McRee

Forever
Hachette Book Group USA
237 Park Avenue
New York, NY 10017
Visit our Web site at www.HachetteBookGroupUSA.com

Forever is an imprint of Grand Central Publishing. The Forever name and logo is a trademark of Hachette Book Group USA, Inc.

Printed in the United States of America

First Printing: September 2008

10 9 8 7 6 5 4 3 2 1

To my incredible agent Jenny Bent
for believing in this trilogy and my twisted mind,
and to my fabulous editor Michele Bidelspach
for her great insight and for joining us
on the dark side . . .

Acknowledgments

Also, I have to thank my critique partner Stephanie Bond for her never-ending encouragement and feedback. Thanks to Jen, Jenni, Susan, and Deb for adding their two cents. And to my husband for loving me and supporting me through the insane process of writing.

INSATIABLE
DESIRE

PROLOGUE

The deep shadows of the Smoky Mountains hid monsters. Beasts and evil that fed off the weak. Creatures not quite human.

Ten-year-old Vincent Valtrez knew because his father was one of them.

Vincent tracked him now, the fierce wind battering his face and hands as he wove through the densely packed woods to save his mother.

His mother, an Angel of Light, he'd once heard his father call her.

But that was before his father's dark side had won and the evil had completely possessed him.

Yellow, piercing eyes seared Vincent with each turn through the forest. His breath caught painfully as he stumbled over a splintered log, falling into briars and other, ice-covered logs. Pine needles stabbed his palms, and splinters clawed at his fingertips. Pushing up on his knees, he searched the deep pockets of leaves and underbrush, knowing his father might be watching him, waiting, ready to strike any second.

A black bear growled nearby, and a wolf howled in the distance, its attack call sending a chill through Vincent that made him lurch to his feet and run faster. But his feet sank into the ankle-deep snow, slowing him, and the wind swirled flakes in a blinding fog, obliterating his vision. He plowed on, sweating as he climbed the rugged hills, shoving away tree branches that slapped his face.

He had to hurry. Had to find the cavern his father had once shown him. It was somewhere in the heart of the Black Forest. A place where no light remained. The land of the dead, where only inhuman creatures existed.

The gathering place of the demons, where his father sometimes worshipped.

The hellhole where he would take his mother to torture her.

Emotions threatened to choke Vincent as his mother's cry reverberated through his head. She had been trying to protect him. That was the reason his father was going to destroy her.

Vincent had to stop him.

Storm clouds rolled ominously across the darkening sky, the scent of blood and death thick and acrid as he drew nearer the black poplars that lined the path to the Black Forest. Vincent tasted the bitterness of his own fear as he entered, heavy winding vines clawing at him when he stepped beneath the black cloud.

Below his feet, the ground suddenly swirled and hissed, a bed of snakes nipping at his heels and winding around his legs. He kicked at them, slinging his pocket-knife in a chopping motion and stirring their anger more.

They sucked at him, trying to frighten him into succumbing to his fear, but he refused to relent. Instead, he roared with fury, slung the knife again, and sent a dozen vile creatures flying through the darkness. More attacked him from the gnarled branches, while batlike creatures screamed and dove toward his eyes.

He battled them away and plunged through the miles of demonic creatures, until he finally reached the cavern. It was a mammoth-size indention in the hollowed-out side of the mountain.

The opening swallowed him like a black abyss, the emptiness echoing with horrific sounds of terror. Hate swelled inside him, and he cloaked himself in rage, knowing it would bolster his courage.

"I knew you would come, son."

Vincent froze at the sound of his father's menacing tone. "Father, please, let Mother go. She loves you."

"Vincent, run!" his mother shouted. "It's a trap."

Her shrill cry rent the air as his father flicked his hand and shot fire around her. Vincent spotted her then, wearing nothing but a thin white cotton gown, her face, hands, arms, legs bloody where he'd tortured her.

Emotions choked him. She'd rocked him when he was little and sick, had read him Bible stories, had sung to him when he'd been frightened of the dark.

Now she'd been beaten and tied to a wooden stake like a sacrificial animal.

"Run, son, save yourself!" she screamed. "You can't give in to the dark side, or you'll be just like him."

Vincent's father laughed, knowing he had won. Vincent would not leave his mother to die like this, even if it meant he died with her or was destined to the dark side forever.

The flames created a halo around her angelic face,

the amulet she always wore around her neck for protection glowing against her pale skin. The fire circled her, dancing into the shadows and chewing at her bare feet. He lunged forward and leapt through the fiery embers. Reaching out with his knife, he was just about to cut her ropes when his father snatched him back. Vincent reached for her again and managed to grab her amulet. The gold medallion imprinted with angel wings seared his palm as his father yanked it from his hand and tossed it back into the blaze.

Vincent kicked, shouted at his father, but his father knocked him to the ground. "Fight me, son. Fight me and maybe I'll let you save her."

His mother's scream pierced the air. "No, Vincent, don't give in to him."

But rage heated his veins, and Vincent raised the knife and catapulted into motion. Outside the wind roared, and cold air swirled through the cavern as he jabbed the knife at his father. His father flung his hand like a savage and grabbed the weapon from Vincent. One slash and the knife sank into Vincent's arm. Blood spurted from the cut, sparking his father's laughter.

Vincent let the pain drive him as he lunged toward his dad again. Hitting him with all his force, he knocked him to the ground, and they rolled and fought on the rocky floor. The knife sliced his thigh, his cheek, his hand, then ripped into his gut. Vincent spat blood, clutching his abdomen as he rolled sideways to dodge another blow.

A scream from his mother made him jerk his head to the side, and he saw the flames consuming her. Her eyes widened with terror and regret, with the certainty that she was going to die and he would be left with this monster.

Fury and rage heated Vincent's blood. Her body jerked as the fire ate it: then her hair swirled and caught. Vincent cried out in horror and tried to crawl toward her, but she took her last breath and the fire consumed her. The wooden stake she was tied to splintered into pieces from the flames, shooting sparks across the black floor. Vincent grabbed one, swinging it like a torch.

His father's evil eyes rounded with the challenge, and he dove toward Vincent with the knife again. Vincent wielded the stake like a sword, raised it, and jabbed it straight into his father's cold heart.

Shock registered on his father's face, then a look of pure malevolence as his vile laugh echoed through the black walls.

Bile rose to Vincent's throat. Even in death, his father had triumphed.

"You're just like me, boy—you got bad blood," he muttered as his last strangled breath shuddered from him.

The world spun sickeningly, but Vincent crawled toward the flames and latched his fingers around the amulet. The hot metal seared his palm, but he refused to release it. Exhausted, Vincent collapsed onto the dirt and faded into the darkness, his father's dying words echoing in his head. *Bad blood, bad blood, bad blood . . .*

He hoped he died now, too. He didn't want to grow up to be an evil monster like his father.

But he had just lost part of his soul, because he'd made his first kill.

Which meant the evil already had its tentacles deeply embedded in him.

Helzebar, the leader of the demon underworld, stood by, clapping as flames consumed the man and woman and the boy choked on his own blood.

Zion had passed the greatest test by killing his wife, the angel. One less do-gooder on Earth to interfere with his business.

Victory tasted sweet. Not just one soul captured, but two in one evening. The father's and son's.

There would be a celebration in the underworld tonight.

But had he really won the son's soul?

He glanced at his minion, one of his many Soul Collectors, but his empty eyes bulged white.

"The boy is not completely with us yet," the Soul Collector concluded. "He killed to save another, not for the sheer pleasure of it."

Helzebar shuddered, repulsed at the mere idea that good existed at all. Vincent was a Dark Lord—the special ones bred from both good and evil. His mother had been an Angel of Light, goodness. His father, Zion, had been a Dark Lord before they'd turned him.

Yet Zion had failed because he had not completely turned Vincent evil.

If Vincent chose good, he would be the fearless leader for the other Dark Lords one day.

Would Vincent pass the test when the time came?

Helzebar waved his fiery sword in disgust. "We need his power. Twenty years from now, Zion will rise from the grave to assume leadership of the underworld. To win over his son, the Dark Lord, will multiply his strength tenfold."

Then Vincent would bring others with him to glorify Zion's kingdom. An army of soldiers for evil.

Helzebar dropped a small piece of black rock beside the boy, a token of his presence, a symbol of the black rock from which his palace on Earth was being built.

The earth trembled as if all the gods had combined their powers, and the Fates laughed as they began to spin the linen thread to measure how long each mortal would live. Ares would cause war throughout the world, destroying thousands. Aphrodite and Eros would lose, and love would die. Eventually all good would be buried beneath the rubble.

Only evil and chaos would survive, just as Satan intended.

CHAPTER ONE

Twenty years later: six days until the rising

The first fuck was always the best.

Not that Special Agent Vincent Valtrez ever bedded the same woman twice.

No, twice meant they might misconstrue his intentions. Get involved. Expect something from him.

But he had nothing to give.

Sex was sex. An animal's primal need. The one he fed willingly.

Unlike the evil bubbling inside him that he fought daily.

The motel room's bedsprings squeaked as he ripped open the woman's blouse, and he stared at her breasts spilling over the lace. Heat surged through his loins at the way her nipples puckered, begging for attention. A martini at midnight, and she'd easily become putty in his lust-driven hands.

He straddled her, then released the front clasp of

her black bra, his cock twitching as her plump breasts filled his hands. Moaning, she traced a finger along his jaw, then dragged his face toward hers and nibbled at his lips. Their tongues danced together, and she slid her foot along the back of his calf, driving him crazy with desire.

Clouds shifted outside, moonlight streaking the room with shards of light, illuminating her flushed face and the splay of her fingers as she tore open his shirt and stroked his chest.

Vincent had felt the evil pulling at him for years, ever since his parents had disappeared. That night he'd been found on the edges of the Black Forest, bruised and beaten, and so traumatized he'd lost his memory.

Although he feared his father had killed his mother . . .

The woman's blood-red fingernails clawed his bare skin. A droplet of blood mingled with the sweat, exciting him, blurring the lines in his mind between himself and the killers he hunted.

For an instant the beast inside him reared its head. He imagined sliding his hands around her slender throat, digging his fingers into her larynx until her eyes bulged, watching the life drain from her.

He hissed a breath between clenched teeth, forced himself to pull away. The dark side, the black holes, tugged at him again, trying to take control . . .

He couldn't give in to the darkness. He was an FBI agent. Had sworn to save lives, not take them.

Oblivious to his turmoil, she jerked him back to her, took his hand and slid it between her thighs. She was so hot. Wet. Ready.

Raw need swirled through him. With a groan, he

shoved the darkness deep inside, then bent and sucked her budded nipple into his mouth. She purred like a hungry cat, then parted her thighs in invitation, arousing him as she cradled his erection. He cupped her mound, pushing aside the edges of her panties to sink his fingers into her damp flesh. Her sigh of pleasure shattered his resistance, and he tore off her bra and underwear, then shoved her skirt up to her waist. A tight skirt that had drawn his eyes to her ass and made him horny as hell when she'd walked into the bar.

His jeans and boxers fell to the floor, socks into the pile. Then the condom—always the protection. He couldn't chance continuing the Valtrez name with a child.

Growling in anticipation, he shoved her hands above her head, pinning her beneath him as if she was a prisoner of his desires.

She struggled playfully, but her eyes flashed and smoldered as he rubbed his throbbing length against her heat. She licked her lips, then bit his neck, and he groaned again, then flipped her to her stomach. He didn't like to look at their faces, didn't want any emotional connection.

His hands skated over her bare shoulders, slid down to massage her butt; then he lifted her to her knees. She braced herself on her hands and moaned, rocking forward, twitching against him.

"I want you inside me, Vincent," she whispered raggedly. "Take me now."

The flames of lust grew hotter as his cock stroked her ass, and the tip of his sex teased her center. Sliding in her moist channel a fraction of an inch, then retreating, then back again, taunting them both.

"God, sugar, please . . ."

He liked it when they begged.

She spread herself for him, and his control snapped, the vision of her offering setting his body aflame. He thrust inside her, ramming her so hard she cried out his name and dug her hands into the sheets, twisting them between those blood-red fingernails. He gripped her hips and began to pound her, deeper, faster, sweat beading on his body as the blood surged through his penis. Her body tightened around him, squeezing, milking his length, and delicious sensations built inside him. Panting, he increased the tempo, closed his eyes, heard her raspy breathing, his own chest heaving as he fought to hold back his orgasm. Pleasure was not an option, but release was imminent.

Another thrust and he tilted her, pressing her back against his chest as he stroked her nipples between his fingers. That sent her spiraling over the edge, and her body quivered, then spasmed around his. Relentlessly he hammered into her as sweat slid down his brow and the sound of their naked bodies slapping together mingled with the wind.

Vincent never lost control.

Except in the throes of his release, and even then, he held on to his emotions. A guttural groan erupted from deep inside him, and he ground himself deeper, biting back a shout as his orgasm spurted into her.

Outside the moon shifted, slid behind the clouds, vanishing completely. A black emptiness crept over the room, beckoning. The wind suddenly roared, rattling the walls, and he tensed, his senses honed, warning him that the devil had risen again to wreak havoc.

A second later, his cell phone jangled from the nightstand, saving him from the awkwardness after.

He released the woman so abruptly she fell forward, still trembling with the aftermath of her release. He tore off the condom and climbed away from her, hating himself. God, what had happened to him back there? He'd imagined killing her.

She caught his arm and tried to pull him back to her. "Don't answer the phone."

He had to leave. It was the only way she'd be safe. "Duty calls."

Her eyelids fluttered wildly, and she ran a finger over his cock, raking a drop of come off the tip and sucking it into her mouth. "But I want you again already."

"Tell the criminals to take a night off, then," he growled.

She sighed, but he firmly ignored the disappointment in her eyes, the needy look suggesting that she wanted more than a lay, that she wanted to cuddle, to *talk*.

Instead, he reached for the phone, silently relaying what he didn't want to have to say out loud. She was an okay fuck, but anything else was not in the cards. No use telling a lie. She had simply been a momentary reprieve between cases.

She clamped her teeth over her lips, then offered a disappointed smile and reached for that seductive skirt. Still he didn't make excuses; he simply couldn't give what he didn't have.

A heart.

The silhouette of the woman's skeletal remains swung from the Devil's Tree in Clarissa King's front yard.

She shuddered, battling the urge to grab an ax and chop it down. She'd tried that before, but the tree was petrified and held some kind of supernatural power. The moment she cut off a branch, it grew back, yet no grass grew beneath it, and in the winter the moment snow touched the branches, it melted. Mindless screams echoed from the limbs, as well, the screams of the dead who'd died there in centuries past.

The screams of Clarissa's mother as she'd choked on her last breath in the same tree mingled with the others.

Forcing herself away from the window, she hugged her arms around herself to gather her composure. Night had long ago stolen the last strains of sun from the Tennessee sky, painting the jagged peaks and ridges of the Smokies with ominous shadows. Wind whistled through the pines and scattered spiny needles, dried and brittle from the relentless scorching heat that drained the rivers and creeks, leaving dead fish floating to the surface of the pebbled beds, muddy wells, and watering holes.

The grass and trees were starved for water, brown and cracking now with their suffering, and animals roamed and howled, searching for a meal in the desolate miles and miles of secluded forests.

There were some areas she'd never been because the infamous legends had kept her away. The Black Forest was one of them. Stories claimed that in the Black Forest, sounds of inhuman creatures reigned, half animal, half human—mandrills with human heads, shapeshifters, the unknown.

The few who'd ventured near had seen sightings of predators without faces, floating eyeballs that glowed in the dark, creatures that weren't human. No light existed inside that forest, no color. And any who entered died a horrific, painful death at the hands of the poisonous plants and mutant creatures that fed on humans.

The whispers of the ghosts imprinted in the land chanted and cried from its depths. And nearby lay the Native American burial ground where screams of lost warriors and war drums reverberated in the death-filled air, where the ground tremored from the force of decades-old stampedes and battle cries.

Clarissa shivered and hurried to latch the screen door of her cabin that jutted over the side of the mountain. Useless, probably. The ratty screen and thin wooden door couldn't protect her should the demons decide to attack.

The year of the eclipse—the year of death—was upon them.

Night and the full moon had brought them, stirring the devil from the ground, the serpents from the hills, the dead from the graves. Granny King—"Crazy Mazie" some had called her, God rest her soul—had taught her to read the signs. The insufferable heat, as if Hades himself had lit a fire beneath the earth, one to honor his kingdom. The blood-red moon that filled the sky and beckoned the predators to roam. The howl of Satan announcing his time for vengeance.

Yes, her once-safe hometown was full of evil, and no one could stop it until the demons fed their hungry souls with the innocents.

Yet the pleas of the women who'd died this week echoed in her head. She'd told the local sheriff her suspicions, that the deaths were connected.

That they were murders.

He'd wanted to know why she thought they were connected, and she'd had to be honest.

The victims had told her.

At least their spirits had when they'd visited.

Thankfully, Sheriff Waller had known her family and hadn't laughed but had listened. Her grandmother had had the "gift" of communing with the dead, and so had her mother. Granny King used to read the obits daily over her morning herbal tea and confer with the deceased as if they were long-lost buddies. Everyone in town had thought she was touched in the head. But she'd been right on so many occasions that most folks believed her.

The rest were scared to death of her.

Clarissa's mother had also been a psychic and an empath, only the constant barrage of needy souls had driven her insane. So insane she'd finally chosen to join them in death . . . instead of living and raising her daughter.

Bitterness swelled inside Clarissa at the loss, eating at her like a virus. She'd been alone, shunned, gossiped about, even called wretched names and cast away from certain families who thought she, too, was evil.

Her mother had visited Clarissa once after her death, ordered Clarissa to suppress her powers. And she had done so most of her life, trying to be normal.

She was anything but normal.

So she'd returned to the one place a few people accepted her. Back to Eerie.

Staying in her granny's house seemed to have unleashed the spirits, as if they'd lain in waiting all these years for their friend to return, and she could no longer fight their visits.

Outside, the wind howled, a tree branch scraped the windowpane, and ominous storm clouds hovered with shadowy hands that obliterated the light. Even with the ceiling fan twirling, the oppressive summer heat robbed the air, stirring cobwebs and dust that sparkled in the dark interior like white ashes.

Wulf, the German shepherd mix she'd rescued last year after he'd been hurt in a collapsed mine, suddenly growled, low and deep as if he sensed a threat, too, then trotted to the window and looked outside in search of an intruder.

Anxiety needled her as she contemplated the meeting she faced tomorrow.

Vincent Valtrez was coming to town.

She'd thought about him over the years, had wondered what had happened to him. Both outcasts, her because of her gift, him because of his violent father, they'd formed an odd friendship as kids.

But when she'd offered to see if his mother had passed, had suggested she could talk to her from the grave, he'd called her crazy and pushed her out the door. He told her he never wanted to see her again.

She couldn't believe he was an FBI agent now. He probably wouldn't be any more open to her psychic powers now than he had been back then.

She had to talk to him anyway. Convince him to listen. She hadn't asked for this gift, but she couldn't deny it, either. Not when others' lives were at stake.

Because this killer wasn't finished. And she didn't want the women's lost souls upon her conscience.

❧

Pan, the god of fear, studied the town of Eerie, his plan taking shape in his demonic mind.

Six days until Zion rose from the dead for the

coronation. Six days until their new leader assumed control.

The underworld buzzed with excitement and preparations. Legend told that Zion would be the most evil leader they had ever known, that he showed no mercy upon any soul.

Just as he hadn't toward his wife and son.

In anticipation of his rising, demons met to plot and scheme, desperate to ingratiate themselves into their new master's graces and raise themselves from their lowly levels to higher realms within the underground. Others forged secret plans, vying to outbid one another to sit at Zion's right-hand side.

Pan had burrowed from his lowly chamber and accepted the challenge. A mere minion, punished to the fiery blazes of the lowest level, he had to collect enough souls to impress the new leader.

Seven souls and he would win great favor.

Mere days ago, fellow demons had fought the Twilight Guards, the ones who guarded the realm between mortals and the supernatural world, and had opened a portal for the demons. Pan had orbed through the dark planes of time and space, through the portal, and floated above the town of Eerie. There he'd watched the mortals and had chosen the face of one to borrow for his bidding. A face that no one would suspect hid a demon.

Two women had died at his hands so far.

One touch and he knew their greatest fear.

Then he'd used it to kill them.

Laughter bubbled in his parched throat. But killing the women and stealing their souls was a minor part of the larger picture. He'd specifically pinpointed the town where Vincent Valtrez had been raised, because he knew the local sheriff would call him.

And he'd chosen Clarissa King to taunt with the voices of the dead, because she was Valtrez's Achilles' heel.

As a boy, Valtrez had protected her from his father. She would be the perfect means to trap Vincent.

Pan had already pressed his hand to her and knew her greatest fear: that the dead she communed with would drive her insane. He would target her friends for his kills, then use their voices to torment her.

He raised his black palm and began to chant, to summon the demons to torture her:

> *"I call to you,*
> *Spirits far and wide,*
> *Rise from the dead*
> *To the medium's side.*
> *Let your cries*
> *Fill her head*
> *So she may join*
> *You and the dead."*

If Valtrez still had a weakness for the woman, when she broke, he would try to save her.

Then Pan would turn the Dark Lord and bring him to the new master.

CHAPTER TWO

Vincent picked up the phone, turning his back on the woman as she dressed and let herself out. "Valtrez."

"It's McLaughlin. Sorry to disturb you, man, but you've got an assignment."

"Where to?"

"A small town in the Smoky Mountains, Eerie, Tennessee. The local sheriff is recovering from a mild heart attack and requested our help, specifically yours. He thinks he has a serial killer in the hills, and the chief wants you to get up there first thing tomorrow."

The Tennessee mountains. Shit, that was the last place he ever wanted to go back to.

"Why me?"

"Because you grew up there. You understand the town, the area, the people." McLaughlin coughed. "Said something about you going into the Black Forest and coming out alive. That no one else ever had."

Vincent rubbed a hand over his bleary eyes. Hell, yeah, he'd survived, but he'd blocked out what had happened inside the forest.

But he knew evil lived in the mountains and that his father had been a violent man.

Maybe it was time he did return, put his past to rest. He had a nagging feeling the blackouts he'd experienced lately had something to do with that hellhole he'd grown up in. With the memories he'd repressed . . .

"Valtrez? You listening?"

"Yeah." He cleared his throat. "How many murders so far?"

"Two." McLaughlin hesitated. "Although the MOs are different, Valtrez. They don't appear to be related. The first one is a drowning victim, the second, multiple spider bites."

"Why does he think the spider bites are murder?"

"There were multiple bites." McLaughlin hesitated. "Dozens and dozens, as if someone had planted the spiders in the woman's bed."

Vincent chewed the inside of his cheek, conceding that sounded suspicious. "What makes this sheriff think the deaths are connected?"

McLaughlin hesitated again.

"Spill it, McLaughlin. What am I up against? Some small-town morons?"

A wry chuckle rumbled over the line. "Maybe. This guy claims their resident town psychic told him the women are being murdered."

Vincent scrubbed a hand over the back of his neck. "Don't tell me. Her name is Clarissa King."

"How'd you know?"

Shit. "Everyone in the area knows about her family." A childhood memory taunted him. Clarissa had been tiny and frail-looking in her homemade checkered dress. They'd forged an odd, awkward friendship.

One day the kids had picked on him at school, and she'd taken up for him. He'd told her he didn't need her help and stormed away. But she was a stubborn little thing and had followed him home.

Humiliation washed over him. His father had found him wearing the angel amulet, yelled at him that it was for girls, and had ripped it off his neck. Then his father had caught Clarissa looking through the window and had snatched her up. Vincent had stepped in the middle to protect her. His father had laughed, shoved her outside, and told her not to come back—then he'd beaten Vincent senseless.

"Look at it this way," McLaughlin said, interrupting his thoughts. "You can meet with the sheriff, brush him off, then relax in the mountains for the weekend. Maybe go fishing."

Vincent laughed sardonically. He didn't want to relax. Hell, he couldn't. The only pastime he had other than work was screwing women.

His gaze zeroed in on the blood the woman had drawn from his arm when he'd fucked her.

Bad blood, *bad* blood, *bad* blood . . . He'd inherited it from his father.

He couldn't change what he was. A bad-to-the-bone bastard. He wouldn't make excuses for it, either.

First thing tomorrow, before he headed to Tennessee, he'd stop by BloodCore, that research center, and offer a sample for analysis. They were researching deviant and abhorrent behavior, searching for genetic markers to pinpoint and predict tendencies toward aggression, violence, and criminal behavior, specifically in sociopaths and serial killers.

All in hopes of finding a cure, so doctors could change a person's genetic makeup to alter that behavior.

He hoped to hell they found one. Vincent would be first in line for treatment. It might be the only thing that could save him.

───◆───

An icy chill engulfed Clarissa. This morning she'd heard another cry. The woman's spirit hadn't gained enough energy to materialize yet, but Clarissa had been tormented by her distinctive wail of terror in the predawn hour. Wulf had heard it, too, and howled in recognition.

She'd phoned Sheriff Waller immediately and asked him if anyone in town had been reported missing. So far, nothing.

But they would. Her premonitions rarely failed her.

As if Clarissa had summoned the spirits, a chill in the air swirled around her, a hint of jasmine mingling with the humidity.

In the shadows of the woods behind her property, a ghostly image drifted toward her, then shimmered inside against the knotty-pine-paneled walls. Its tormented mass filled the silence with shock and the trauma of just being taken.

She recognized the spirit immediately. Billie Jo Rivers, a teller at the bank. She'd drowned in Redtail Creek three days ago.

Now, she stood pale-faced, a white skeleton with soaking wet clothes, drenched tangled hair, mud-stained limbs, and distorted features, lost in her own bed of horrors.

Clarissa wanted to reach out and hug her in comfort,

but that was impossible. But she could help find her killer so Billie Jo could cross into the light.

Beside Billie Jo, another spirit appeared, shimmering against the darkness. This one, twenty-five-year-old church director Jamie Lackey. Her pale green eyes stared back, gaunt with pain and terror in her skeleton. Swollen and discolored patches marred her body, and her black hair swirled around her face, wild and tangled, a half-dozen brown recluse spiders crawling through the tresses, others spinning a web on her arms and legs.

Clarissa shivered. She had to help the girls. Had to convince Vincent that she was telling the truth. That the people of Eerie needed help. That a monster was here, preying on women. But how?

"I need more from you," she pleaded into the darkness. "Some clue, something I can tell the police to help them find out what happened to you."

Both women's spirits reached for her with outstretched brittle fingers, but when they tried to speak, only a strangled sound of agony pierced the air. It was too soon. They needed more time to acclimate into their astral spirits; then they would be able to communicate.

Exhausted, and knowing she needed her strength for the next day, Clarissa climbed in bed, then closed her eyes and silently willed the spirits to rest and let her sleep. She didn't want to see them anymore tonight. To hear their shrieks of terror.

But hysterical laughter bubbled in her chest as she felt the whisper of the spirits' breaths on her neck. Their cackles of agony splintered the silence. She'd *never* be free of them. No matter where she'd run these past few years or how hard she'd tried to escape, the spirits begged her to listen.

Outside, the clouds shifted to hide the moon, and a sea of darkness engulfed the room, the whisper of more danger breathing through the air. In less than a month the eclipse would occur.

The time when demons rose to wreak havoc.

The people of Eerie had to be ready. Her destiny lay in helping those who needed her.

Even if it meant she would be alone forever.

And that she'd end up hanging from the Devil's Tree just like her mother.

Fear clawed at Tracy Canton. She was going to die here in the woods, alone where no one would find her.

Bugs nibbled at her flesh, and tears rolled down her cheeks, mingling with the sweat and blood running down her face. Blood the monster who'd attacked her had smeared on her after digging the knife into her wrists.

She'd tried to scream for help, but the sound had died in her throat, as if her voice was paralyzed, just like her body.

One touch of his hand and she had been immobilized by fear.

How had he done that? Why? God, why? She was too young to die.

She squeezed her eyes shut, tried to remember why she'd climbed in the car with him. Her car had broken down . . . she'd needed a ride. She knew him, had trusted him. His eyes had been kind.

Nothing like the evil of the hideous creature mauling her now.

Pine needles stabbed her back and head as he pressed his weight on her with one knee and twisted the knife into her thigh. She gasped, inhaling his rancid breath as pain exploded in her leg. Unable to scream, she shook with sobs, trying desperately to fight him, but her limbs refused to cooperate. Instead, she lay like a limp doll below him, helpless to stop him from carving her into pieces.

He waved the knife in front of her, the bloody tip glinting with drops of crimson. Her body spasmed with nausea. Through the fog, his eyes turned a yellow, ghoulish color, piercing her. Then he flicked a drop of blood with his finger and painted her lips with the sticky substance.

She gagged, choking on the coppery taste as the world spun sickeningly. Knowing she was going to pass out, she closed her eyes again, praying for him to end this torture.

Despair and sadness washed over her. Yesterday her entire life had loomed in front of her. She wanted to get married one day. Have babies. Attend college.

None of that was going to happen.

He plunged the knife into her shoulder, and her body jerked in agony. In a last-ditch effort to save herself, she silently begged him to let her go.

But his vile laughter echoed off the mountain as he raised the blood-soaked knife again and sliced her throat. Blood gurgled and spewed, her choked scream dying in the air.

Finally, the black abyss of death swallowed her.

CHAPTER THREE

Five days until the rising

Vincent studied the questionnaire at BloodCore, debating how much information to reveal. If the bureau discovered he was here, they'd ask questions.

Questions he didn't want to answer.

Maybe it had been a mistake to come.

"Mr. Valtrez?" A slender female doctor who looked to be in her midthirties approached him. "Hi, I'm Dr. Marlena Bender. Come this way."

Shoulders rigid, he followed her into a small laboratory, where she proceeded to explain the project in more detail.

"This research is privately funded, and it's one of my personal pet projects," she said. "The age-old question of nature versus nurture. It especially intrigues me, as I was a product of a rape myself and feared that my genetic father passed his violent tendencies on to me. I've always struggled with that fear and decided to make it my life's work."

Vincent relaxed slightly.

"I'm sharing my story because most patients in the study are reluctant to reveal their histories. But rest assured, your records and tests will be kept strictly confidential." She explained how she used encrypted codes to prevent hackers from accessing the data. Feeling marginally better, he admitted that his father had been abusive and had murdered his mother.

"It's admirable that you've chosen to be a federal agent," she said. "Seems we're both fighting our pasts. Just think, if we could pinpoint genetic markers to identify aggression, tendencies toward violent behavior, and mental disorders, we could test fetuses or newborns and treat them early on and possibly eradicate criminal behavior."

Her enthusiasm seemed sincere, although Vincent doubted they'd ever be able to prevent criminal behavior completely. There were too many variables.

"The agency is not aware that I'm participating in this," he said. "My anonymity has to be kept."

"Absolutely." She arranged several test tubes on the counter, tied the tourniquet around his arm, and inserted the needle. He stared at his blood as it flowed through the tubing, his anxiety mounting.

Was violence genetic? Had he inherited his father's violent tendencies?

Worse, would he someday succumb to the darkness within him and let it consume him, as his father had?

❧

The graveyard always drew the ghosts.

Clarissa tried to avoid it, but her family was here, and

she forced herself to visit and bring flowers at least once a week.

She'd been awake half the night, haunted by Billie Jo and Jamie's whimpers. She had no room in her cluttered mind for the other spirits rising from their graves, crying out for her.

A scraping sound jarred her, and she pivoted, then noticed Hadley Crane digging a grave for a burial. Probably Jamie Lackey's.

As if he sensed her watching, Hadley lifted his gaze to her and tipped his baseball hat. She flicked her hand up in greeting. Although he was nice-looking, he'd always seemed strange, talking to himself constantly.

Of course, most people thought she was strange, too.

Shaking off the thought, she knelt, gently placed the flowers in the respective vases. Needing solace from someone who understood her, she summoned her grandmother's spirit.

She'd long ago stopped calling for her mother. The night she took her own life, she appeared to Clarissa, whispered that she loved her and that she was sorry for leaving, but that she wouldn't visit her from the grave, because she wanted Clarissa to stifle her ability, to have a normal life free from the voices. True to her word, she hadn't visited since.

"Grandmother," she said softly. "I'm here."

"I know, sweetness." Her grandmother's voice sounded distant and low, like an ocean breeze ruffling the water. "I knew you were coming."

"Then you know about Billie Jo and Jamie, that I need to help them cross into the light."

"Yes, dear. But I'm afraid there will be more victims of this evil." Her voice warbled. "There is talk that a new leader is rising from the underworld. A band of Soul Collectors has dispersed across the Earth to claim souls for the offering at his coronation."

"Will I recognize him?"

"Maybe, maybe not. Some demons can shape-shift, possess a human's body and walk among you."

Clarissa swallowed. "What can I do to stop him, Grandmother?"

"Trust your instincts, and help the lost cross over," her grandmother said.

Clarissa nodded. She'd accepted her destiny years ago.

"There is one who comes to town," her grandmother continued, "one you must be wary of."

Clarissa knotted her hands. "You're talking about Vincent Valtrez, aren't you, Grandmother?"

Her grandmother sighed. "Yes. He is dangerous, possesses a darkness as his father did."

Clarissa waited for more, but her grandmother's voice faded, and so did her image. Fear blanketed her as the mist of morning dotted the tips of the mountain ridges and animal life scurried through the forests.

She shivered.

She wasn't a child anymore or a fanciful teenager. This time she'd heed her grandmother's warning and protect herself from Vincent.

Troubling thoughts pounded at Vincent as he drove through the Smokies to Eerie, Tennessee. The mountain ridges jutted around the ghostlike town like soldiers guarding an ancient tomb, a tomb of lost souls and malevolence.

McLaughlin's words about relaxing while he was here taunted him. This was not a place to relax—it was a place that bred trouble.

Storm clouds rumbled above the tall ridges, the spiked, jagged cliffs offering the perfect place for a madman to hide. Childhood memories of hiking through a similar area flashed back, making him break out in a sweat.

The insufferable heat choked him, the crunch of leaves and animals scurrying for safety echoing in his head. He inhaled the loamy scent of the earth, the rotting vegetation, the stench of an animal's blood where nearby vultures gnawed at the carcass already too mauled to identify. He heard his father's breath coaxing him on, driving him into the woods, teaching him to aim at his target, telling him to shoot.

Kill or be killed . . .

He banished the memory. The past did not matter now.

He was here to do a job, and he'd do it, then go home and on to the next case.

But a frisson of anxiety ripped through him. He had lived in these mountains near Eerie when he was young, then in that juvenile facility on the other side of the Black Forest as a teenager. Would people here remember him?

Praying they didn't, he wheeled into the police station entrance and parked, dust spewing from his boots as he strode into the mud-splattered adobe building. This meeting would be a waste of time. Time he'd never get back.

Time he could have used on a *real* case, not on speculations made by a psychic.

A short, burly man with wiry graying hair lumbered up from behind a metal desk, a cup of coffee in one stubby hand. "Sheriff Dwayne Waller. Thank you for coming. Do you remember me, Valtrez?"

Vincent gritted his teeth. Hell, yeah, he did. Waller had been young and cocky years ago, had come out to his house on a couple of domestic calls. "Yes. That was a long time ago." *And I'm not my father.*

They shook hands, then the sheriff gestured for Vincent to follow him into a cramped, sweltering office overflowing with paperwork, dirty coffee cups, and Dolly Parton memorabilia. The aroma of bacon filled the air, along with strong chicory coffee.

Vincent fought a caustic remark, but the comment died on his tongue as his gaze shot to the woman seated in one of the caned straight-back chairs to the side. Damn.

Clarissa.

Not a frail-looking kid any more.

Yet those eyes . . . they were still huge in her heart-shaped face. Soft. Troubled. Mysterious. The color of burnt copper.

She stared up at him with a fierce expression of bravado, like an enemy warrior braced for attack.

Except this soldier had curly auburn hair that cascaded over slender shoulders. Skin like hot honey. And a body that was sinfully curvaceous.

His mouth watered as he pictured the womanly Clarissa sprawled beneath him, naked and begging him to bed her.

He had a habit of imagining a woman naked the first time he saw her. Liked to guess at the color of her nipples. Clarissa would have large areolas, golden brown tipped in bronze. He could almost see them hardening beneath his gaze, imagined wetting them with his tongue.

He hadn't believed she could talk to ghosts when he was young. Then she'd freaked him out when she'd offered to commune with the spirits to see if his mother had passed . . .

Time to get this meeting over with. He cleared his throat. "Clarissa?"

Her gaze remained steady, soulful like an exotic gypsy's, as she extended her delicate hand. "Special Agent Valtrez."

He clenched his jaw as he accepted the gesture. Her palm would have fit inside his hand twice, her skin soft next to his callouses.

Heat seared him at her touch, making his body harden. Had she felt it, too?

A cool look slid onto her face, masking any emotion, giving him his answer.

Against his will, though, that aloofness turned him on. He'd like to do her right here in the office up against the wall with Dolly Parton watching.

But that mysterious, almost eerie look settled back in her eyes again, sucker punching him, and he realized that once with her might not be enough.

She'd want more. She'd pick at a man's soul with those probing deep eyes, weave a magic spell around him with her sultry voice.

His jaw tightened, and he pasted his professional mask in place, reminding himself why he was here.

To check out the possibility of a serial killer. Nothing more.

CHAPTER FOUR

Clarissa took one look at Vincent and a tingle rippled through her. He had been a tough and lonely little boy, mad at the world, and he had grown into a tougher man, big and broad shouldered, all dark, brooding, and sexy.

In fact, he was absolutely breathtaking now.

He stood well over six feet. His muscles had become defined and pronounced, his jaw square, and a few lines had started to fan around his eyes. His black hair was thick and layered and shadowed dense brows, deep-set eyes, and a slight scar on his forehead.

Tension vibrated between them as those intense black eyes bore into hers. They were blacker than she remembered, angry, as if he was void of a soul.

Maybe it had been ripped out by all he'd seen as a kid and since he'd left Eerie.

God knew that living with the victims' spirits had robbed her innocence. Their suffering—the mind-numbing fear that had frozen them in place and kept them from escaping their tormentor—ate at her. Sometimes their final thoughts as their last breath shuddered from their failing bodies haunted her at night, especially those not ready to pass. And then there were the ones with so many sins they'd never make it into the light.

Fear of not being able to help the victims barreled through her. Sorrow rolled in on the last train in that car. She couldn't fail. Billie Jo and Jamie were depending on her. And so was this other woman.

"Sheriff Waller requested the FBI's assistance because of information you've supplied, Clarissa?" Vincent's husky tone dripped sarcasm and male sexuality.

"Yes. Thank you for coming."

He claimed the other metal chair, his impressive height towering over her, his intimidating look pinning her to the seat. He fully intended to discount any information she offered, that was obvious.

She forged on anyway, determined to convince him to investigate. She didn't care what he thought of her personally anymore, but she had to help the ones in limbo.

"Let's review the facts. You're a grief counselor now?" he asked.

"Actually, I'm a family therapist here in town, but I specialize in grief counseling. I've spoken with each of the two families who lost loved ones."

He gave a clipped nod. "I've studied the files on those cases, and I don't see anything to indicate they're connected." He consulted the folder in his hand. "In fact, both the drowning victim and spider-bite victim appear to have died from accidental causes. And according to the lack of evidence of a struggle or footprints, the drowning might have been a suicide."

"Billie Jo Rivers did not kill herself," Clarissa stated with conviction. "She had just gotten engaged last week and was excited about planning her wedding."

Vincent glanced at the sheriff for confirmation.

Sheriff Waller nodded. "I talked to Billie Jo's mama. She said she and Billie Jo were supposed to go dress shopping the next day, that Billie Jo couldn't wait." Sheriff Waller hooked his thumbs in his belt loops. "There was no suicide note, either."

Vincent arched a thick black brow. "Maybe she discovered her fiancé was cheating and was distraught."

"No," Clarissa argued. "Curtis Riggs worshipped that girl. He's not the cheating kind."

Vincent leaned back, his crisp shirt stretching across massive, powerful broad shoulders. "What about defensive wounds?"

Waller hesitated, then scratched his head. "That's what makes this so danged confusing. There weren't any. And Billie Jo was a strong girl—she should have fought back."

"Any markings around her neck or head where someone held her underwater?" Vincent asked.

Waller shook his head again. "No. And she didn't have any enemies, either. Everyone in town loved Billie Jo. That girl was sweet as molasses."

"You questioned the fiancé?"

"Yep. Standard police work." Waller's tone held a defensive edge to it. "We may be small-town, but we're competent. Curtis was devastated over Billie Jo's death, cried like a baby."

"He loved Billie Jo," Clarissa seconded. "They were high school sweethearts. I talked to him myself, and he's despondent. He said Billie Jo was afraid of water, too, that she never would have gone to that creek by herself."

"How about alcohol in her system?" Vincent asked.

Waller shifted. "Tox reports showed no alcohol or drugs."

"That's interesting," Vincent conceded, "but what makes you think the spider-bite victim was murdered?"

"Did you see the number of bites she sustained?" Clarissa asked, annoyed. "Her apartment building was new, too. Someone had to have collected those spiders and put them in her bed."

Vincent leaned forward, his jaw set hard and firm. "Even if that were so, what makes you think the two deaths are connected? That they're the work of one person?"

The two women's faces floated into Clarissa's vision, ghostly hues in ethereal, shimmering pale white that screamed for her to speak for them, because they could no longer speak for themselves. They wanted justice and deserved an explanation. So did their loved ones.

Vincent folded his hands, hands that were large and masculine, filled with power and strength. His fingers were scarred now, rugged—she wondered about the scars, then if his hands could be gentle.

He cleared his throat. "Clarissa, answer the question."

"Because Billie Jo's and Jamie's spirits are together, holding hands," she said in a strained whisper.

Vincent's jaw tightened. "If these spirits can talk to you, why don't they tell you who killed them?"

"Because they don't know." She wet her dry lips with her tongue. "When people die from a sudden trauma or violent death, their souls go into shock," she explained. "It takes time to adjust, to accept that they're dead. It may take even longer for them to communicate."

"Why do these spirits appear to you?" he asked.

Clarissa twisted her hands. "Two reasons. I knew both victims. And I'm what's called a safe zone. The spirits know I'm a believer and more emotionally detached than a family member."

His eyes narrowed. "Have you ever been tested?"

"No. I don't need testing. I know what I hear."

"I meant for mental disorders," Vincent said.

Anger and hurt gnawed at her. "I'm *psychic,* not psychotic, Vincent." She glared at him. "I understand that believing in the supernatural is difficult for some people, especially those who don't have an *open* mind, but I wouldn't be here if I didn't think I could help."

A flicker of surprise glinted in his eyes, along with anger. "Even if I did believe in psychic powers," he said sharply, "how exactly do you intend to help me if you can't offer any real information?"

"Look, I didn't ask for this gift, to hear from the spirit world, but I can't control when they come to me." Clarissa's voice rose. "If I ignore them, I might as well be putting them in the grave myself."

He stiffened.

"You don't have to believe me, Vincent. You don't have to even like me. All I'm asking is that you investigate." A chill swept over her. "The spirits are here now, I can see them. They need our help so they can cross into the light."

Sheriff Waller coughed. "Her granny was like this—"

Vincent cut him off with a wave of his hand, and Clarissa realized he was getting ready to dismiss her. She grabbed his arm, imploring him to wait. A zing of electricity rippled through her veins, and her pulse jumped.

Vincent dropped his gaze to her hand, then looked

into her eyes as if he'd felt it, too. Judging from the scowl on his face, he didn't like it, either.

"I don't need this bullshit," he said gruffly. "I work with cold, hard facts. Evidence."

"You went into the Black Forest and survived," Clarissa said boldly. "You had to have seen things inside those woods that you can't explain."

A muscle ticked in his jaw. "I don't remember what I saw in there."

She flinched at the anguish in his haunted eyes.

Desperate, she silently willed the dead to talk to her, to give her something concrete, a detail about the killer, that might convince him she wasn't crazy.

"Afraid . . ." Jamie whispered. "Afraid of spiders . . ."

"Their fears," she said, realization dawning. "Billie Jo was afraid of water, of drowning. Jamie suffered from arachnophobia."

"That's true. Jamie was terrified of spiders," Sheriff Waller confirmed. "She was bit when she was a kid and almost died. Her mother mentioned it when we found her body."

The pieces snapped together in Clarissa's mind like a puzzle. "That's how the cases are connected," she whispered. "This madman knows each girl's worst fear, then uses it to kill her."

⌒

Vincent silently cursed. He didn't want to be here and be reminded of his past. Of his father's violent behavior.

He especially didn't want to remember the Black Forest or believe in Clarissa.

But dammit, her angelic voice was convincing. And her eyes were mesmerizing, her body that of a seductress.

"Just investigate, Vincent," she said, near pleading. "Consider that I might be right, that the killer learns the woman's worst fear and uses it to murder her. That the deaths are connected."

He hesitated, then scrubbed his hand over his beard stubble. "All right. I suppose it's possible a psycho is stalking women. If so, we should look at your local residents, someone who befriended each of the girls, someone each girl probably talked to and told her secrets."

Clarissa shuddered. "One of our locals?"

"You'd be surprised at the secrets your neighbors might have." He turned to the sheriff. "Is there anyone in Eerie with a history of violence or mental disease? A stranger in town? A new teacher or businessman, even a counselor or preacher?"

"Offhand, Bo Bennett comes to mind," Waller said. "He did time in the pen for assaulting a woman. He's been clean since he got out, though, runs the tow truck service."

Vincent shifted. "Let's bring him in for questioning, find out if he has alibis for the two cases in question. I'll check national databases and see if there are any cases with similar MO's."

The telephone rang and the sheriff stepped from the room to answer it.

Clarissa turned to Vincent. "Vincent, I told the sheriff that I think another woman is missing."

He arched a dark brow. "Who?"

"I don't know yet."

Her eyes implored him to believe her, then searched his face as if she was trying to see inside his head.

Hell, he should let her see his dark soul. Then she'd run like hell and he'd be done with her.

Clarissa cleared her throat. "What are you afraid of, Vincent? That I might be right? That there might actually be demons or some supernatural explanation for these murders?"

"You've got to be kidding."

"I don't kid about murder."

A sarcastic laugh rolled from him. "First of all, there's no proof of any murders. And second, I'm not afraid of anything. Especially you."

She smiled slowly, then placed her hand on his arm. Heat flooded his veins, sending his pulse into an irregular pattern. "You're lying, Vincent. You're afraid that I'm right. That there is an evil presence here, that it's taken root in the town, and that you can't stop it."

"I know there's evil—that's the reason I became an agent," he snapped.

She leaned closer to him, her breath bathing his neck. That sweet scent enticed him to forget her words and drag her in his arms and taste her.

"Then it's the evil inside you that you fear," she whispered. "That's the reason you left here. The reason you became an agent."

He swallowed hard and shook his head, but her words hit too damn close to home. Worse, her touch made him ache inside, made him want to feel her delicate hands on his flesh, her lips soothing and cool on his skin, her body welcoming his inside her.

Blood surged to his loins, his cock swelling with arousal.

He struggled for control, for a reason why she made him so damn hot, for a reason he shouldn't sleep with her, for rational thoughts to resurface.

Thankfully the sheriff rushed in, and Vincent clawed his way back from the brink of insanity.

"Clarissa, you were right." Sheriff Waller heaved for a breath. "A jogger out at Hell's Hollow just found Tracy Canton's body. Someone slashed her throat and left her at the edge of the canyon."

Vincent fisted his hands. No denying it, this sounded like murder.

Sheriff Waller grabbed his gun and hat and headed to the door.

Vincent followed. "Hell's Hollow?"

"A small canyon between two of our highest ridges," Waller said. "Developers built a bunch of houses there a decade ago, but they burned down one night. Killed all the people home at the time, about a hundred." He wheezed a tired breath and scrubbed a hand through his hair.

"Arson?" Vincent asked.

"Never determined the reason. But since then, two developers have tried to build on that land and stopped."

"Why?" Vincent asked.

"Ghosts," Clarissa filled in as she came up behind him. "People claim they can still smell the smoke and the charred bodies, that they hear screams of women and children dying as they were burned alive."

"The devil's work," Sheriff Waller added. "No other explanation. Grass won't even grow there."

"It was another year of the eclipse," Clarissa said in a cryptic tone.

"What the hell does that mean?" Vincent asked.

"That more deaths will follow," Waller said. "The massacre at Hell's Hollow happened during one eclipse year. And a mine collapsed, killing and trapping dozens during *another*."

Vincent's chest clenched. There had been an eclipse the year his parents disappeared.

The year he suspected his father had killed his mother.

CHAPTER FIVE

The scent of burning cedar and flesh assaulted Vincent as he approached Hell's Hollow. Not a deep canyon, but a groove carved out of the mountains. The earth was dry, the ground hard, the trees bare of leaves as if life couldn't survive on the plot of land. For a moment, he actually paused to listen for the spirits of the dead Clarissa had described, but other than the whine of twigs snapping and the cry of the vultures stalking the hollow as if they smelled fresh blood, the air was eerily silent. And hot, so hot that sweat trickled down his jaw and back, plastering his shirt to his skin. Even the soles of his shoes felt the infernal heat from the ground, as if that fire still burned beneath the soil, ready to strike any second.

Déjà vu suddenly hit him. He'd been here before.

He turned around and scanned the area, his gut tightening. This place was familiar, was where his own childhood home had sat. The house that had become a torture chamber . . .

Sheriff Waller gestured toward a path to the right and a ridge that overlooked the hollow, and Vincent followed him, drawing in the mountain air but smelling the heat and stench of death mingled with dry pine.

Clarissa kept close to his back, her essence sneaking in between the vile odors to throw him off balance. Suddenly she gasped, and his gaze zeroed ahead onto the crime scene. A younger guy, whom Waller introduced as Deputy Bluster, approached, but Vincent barely looked in his direction. Instead, he balled his hands into fists to control his rage. This one was definitely a murder.

The killer had nearly decapitated the woman and had left her bloody corpse at the edge of the mountain ridge next to a camping area, as if to announce his boldness with the extent of his violence and the public location where he'd left her remains.

Her thoracic muscles had been sliced through, so her head dangled sideways; her cotton dress was shoved up her hips, exposing bruised thighs. Cuts and abrasions also marred her wrists, arms, breasts, and legs. Her own blood had been smeared all over her body, as if the killer had had a party with it.

Vincent dragged in a labored breath, battling rage. He wanted to kill the maniac who'd done this and cut him up into a zillion pieces.

Instead, he tugged at his collar, loosened his tie, and inhaled sharply, fighting the darkness inside him. He couldn't afford one of the blackouts he'd been having recently. He'd lost time, woken up in odd places, sometimes with blood on his hands.

The state crime-scene unit roared up, descending upon them, then began to comb the area for trace evidence. Sheriff Waller and Tim Bluster questioned the scant few visitors at the park who'd ventured out this morning. A couple of homeless bums sleeping off their drunk on park benches, a pair of teenagers who'd sneaked out to have sex, and a morning jogger who'd discovered the body.

The young girl hovered next to the boy, who'd turned as pale as buttermilk. "We didn't see anything," the boy whined.

"He's right," the girl said in a haunted whisper. "We fell asleep in our sleeping bag by the creek."

"Buddy, you know Dina's mama is going to skin your hide for sneaking up here with her," the sheriff said.

The boy's knees knocked together. "You don't have to tell them, do you?"

"Please." Dina pulled at the older man's arms. "She'll ground me forever."

Sheriff Waller shook his head. "You're material witnesses, kids. I can't keep this from them."

"But we told you we didn't see anything," Buddy argued.

"You didn't hear someone screaming?" Vincent asked.

The young couple shook their heads vehemently. "She must have been dead already," Buddy said.

"And we had our iPod playing," Dina added with a sniffle.

Sheriff Waller clicked his teeth. "All right for now. Go on home, but I'll talk to you again later."

Hand in hand, they ran down the hill toward the VW they'd parked on the side of the road, and Vincent and Waller approached the jogger. He was slumped on a log, head in his hands, a green cast to his pallor. The stench of vomit drifted over the bushes.

"Who would do such a thing?" he said, mumbling to nobody.

"That's what we intend to find out," Sheriff Waller said.

Clarissa rubbed his shoulder in sympathy. "What's your name?"

"Riley Adams." His face was stark with horror, his lips blue from chewing on them. "I just came for a run and I stumbled over her. God . . ." His shoulders sagged as he dropped his head forward again. "I've never seen anyone dead before. So sick . . ."

"Did you see anyone else in the woods? Hear anything?" Waller asked.

He shook his head back and forth, digging the toe of his sneaker into the dirt. "Just those old drunks."

Vincent stepped closer to examine the area near the corpse. "Sheriff, it looks as if she might have been killed somewhere else, then her body dumped here. See how the brush has been crushed on the path?"

Waller jammed his hands on his hips and studied the scene. "You're probably right. Maybe forensics will find something."

Vincent nodded. Dammit, when the small town heard about the murder, panic would spread. Three suspicious deaths in one week was a hell of a lot. Granted, the heat wave hadn't helped. Just as the full moon seemed to drive out the crazies, so did the high temperatures. But the MOs were all different, so the murders couldn't be connected like Clarissa had said.

Could they?

He glanced at Clarissa, and his gut clenched at the horror etched on her face. Tears streaked her pale cheeks, but she brushed them away as if angry with herself.

Forcing a detachment to his expression, he focused on the crime scene. The amount of blood suggested a sadistic killer who had enjoyed his game of torture. Multiple stab wounds, blood smeared all over the woman's flesh, the depth of the slice to her throat . . .

How could a human do such a sadistic thing to another?

He mentally put together a profile—the killer was male. Out of control. Angry. But he also was a planner.

Clarissa curled her arms around her waist as if to hold herself together. "He's not finished, Vincent."

Worry tinged her voice, fear making it warble. She'd accused him of being afraid that he would never be able to end the evil in the world, but he'd denied it.

But she'd been right.

He heard that same fear in her voice now.

On the heels of that realization, his damn protective instincts kicked in, and he wanted to offer her comfort. Hold her in his arms. Banish that grisly sight from her eyes. Assure her that he would catch this maniac.

But he did none of that.

He couldn't let himself care about Clarissa any more than anyone else on the planet.

Work and emotions didn't mix. Although he didn't have to have emotions to have sex with her.

You're not going there, Valtrez. Not with Clarissa King.

Muttering another curse, he turned back to do what he did best. Leave her to slay her own demons while he forced himself to step into a killer's mind.

Every time he did, it was a test of restraint.

A test to prove that he wouldn't turn into one himself and let the evil in his soul, in his *bad* blood, overpower him as it had his father.

The stench of blood, body fluids, human sorrow, horror, filled Clarissa's nostrils, obliterating the sweet smell of honeysuckle in the air, even the lingering odor of charred wood from Hell's Hollow.

Clarissa shuddered again at the sight of Tracy's mutilated body. What kind of person would do this to another human?

Blood soaked Tracy's gaunt face, and her eyes looked glassy, frozen with terror and shock. Her head hung grotesquely to the side, nearly severed, as if it might fall off if one touched it . . .

And the bugs . . . dear Lord, they were crawling and feasting on her, drinking her blood for sustenance. Above, vultures careened, waiting for their turn, and Clarissa swallowed to keep from losing the contents of her stomach.

A shout erupted from the hill near the road. Pivoting, she saw Ronnie Canton running up the embankment, gravel spewing from his heels as he wove through the trees. The deputy lurched forward to grab him and keep him behind the crime-scene tape.

"You found Tracy?" Ronnie shouted. "My God, is she all right?"

"Hang on there, Ronnie." The deputy shielded Ronnie from the sight of his sister's mutilated body. "You don't need to see this."

But Ronnie spotted Tracy, collapsed onto his knees in the dirt, and howled like an injured animal.

Vincent's jaw tightened as if hardening himself to the man's pain.

Clarissa folded her arms across her chest. Didn't he care about anyone?

"Who is that?" he asked quietly.

"Tracy's brother." Clarissa sprang into counselor mode as she rushed toward the lanky young man. By the time she reached him, the deputy had helped Ronnie to sit on a tree root. His wails echoed off the mountain, shrill and anguished.

"Ronnie, I'm so sorry," Clarissa said gently.

He fell against her, sobbing and mumbling incoherently. His tears soaked her top, and she curved her arm around him, murmuring nonsensical words, assuring him that it would be all right, when they both knew nothing was all right.

"Who could be so vicious?" he cried. "Who would hurt my sister like this?"

"I don't know, but we'll find out," Clarissa promised.

Vincent watched them with a brooding expression, and she shivered. He obviously disliked everything about her. She didn't know why that hurt, but it did.

The heat that had radiated between them when they'd touched disturbed her even more. She didn't want to be attracted to him.

But concern for Tracy and Ronnie erased any personal misgivings. She'd tolerate him, just as long as he helped them stop the killer.

Finally Ronnie's cries quieted. He dragged out a handkerchief and blew his nose, then turned to her. "What happened, Clarissa? Who did this to Tracy?"

She stroked his damp hair from his forehead. "I don't know yet, Ronnie. But Sheriff Waller won't let you down. And an FBI agent is here now, Special Agent Valtrez. He'll find her killer."

Vincent crossed the distance to them, his jaw set tight as he introduced himself. "This woman was your sister?"

Ronnie nodded, rubbing his hand over his eyes as he blinked back more tears, his bony shoulders slumped. "Tracy was only twenty-one. She can't be dead. She was so young . . ."

He scrubbed a hand through his wiry brown hair, making it stick up in all directions. "She hated blood . . . the sight of it," he said raggedly. "She fainted when they drew blood at her physical. I can't believe she died covered like this."

Clarissa jerked her head toward Vincent. "Her greatest fear . . ."

For a moment, his gaze flickered with acceptance of her theory, but a second later, a mask slid over his expression as if that moment had never happened.

"Did your sister live with you?" Vincent asked.

Ronnie jumped up and began to pace, kicking leaves and rocks as his agitation mounted. "She moved into an apartment last week. I go by and check on her every day, but this morning when I saw her car wasn't at home, I got scared. So I drove around town and found it on the side of the road near the bakery. The battery was dead . . ." He paused and sniffed, and Clarissa patted his back, encouraging him to continue.

"I should have installed a new one for her last week . . . but I was going to wait for my next paycheck . . ." He gulped back more tears. "Jesus, it's my fault. If I had, she wouldn't have had car trouble—"

"It's not your fault," Clarissa said softly. "Tracy knows you cared about her, Ronnie. She loved you and wouldn't want you to blame yourself."

Vincent gave her a sharp look, and Clarissa's temper flared. But through the hazy turmoil of her own emotions, she saw a misty gray swirling above Tracy's body.

Loose particles of ectoplasm glittered like tiny diamonds, then slowly congealed to resemble her shape. Even in spirit form, Tracy's head hung precariously to the side, and her eyes were stricken as she watched her grief-stricken brother.

"She was stabbed. Judging from the knife wounds, it looks like the perp used a hunting knife," Vincent said. "Do you know anyone who would have hurt her, Ronnie?"

Ronnie shook his head. "No, no one."

"Was she dating anyone?"

Ronnie shook his head. "Not that I know of."

"Any recent breakups?"

Again Ronnie shook his head. "You have to find the monster who did this."

A muscle ticked in Vincent's jaw, and Clarissa grabbed his arm before he could question Ronnie further. "Vincent, can we talk for a minute?"

"What?" he asked sarcastically. "Do you have more news from the dead?"

Anger sharpened her voice. "Maybe you should crawl back under your rock and request another agent for this case. You obviously don't want to be here."

His black eyes stabbed her. "My job is not to make friends here or coddle the locals," he said in a gruff voice. "It's to find out who murdered this woman."

"At least you could have some compassion for Ronnie."

"Everyone is considered a suspect in a homicide case." The dark aura surrounding him swirled with energy.

"So I'm a suspect, too?" she said.

His eyes pierced her, his voice gruff when he spoke. "No."

Desperate for something concrete to convince him, she turned to Tracy. Billie Jo and Jamie's spirits appeared beside Tracy, and she silently begged them for more information.

Tracy held out a trembling, bloody hand and slowly unfolded her fingers.

Clarissa frowned as the other two women's spirits extended pale, ghostly hands containing the same object.

She studied the rock, trying to understand the significance. "Agent Valtrez, there is something that proves the deaths are connected."

His sigh rasped through the silence. "I'm listening."

Clarissa cleared her throat, certain now she had a clue. "The killer left a small piece of black rock at each crime scene."

His thick eyebrows rode up. "You know this how?"

She opened her mouth to answer, but he shrugged her off. "Never mind. I guess the victims told you."

Her mouth tightened. "Just check the area. See if you find a piece of black rock beside Tracy. Look in her hand."

He didn't comment but glanced back at the scene. "Why am I looking for black rock?"

"The killer leaves it as his signature."

His gaze met hers. Distrustful. Filled with suspicion. And a small flicker of some other emotion she couldn't discern.

He knew something about the black rock . . .

Moving like a giant panther stalking his prey, he strode over to the body and knelt. Clarissa's stomach tightened as he removed the small piece of rock from Tracy's clenched fingers with his gloved hand.

The hairs on the back of her neck bristled, and she glanced up at the imposing ridges surrounding them. In spite of the heat, a stiff wind rattled the trees, a hollow moan echoing as if it had emerged from deep in the mountain. Below her feet, the earth shook as if the ground might open up and swallow her.

This killer was truly evil. Supernatural. He had been here last night in this park, and he was close by now, too.

Ready to strike again and take another life if they didn't stop him.

~

The cycle of the moon—that was Pan's curse. Collect seven souls and he could rise to the next level of the underground. Fail and he would be sentenced to the lowest level, where he would be tortured through eternity.

Pan had killed three times now, but the girls' souls remained in limbo. Though they had begged for their lives, not a one had agreed to be converted. He had the power to offer them eternal life if they joined him on his quest. Once they sold their souls to him, then made their first kill, immortality would be theirs.

He'd known they'd contact the medium, had intended for them to drive her crazy. But she was stronger than he thought. She was trying to help them fight him, to cross into the light.

Still, she was suffering.

Heat beat down on Pan's back as his demonic form watched the humans studying his handiwork. He enjoyed torturing the humans. Would use them to make Vincent more vulnerable.

The woman, Tracy, her blood had tasted like nectar, her fear like a fine wine, rich and heady. The coppery scent still lingered on his hands and in his nostrils, making him shudder with excitement. And what a fitting place to leave her body—Hell's Hollow.

Had Vincent recognized his old homestead? Were his memories of the past and his father's teachings finally returning?

Did he remember where he'd first seen the black rock? Did he understand its significance?

Excitement raced through him. Vincent would remember . . . everything. And soon.

His soul was worth a million others.

Pan would steal it for his master. Then he would bask in the glory.

CHAPTER SIX

Horrific images and thoughts suddenly bombarded Vincent as he held the black rock in his hand. For a brief second, heat seared his palm and the rock actually glowed, launching him back to the past he'd forgotten.

To the cave his father had taken him to in the Black Forest. The cave made of black rock.

The cave where his mother had burned to death.

He swallowed hard, emotions churning in his chest as the memory became clearer.

It had been a hot day, yet another in a series of vicious and cruel beatings. His mother had tried to protect him, but his father had raged and dragged her into the woods, into the Black Forest.

Vincent had been terrified, but he'd chased after them. He had to save her.

His body shook now as the images crashed back—battling his way through the snakes and creatures in the thick forest, fending off animals and dark shadows that he couldn't distinguish.

And when he'd finally reached the cave, he'd found

his mother, bloody and half beaten already, tied to a wooden stake in the center.

Then his father, a black shadow of evil surrounding him, had raised his hands, hands that had been cruel and unforgiving, and pressed his fingertips against the stone walls. As if from the bowels of hell, flames sparked from the rock, lighting up the cavern. Satan's image swam against the jagged stone surface.

His father's hands held that flaming power. And he'd used it to light the torches surrounding his mother and burned her to death.

Vincent had fought him. Fought him and driven a stake into his father's cold heart.

"You have my blood, bad blood," his father had told him repeatedly when he was a child. "You're a Dark Lord."

He hadn't understood the depth of his father's lack of morality until that day.

Sorrow clogged his throat, nearly bringing him to his knees. He hadn't been able to save his mother. He could hear her screams and cries as the flames consumed her.

"Vincent?" A hand touched his arm, fingers gentle and tender, dragging him back to reality.

Still, he shuddered at the power of the memory. He'd always suspected his father had killed his mother, but now he knew.

He'd witnessed her horrific murder and hadn't been able to save her. His right hand went to his pocket, where he kept the amulet he'd pulled from the fire, the only thing he had left of her.

He'd kept it, had known it was important, that she would never have taken it off. Not willingly.

What else had happened in that forest? What exactly

had he seen? And how had he ended up outside the forest afterward?

"What is it about the black rock?" Clarissa asked.

He blinked away the images and glanced into Clarissa's eyes. Eyes that saw too much.

Did she possess a psychic power? Could she see the
darkness inside him?

Tension knotted his neck as he handed the rock to
the crime-scene investigator to bag. He wasn't ready
to reveal what he'd seen. Not yet. It was too personal,
too painful.

Besides, it had nothing to do with this killer.

"I was just wondering if there could be a cave nearby
made of this black stone."

"It's possible," Clarissa said, still watching him
thoughtfully. "The mountains have dozens of caves and
mines interspersed throughout."

He frowned. "I'll have forensics analyze it. Could be
where the killer takes his victims or where he's holed
up."

He remembered Ronnie saying his sister's car had
broken down. Hadn't Waller said Bennett ran a tow
service?

He'd follow up, see if Tracy might have called
Bennett.

Her eyes narrowed as if she suspected he was with-
holding information, but he didn't have to include her in
his investigation, not the details, anyway. She was nothing but a distraction.

And the only person he'd ever been tempted to confide in about his father's cruelty.

"Why don't you take the brother home while we finish up?" he suggested.

A heartbeat of silence yawned between them, filled with tension. "You want to get rid of me? Why, Vincent? Afraid I'll slip into your head and see something you don't want me to see?"

His jaw clenched. "I thought you talked to ghosts. I didn't know you read minds of the living, too."

Her lips tilted into a smile. "You don't have to be a mind reader to understand some people."

He arched a brow, injecting cynicism in his voice. "And you think you understand me?"

She shrugged. "You act tough. You want people to think you don't care, that you don't have a heart. But if you didn't, you wouldn't have chosen to save lives for a living. You protect and fight for innocents."

He hissed a breath as he leaned forward, so close to her he inhaled her scent, so close he felt her breath on his face. Heat still curled inside him where she'd touched his arm.

Goddammit, he didn't want her touch or her voice tempting him.

He wanted her to feel the danger radiating off of him as he stared coldly into her eyes. Wanted to make her run far away so he wouldn't have to be tempted by her big eyes. "I do this job because I understand the need to kill," he murmured. "Because I'm just like these monsters."

***

Vincent's masculine scent taunted Clarissa as he leaned closer to her.

Darkness swirled around them, cocooned them as if they were alone at the precipice of the mountain. His breath against her face was intended as a warning, just as his cold statement was. He wanted to scare her.

For a brief moment, fear tickled her nerves. Yet at the same time the power and intensity in his gaze sent heat and hunger splintering through her.

She constantly dealt with tortured spirits and refused to let Vincent intimidate her. If she ran from him like a frightened child, he'd never take her seriously.

Besides, her instincts and counseling experience told her that he wore a cold shield around himself as a protective device. Though she had no idea what a tough man like him could be afraid of.

Maybe that his secrets would be exposed.

The man had those; she saw them hidden in the depths of his eyes.

But she would be a glutton for punishment if she allowed herself to fall prey to his sexuality.

Before she had a chance to recover, he pivoted and strode away from her, cornering one of the crime-scene investigators, who'd found a small piece of blue fabric caught on a low branch.

She walked over to examine it and touched the branch. Suddenly, images bombarded her. Tracy crying for help. Silently pleading for the killer to stop torturing her. A faceless monster sinking the knife into her.

A man digging a grave. A grave meant for Tracy.

Or for her?

Ronnie sniffled and shuffled up to her. "Clarissa, I gotta go tell Mama 'bout Tracy . . ."

Clarissa's heart bled for him and the pain Tracy had endured. No mother wanted to hear her baby girl had been dealt such a horrible fate. "I'll go with you, Ronnie. Eloise might need me."

Gratitude softened his haunted eyes as she folded him in her arms and hugged him. "Go back to your car and wait for me. Let me tell the sheriff and Agent Valtrez that I'll drive you home."

He nodded, his bony frame trembling, and she gave him a slight push for encouragement. He took one last look at the gruesome scene, swayed, then ran through the path to his rusted Malibu.

Clarissa drew a deep breath, watching Tracy's spirit as she extended a trembling hand toward her brother. As much as Clarissa's ability troubled her, she found solace in the fact that she eased the transition for the deceased and their families. Although at times, their suffering tore at her, as it must have her mother.

Would it eventually eat away her sanity, too?

No. She wouldn't let it.

Aware the Cantons needed her, she hurried to inform the sheriff and Vincent where she was going.

The two of them stood by the body, discussing the crime scene. Before she reached them, Deputy Bluster approached her. She'd had coffee with him a couple of times, even dinner once. Odd how when most men gave her a wide berth, he had pursued her openly.

"Hey, Clarissa." His brown eyes softened as he touched her arm. "You shouldn't be here. It's too gruesome."

As if communing with the dead wasn't. "My heart breaks for Tracy and her family."

"Damn shame," Tim said quietly. "How did you find out, anyway?"

"I was at the sheriff's office when your call came in."

He darted a glance at the sheriff and Vincent. "Can't believe Waller called in a feebie."

"Tim, there have been three murders in the past two weeks. We need help around here."

He twisted his mouth sideways. "What do you mean— three murders?"

"Billie Jo Rivers and Jamie Lackey. I think they were murdered, too."

He kicked an ant pile at his feet and dozens of fire ants scattered. "You know something we don't know, Clarissa?"

She shrugged. Even though Tim probably had heard rumors that she communed with the dead, they'd never discussed it.

"A hunch," she said, glossing over the truth. He didn't have to know the details.

"We don't need his kind," Tim said more harshly. "Sheriff and I are perfectly competent."

The anger in his tone surprised her. "But if he can help, Tim—"

"Why some hotshot FBI guy? Does Waller think he's better, smarter?"

"He called him because Vincent grew up around here, Tim. He knows the area."

"Vincent?" Tim said sarcastically. "So you know him?"

"I did when I was young. Then he moved away."

"Well, I don't like him. Stay away from him, Clarissa."

She couldn't do that. "Tim—"

He gripped her hand. "I'm concerned about you. Especially in light of Tracy's murder."

Clarissa shrugged off his concern. "Don't worry. I can take care of myself."

"Tracy probably thought that, too."

A chill slithered through her, and she pulled her hand away, taking a step backward.

"I'm sorry, I didn't mean to scare you," he said, lowering his voice. "But I'm not sure it's safe for you, living in that old log house on the mountain all alone."

She wasn't alone, she wanted to tell him. She had the spirits. "I have Wulf," she said instead.

He smiled slowly. "I could stay with you."

Clarissa heaved a breath, using one hand to rake her hair from her forehead. Perspiration dotted her neck, and flies buzzed around her ankles. "Thanks, but I'll be okay. Listen, Ronnie's waiting. Tell the sheriff I'm driving him home. I figure someone should be there for support when he breaks the news about Tracy to their mother."

He studied her for a long moment, then tipped the brim of his hat. "Good idea. I heard she has a bad heart."

"Then I'd better go."

"I'll tell the sheriff for you."

"Thanks."

Vincent's cold gaze pierced her, and she nodded, conceding for the moment. She'd stop by her house and take care of Wulf first, then go to the Cantons. Comfort the Cantons tonight, but she would talk to the sheriff and Vincent later. She knew these murders were related, and she had to make sure they found the killer before he stole another life.

Three spirits were depending on her.

Out of the corner of his eye, Vincent watched Clarissa weave back through the woods. The deputy stared after her, his tongue dangling like a dog in heat. His reaction would have been laughable if they weren't standing in the middle of a brutal crime scene.

As if the man sensed Vincent's scrutiny, he tilted his head sideways and met his gaze. Tension sliced the air between them. Either Deputy Bluster didn't want him here professionally, or he didn't want him looking at Clarissa.

Tough shit. Vincent didn't give a damn. He'd do what he pleased, and this pissant wouldn't stop him.

Bluster strode toward him, rolling his shoulders back to sharpen his height. Still, Vincent's six-three towered over him.

Waller glared at him for a tension-filled minute as the stench of death and blood rose around them, then Bluster directed his comment to the sheriff as if purposely leaving him out of the investigation.

"Sheriff Waller," Bluster said. "Clarissa's going to drive Ronnie home to tell his mama about Tracy."

"Eloise will take it hard," Sheriff Waller said in a gruff voice. "I'll stop by and see her myself later."

Vincent cleared his throat. "We need to question her. Find out if she knew if Tracy was seeing anyone."

Waller nodded.

"And we should bring Bennett in right away," Vincent said. "I'd also like to question the family and friends of the other two cases."

"Folks around here don't always take kindly to

strangers," Bluster cut in bitterly. "It'd be best if the sheriff and I handle the locals."

Vincent wanted to choke the bastard. Granted, he hadn't asked for this assignment, wasn't convinced the three cases were related, but he sure as hell wouldn't allow this dickhead to run him off. "I was called here to do a job, and I'll question whomever I damn well please."

Bluster's cheeks ballooned out as he worked to control his temper. "We don't need your help."

"Bluster," Waller growled. "I requested his assistance."

The deputy's eyes flashed with fury. "Why? What can he do that we can't?"

"He has access to state and federal databases, is more experienced in serial-killer cases. We have three deaths now, Deputy. I don't want any more."

"Three that aren't related," Bluster argued.

"That's not what Clarissa thinks," Waller said.

A range of emotions paraded across Bluster's face. His feelings for Clarissa had been evident when he was talking to her earlier, and he didn't want to refute her opinion. But Vincent saw the question, doubt in the man's eyes.

"Bluster, if you want to help, go pick up Bo Bennett," Vincent said. "And get his phone records. Let's see if Tracy Canton called him when her car broke down. Also get a mechanic to check her car, make sure the battery really died. Maybe the car was tampered with."

"You're thinking Bennett could have set her up?" Waller asked.

"It's a possibility," Vincent said.

Bluster glared at Vincent but nodded, silently conveying

his acceptance of the situation, although belligerence laced his acceptance.

"Sorry about that," Waller said as Bluster headed to his car. "But he's right. Sometimes the locals don't cotton much to big-city cops coming in and trying to take over. Especially ones who left and come back."

Vincent fisted his hands by his sides. *And ones with my past.*

"I don't give a damn who likes it," Vincent said. "Tell them if they want to find this girl's killer, they'd better cooperate. If they don't, it'll only make them look suspicious."

Waller frowned but nodded. "How about we round the families and friends of the other victims up tomorrow? That soon enough?"

"All right, but we need to talk to this girl's mother tonight."

Waller nodded again and pressed his hand over his chest. Vincent remembered he'd had a mild heart attack and wondered if the old man was all right.

The coroner finished, and they loaded Tracy's body to take to the morgue. Then they'd transport her to the state medical examiner's facility for an autopsy.

Hopefully, forensics would do their jobs and find conclusive evidence to link to the killer.

But that would take time. Time they might not have before the killer struck again.

He opened his palm and studied the imprint of the angel wings that had branded his hand from his mother's necklace. It had faded over the years and was so faint that people rarely noticed.

Yet now he knew how he'd gotten the scar.

The black rock had lit up when he'd closed his fingers

around it, just as the cave of black rock had lit up when his father touched the rock the day he killed Vincent's mother.

He blinked, his vision blurring.

His father had been a monster, and that evil had given him the power to turn the black rock to fire. Another memory gnawed at him—twice he'd shattered something with his hands, caused an object to explode without touching it. Each time he'd been driven by anger.

A Dark Lord . . . It meant he had evil in him, just like his father.

He felt it now, the incessant desire for blood, the consuming darkness clawing at him, just as he heard the echo of his father's voice ordering him to succumb to the call. His finely tethered control slipping . . .

He'd told Clarissa that he was just like the monsters he chased.

She'd better heed his warning and stay away from him, or she might end up dead at his hands just as his mother had his father's.

Pan momentarily shifted his demonic body from the human's. He thirsted for more. For another kill.

Then he'd send the dead's voices to taunt Clarissa until she went completely crazy.

He waved a hand and morphed down from the mountain, landing in the town square, a ghostlike maze of old buildings, family businesses, and ancient customs passed down through the generations. Smiling, he walked down Main Street, his senses honed as he searched for his next victim.

Since he'd been in town, he'd borrowed a body. To

others, he looked normal. A human. One among them.
Disguise made it easy. They trusted him, allowing him
to get close to his prey.

But now, in his demonic form, he slid into the shadows, invisible when he wanted. A pretty redhead he'd
heard someone call Sadie Sue rushed toward the small
diner, Hell's Kitchen, and he followed her, the scent of
her sex causing his cock to twitch.

He grinned. All good had to be destroyed. One touch
was all he needed. Then he would know the redhead's
darkest secrets.

And the perfect way to put an end to her miserable
existence.

First the touch, then the taunt, then the kill . . .

Pan knew exactly when to strike. When the near-dead
begged for another moment of life, when they would do
anything he asked, when they would make a deal. The
ones with the *bad* blood, the weak, the greedy, accepted
his terms at all costs.

Zion would not only survive but thrive, feeding off
of each kill. For each soul he collected heightened his
power.

Pan brushed the curve of her back. A cloying, sweet
perfume rocked his libido, and he licked his lips.

As his hand lingered, her mind became an open book,
and he skimmed the pages, searching through the cluttered lines. She'd never known her old man. Her mama
had died from emphysema four years ago. She had a son
named Petey.

Aha . . . there, he'd found it. Her greatest fear.

Snakes. She had fallen once in the woods and a rattler
had bitten her, and she'd nearly died.

Laughter mushroomed inside his chest—Eve had been

tempted by the forbidden fruit, tricked by a serpent, and this sinner would die at the hands of one herself.

His pulse thrummed double-time as his gaze veered toward the jagged mountain peaks surrounding Eerie and its miles of forest. Snakes abounded in those hills.

Pan would watch the terror freeze her veins as the snakes slithered across her naked body.

Then those snakes would suck the life from her as they fed on her.

He could hear her silent screams, her pleas for help, see her eyes begging for salvation.

Maybe this one would trade her soul for the chance to remain alive. And when she made her first kill, she'd be his servant forever.

CHAPTER SEVEN

No, no, you're lying! My little girl can't be dead . . ." Eloise Canton raced to the oak desk in the kitchen corner, picked up a photo of Tracy at her high school graduation, and waved it at Clarissa. "See, there she is on graduation night. Isn't she just beautiful?"

"Yes, Mrs. Canton, but—"

Tracy's mother cut her off. "And now she got herself a good job teaching preschool. Gracious, the little children just love her."

Clarissa fought tears of sympathy as sixty-year-old Eloise continued to babble in denial.

Ronnie reached for his mother, extracted the photo, and set it on the desk. "I'm so sorry, Mama, but you have to listen to me. It's true about Tracy. Someone killed her."

Eyes wild, Eloise jerked Ronnie by the collar and shook him. "What kind of mean-hearted joke are you trying to pull? My Tracy is coming back. She just moved out, but she'll be here for dinner later on. She promised."

She released him, whirled around, wiped her hands on her apron, and turned back to the scarred counter. "I'm making her favorite, country fried chicken. And I just popped a peach cobbler in the oven. Why don't you get the ice cream churn and we'll make some homemade ice cream to go with it." She threw a quick glance over her shoulder. "You can stay if you want, Clarissa. I always cook plenty."

"Mama," Ronnie said in a fragile voice. "Mama, I'm not trying to be mean or playing a joke . . ." His voice cracked and tears rolled down his cheeks. "I saw her, Mama, she's dead . . ."

Eloise shook her head in denial, pain and shock glazing her eyes, eyes the same color as her daughter's. Clarissa would never forget the way they'd looked in death, wide and staring.

And all that blood . . .

She banished the images. Had to help this woman cope with the truth.

Eloise poured oil in a cast-iron skillet, turned on the stove to heat the pan, then hastily scooped flour into a bowl. She reached for a chicken breast to dip it in egg, but Clarissa flipped off the heat and cradled the woman's hands in her own. Eloise's body tensed, her fine bones cracking with tension.

"I'm so sorry, Mrs. Canton," Clarissa said softly. "But it's true. Ronnie and I just came from seeing Tracy. Sheriff Waller is with her now."

"No, no . . . Please stop this, Clarissa." The older woman trembled with the realization that she had to face reality, a reality that was every parent's worst nightmare.

Clarissa simply waited, allowing her the time she needed to accept the truth.

"I can't lose my baby," Eloise cried. "I gave life to her; she can't be gone."

"I wish it wasn't true," Clarissa said, giving Ronnie a compassionate look as he dropped into the straight chair at the table and lowered his head into his hands again.

"The sheriff is going to stop by later," Clarissa said. "He'll need to talk to you, Eloise. And once the coroner finishes, he'll send Tracy to the funeral parlor; then you can see her."

"The ME?" Her voice broke, sounded distant. "You can't let them cut up my baby."

Clarissa swallowed. "Eloise, I'm sorry, but Tracy was murdered. An autopsy will help find her killer and put him away."

Eloise's eyes dulled as reality interceded, and her legs buckled. Clarissa caught her just before her bony knees hit the wood floor. Panicked, Ronnie lunged up and helped Clarissa carry her to the sofa, where she curled into a fetal ball, her horror palpable as her anguished sobs echoed through the room.

Vincent's agitation with the deputy intensified as the hour wore on. He didn't care what the homeboy thought—he hadn't chosen to come to this podunk town and join this case, but he would damn well find the sadistic animal who'd carved up the Canton girl and played in her blood.

Irrational jealousy snaked through him though as he remembered the possessive streak Bluster had for Clarissa, but he shoved it away. Vincent didn't do jealousy.

Didn't allow himself to care about a woman enough to let her relationships with other men bother him.

He couldn't care about Clarissa, either.

"You ready?" Sheriff Waller heaved a breath, his belly shaking with the effort. "CSU is finishing up."

Vincent nodded. "I guess we've done all we can here. The forensics team had better be thorough."

"We're not backward like you guys from the FBI think, if that's what you mean. We have a decent unit," Waller said with a scowl.

Apparently Bluster was right. Folks were sensitive around here. But they'd asked for his help, and if he had to insult a few locals to do it, so be it. As long as he solved this damn case. Because as much as he hated to admit that Clarissa might be right, three deaths in the small community within this short time frame raised suspicion.

"Are we stopping by the vic's house?" Vincent asked.

Waller frowned. "Her name is Tracy, not the vic," he muttered as he tugged his uniform khakis up to meet his belly. "Around here, everybody knows everybody else, so you'd do good to use her name."

Vincent's jaw tightened. He'd long ago stopped referring to victims by name. Keeping them impersonal was a survival tactic that had kept him alive and sane.

He contemplated the facts so far. It was possible the deaths were related, or that a single killer might have used another death to distract the police and cover for a murder. He had to interview each of the victims' families and friends, look for a motive.

He also wanted to know why the killer had left that piece of black rock as his calling card.

Night cast its claim on the sky and land, painting shadows along the path as he and the sheriff headed to the squad car. A red-tipped hawk with a breathtaking wingspan soared above the ridges, and Vincent paused to watch it. When the bird found its prey, it would swoop down and tear it apart with its sharp talons. The low growl of a mountain lion echoed from a distant peak, its hunger call warning smaller animals to run for their lives.

Just as a killer was out there hunting for his next victim.

As he climbed in the car, and Waller guided the vehicle around the curvy mountain roads, the darkness beckoned him, drawing him into his seductive lair. He had to climb into the killer's head to discern his motive, understand his past, the reasons he chose to kill.

The reason Vincent was good at his job. He understood the drive, the hunger, the bloodlust that drove these crazies.

A sinister laugh caught in his throat, burning like acid eating at his control. His father had told him he had bad blood, that he was just like him.

If he allowed the dark side to win, would he become as cruel and violent as his father?

>———

Clarissa buried her head in her hands and tried to drown out the voices. A dozen more dead had risen, crying out to her, but she had to shut them out. Had to focus.

Why were they all bombarding her now? Normally she could control them. She avoided the graveyard and the mines where so many had died. But the past two days, her head had been filled with tormented pleas.

Doc Pirkle, the town's resident physician, stepped from Eloise's room with a frown. "Are you all right, Clarissa?"

She nodded, her head throbbing from the incessant cries. But she couldn't complain, not when Eloise was suffering. "Yes. How is she?"

"Struggling. But I gave her a sedative, so she should sleep through the night."

He glanced toward the back. Ronnie had disappeared outside to work on the back porch he was building for Eloise's weathered house. The sound of him pounding nails into wood drove home the force of his anger, but the chore was therapeutic, a coping technique.

A picture of Tracy sat on the counter, and she ran a finger over it. Another image flashed in her head. Tracy climbing into a faceless man's car. The terror in her chest when she realized the man was dangerous.

"I'm worried about them," Doc Pirkle said.

"I'll take care of them tonight," she said softly.

He squeezed her hands. "Your grandmama and mama, God bless their souls, would have been proud of you."

Clarissa tensed, willing herself not to react. Her grandmother yes, her mother—no. Clarissa had tried to forgive her mother for leaving her, but the ache of being alone all these years haunted her constantly.

She had to be alone, though. No one else would understand her. Accept that her nights often meant communing with the dead. That sometimes she related to them more than the living.

The doctor let himself out, and she started to make tea, but a knock at the door made her rush to answer it.

Sheriff Waller and Vincent stood on the front stoop, both looking tired. Waller mopped at his forehead while Vincent simply let the sweat trickle down his jaw without bothering to stop it, a cool expression on his face as he met her gaze.

"We came to speak to Mrs. Canton," he said without preamble.

"It's not a good time," Clarissa said. "Doc Pirkle gave her a sedative. She may be out for the night."

"It'll just take a minute," Vincent said. "I thought you wanted to find this killer."

"I do, but Eloise Canton is in shock and can't tell you anything tonight that she can't tomorrow." She jammed her hands on her hips. "For heaven's sake, I don't want her having a heart attack. I don't want to live with her death on my conscience."

For some reason she didn't understand, coldhearted Vincent took a step back. Only a fraction of an inch, but an emotion akin to pain darkened his soulless eyes before he masked it.

"If Doc thinks it best, we'll come back in the morning," Sheriff Waller said.

Vincent glanced inside the house. "Do you know if Tracy had a computer or cell phone?"

Clarissa frowned. "I don't know. You might check her apartment."

Sheriff Waller rubbed the back of his neck, then turned to Clarissa. "Do you need a ride home?"

"No, thanks. I'm staying with Eloise and Ronnie tonight."

"All right, but call if you need anything." The sheriff gave her hand a squeeze, and she smiled in gratitude, knowing she had her work cut out for her. Eloise would likely wake with nightmares, and Tracy's ghost would probably haunt her all night.

Tracy needed help to move on.

If she hadn't fully realized her fate, finding Clarissa there with her grieving mother and brother would force her unfortunate destiny to sink in. Then her wails of sorrow would begin.

And the only way to end them was for Clarissa to see that Tracy's killer paid. Doing that meant working with the sheriff and Vincent, a man who had his own dark secrets.

A man who made it obvious he didn't want anything to do with her.

~

"We need to go to the girl's apartment tonight," Vincent said. "And call a CSI team to examine Tracy Canton's car."

"Can't it wait until tomorrow?" Sheriff Waller asked. "I'm dead on my feet."

"You want to find Tracy's Canton's killer, then it's tonight. By tomorrow the scene and her car might be contaminated. The killer could have destroyed any link to him he might have left behind."

Waller heaved a weary sigh and then phoned for a team to confiscate the car and another one to meet them at Tracy's house as he drove to a run-down apartment complex on the outskirts of the town.

"I want this place dusted for prints," Vincent told the CSI. "Anyone and everyone who has been in here needs to be accounted for."

The crime scene investigator nodded and the two young men went to work.

"All right, Waller, let's tear this place apart," Vincent said. "Look for notes, phone bills, journals, calendars, a computer, cell phone, anything that might offer a clue as to who Tracy might have met up with lately."

Waller rubbed his chest, his ruddy cheeks showing his age and failing health, but nodded. He might not like to take orders, but at least the man had enough sense to admit he was in over his head and to ask for help.

Which meant he was smarter than that worm of a deputy who had his dick in a knot over Clarissa.

Shit. He had to get his head back in the case and forget about Bluster. It was possible a local might have snapped and turned into a killer. A local whom no one would suspect, whom the girls might willingly trust.

He spotted the computer in the alcove to the left, strode toward it, then sifted through the mail on the small desk. "Here's her cell phone bill."

Sheriff Waller glanced at it and grimaced. "Don't see anything suspicious."

"Maybe not, but let's cross-check the numbers with the other victims' phone records, see if they had any friends in common. Check their landlines, too. Maybe we'll find a connection."

Waller scratched his chin. "I'll request the landline records first thing in the morning."

"While you're at it, get Bennett's. We need to know if Tracy called him when her car broke down," Vincent said. "I'd like to take the computer and examine it."

Waller nodded, and Vincent carried it to his car. If Clarissa was right, and the unknown subject—UNSUB—used the victim's greatest fear as his MO, he could glean that information by asking questions. Reading a journal. Talking to her or e-mailing her. Hacking into a chat room. The possibilities were endless.

They spent the next hour searching and found no leads, no journal with personal dates, just Tracy's school planner, a calendar listing doctor and hair appointments, and a neat, orderly apartment. He did find service records on her car, work that had been done at the dealership where she'd bought it, not at Bennett's garage.

Waller's cell phone rang, and he answered it, mumbling beneath his breath. A minute later, he disconnected and turned to Vincent. "That was Bluster. He brought Bo Bennett in for questioning."

Vincent nodded. "Then let's go have a chat with Mr. Bennett."

＞

As Vincent and Waller entered the police station, the sound of cursing echoed through the halls.

"What do you mean dragging me in here, Bluster?" Bennett growled. "I told you where l was last night."

"Just settle down, Bennett," Bluster ordered.

Vincent studied the suspect. Bo Bennett was a meathead thug with prison tattoos and a bad attitude. His dark eyes narrowed with accusations as Vincent leaned against the scarred table where Bo was seated, his beefy body swelling over the wooden slatted chair.

"We just need to ask you some questions, Bennett," Vincent said.

"Who the hell are you?"

Vincent flashed his ID. "Special Agent Valtrez, FBI."

"He's here at my request," Waller cut in. "Tracy Canton was murdered last night. Where were you, Bennett?"

Bennett released a string of expletives. "Just because I have a rap sheet, you're going to blame every shitty thing that happens around here on me."

"It's a fair question," Vincent said calmly. "Answer it."

Bo scrubbed a scarred hand through his buzz cut, sweat beading on his forehead. "Like I told the deputy, I was with my girl. She'll verify it."

Vincent leaned toward the man, his tone lethal. "She wouldn't lie for you, would she?"

A sinister smile slid across the man's chiseled jaw. Then he shrugged.

Vincent shoved a pad of paper toward him. "Write down her name, number, and address."

Bennett cursed again but did as he was requested, then shoved the pad back toward Vincent. "She knows I'm trying to make an honest living with the tow service." A lecherous grin lit his eyes. "Besides, she keeps a tight rein on me, if you know what I mean. Don't want any of the other women stealing me away."

"Yeah, 'cause you're such a catch," Vincent muttered sarcastically.

Bennett chuckled, then stood. "Now I've answered your question. If you aren't going to arrest me, I'm out of here."

Waller held up a hand. "Let me call and verify your alibi first."

He stepped from the room to make the call, and Vincent crossed his arms. "One more thing, Bennett. Tracy's car broke down last night. Did she call you for help?"

Bennett's eyes narrowed to slits. "What? You think she called me to tow her car and I killed her?"

Vincent simply arched a brow.

A vein bulged in Bennett's jaw. "Listen, I paid my dues. I'm trying to make an honest living with my garage. I wouldn't jeopardize it for a piece."

Waller walked back in with a scowl. "All right, Bennett, you can go for now. But don't leave town."

Bennett stalked to the door, but Vincent caught the man by the collar. "If I find out you killed Tracy or any of the other girls, I'll see that you pay." His gaze shot to the scars on the man's hand and face. "And those will look like child's play."

For a brief second, fear flickered in Bennett's eyes, but he masked it. "Fuck you."

Vincent grinned and watched him go, although he felt the darkness in him begging to be unleashed.

He hadn't been lying. He didn't like the SOB one bit. And if Bennett had mutilated Tracy, he'd show him what it felt like to have someone carve his flesh into pieces and play in his blood.

~

Bluster muttered a curse as he headed back to the cabin he'd rented north of Hell's Hollow, parked, and let himself in. He didn't want the feds here in Eerie, not poking into his business.

Didn't want Valtrez looking into his past or knowing that he had dated all three of these victims.

Dammit. There was definitely something between Valtrez and Clarissa.

He grabbed a beer and booted up his computer.

The fed's files were sealed, but he dug around and stumbled on an article about his parents. At age ten, Valtrez had been found outside the Black Forest covered in dirt and blood.

He'd claimed he didn't remember what had happened, that he thought his father might have hurt his mother.

The authorities checked their home but the parents were gone, so the courts ruled child abandonment, and Valtrez was sent to live in a foster home.

Bluster rocked back in the wooden chair. Did Clarissa know about this?

He had plans to see Sadie Sue tonight, but he had to talk to Clarissa first. Find out what she knew about Valtrez.

And just how much she knew about these recent murders.

⤙

Sadie Sue LaCoy devoured a bowl of chicken and dumplings, washing them down with a jelly jar of sweet tea, then left Hell's Kitchen. A place where she felt safe, where she could hang out with Myrtle, the head waitress who'd been like a big sister to her ever since Sadie Sue had got pregnant at sixteen and her mama had thrown her out. A place where she ate comfort food and pretended that she was going home to her baby boy to read him bedtime stories instead of heading to work at the Bare-It-All Truck Stop, where she read a different type of bedtime story to the locals. Men who cheated on their wives, and the truckers and out-of-towners who stopped off the expressway for a cold beer and a tittie show.

At least God had gifted her with big breasts, and at her age, they were still perky and high and bounced all over the place, which earned her far more tips than she could get slaving as a waitress at the Kitchen. Knowing she'd work off those dumplings dancing the next three hours, she didn't skimp on dinner like some of the young girls did. 'Sides, from her experience, men didn't want to bang a bunch of bones but appreciated curves and enough ass to grab hold on when they rammed inside you.

Earning a little extra cash on her back had first made her feel cheap, but she needed the money too damn bad to turn it down. After the first few times, she'd gotten used to the sex, and when she closed her eyes, every man looked and felt pretty much the same.

Except for the ones who wanted to slap her around. Those she got away from fast. Her mama might have thought she was stupid, but she wasn't.

Sadie Sue had learned a lot about survival in the past few years, and she was nothing but a survivor.

She slipped through the back door of the Bare-It-All, hurried to the dressing room, and began to strip. What should she be tonight? The French maid? Town saloon girl? Motorcycle babe?

Donning a robe, she tiptoed to the back of the stage and peered through the curtain. Saturday night, the house was packed. Some regulars, a couple of leather-clad bikers, a man wearing a black cape, his face in the shadows.

Maybe the Little Red Riding Hood costume tonight. After all, men were animals. She'd play the innocent little girl the wolf wanted to eat.

As long as he had cash, she'd let him have her.

CHAPTER EIGHT

Vincent's dark side always emerged at night.

He tried to ignore the incessant draw as he and the sheriff settled into Hell's Kitchen.

Waller scribbled down the name and directions to a mountain lodge that would rent him a cabin to stay in while he was working on the investigation.

Vincent hoped to hell it wasn't long. He didn't like this damn town, didn't like the mountains or the mines and caves that held secrets. Didn't want the reminders of his childhood and his father, or the echo of the wild in the dark recesses of the woods, of the Black Forest, calling him to join them. To find out what had happened there and how he'd survived it.

Tonight his blood sizzled in his veins, his temperature rising as if an inferno burned deep in his soul, and the allure of the hunt tugged at his sanity.

As did his primal urges. Man was, after all, part animal. He had needs. Cravings.

Vincent needed sex. Craved the feel of his cock pump-

ing in and out of a female body. Needed the release of
his seed spurting into the warmth of a willing woman.

He would not have that release tonight. Not here in
Eerie while he was on a case. Not when the woman he
hungered for was Clarissa.

God, he'd never expected to want her so badly. But
fantasies of her filled his head, images of her tender lips
on his flesh, milking him. The feel of her skin, hot and
tingling beneath his hands as he stroked her to orgasm.

He'd expected that same little homely kid when he'd
arrived, not a sex siren. The moment she'd opened the
door at the Cantons', his eyes had zeroed in on that lone
droplet of perspiration trickling down her neck into that
sweet spot between her breasts. He'd watched it disappear beneath the thin layer of her tank top, and his
tongue had flicked out to lick it off.

He fisted his hands. Hellfire and damnation. He was
losing control. He had to get a grip. No blackouts while
he was here. No sex, either. At least not with a woman
who talked to ghosts.

He saw enough of the dead in his line of work, didn't
need her telling him what they said.

Or hinting that she could talk to his mother.

Then she'd know he was evil like his father.

Waller swerved into Hell's Kitchen's parking lot, the
red flaming sign spiking upward in an arc with the name
painted in bold yellow. Several cars crowded the lot,
and as the men climbed out, complaints about the heat
wave—and the danger a drought posed to the streams,
the river, and the locals' gardens—rumbled around him.

Others huddled, whispering and worried about the
recent deaths of the young women, and Tracy Canton's
murder. Two blue-haired women in contrasting knit

jumpsuits gave him a wide berth as he entered with the sheriff, as if he might be a suspect, not here to help.

Or maybe they sensed his darkness.

Inside, the red and yellow decor mimicked the devil's lair. Why did these people frequent a place that served as a reminder of Hell's Hollow, where so many of their loved ones had died?

"That's Myrtle." Sheriff Waller gestured toward a heavyset woman with spiked orange hair. "She makes the best country fried steak and fried green tomatoes in the county." He handed Vincent a menu. "Plus a mean rattlesnake stew—that is, if you don't mind setting your throat on fire."

He didn't care what he ate, foodwise. Waller ordered the stew and he ordered a burger, ignoring Waller's scowl as he requested it rare.

"So what's the plan for tomorrow?" Waller asked.

"I'm going to check Tracy's computer tonight, see what I find. If she has a MySpace or Facebook page, e-mails, if she might have joined an online dating service."

"I doubt Tracy Canton did any of that. She was a country girl, didn't have much money for extras."

"Listen, Waller, we have to check every avenue. You'd be surprised at how technologically adept kids and young people are today."

Waller conceded and sipped his sweet tea, then dug in to his food as if he hadn't eaten in a decade. Vincent bit into the burger, savoring the blood-red meat.

"Let me see the files on the other two girls' deaths, then I'll review them tonight and we can meet tomorrow and regroup."

Waller nodded again, his expression grave. "I want folks to feel safe around here. But I have a bad feeling."

"How long has Bluster been with you?" Vincent asked.

Waller frowned. "Actually, he just came on board. Transferred here from Nashville. Why?"

"Just curious." He hadn't pegged Bluster for a suspect, but if he was new in town, maybe he should. After all, everyone in town would trust the deputy.

Waller slathered butter on a biscuit. "You know, there is another new resident I forgot about. A real-estate developer. Bought up some property and built a development on the outskirts of town. Think he owns the apartments where Tracy lived."

Vincent's fork clattered. "Have you questioned him?"

"No, but I'll bring him in first thing tomorrow."

"Good. Is there a place in town the young people go to hook up? A bar, club, maybe?"

Waller seemed to ponder the question. "Well, some of 'em ride up to Hawk's Ridge to hang out. It's a lookout spot over the mountain. And a few go bowling or to Six Feet Under, a bar down the street. But ones looking for some T and A go to the Bare-It-All club on Wiley Street."

Vincent's body twitched at the thought. The temptation to take a trip there tonight made him itch to leave.

But the case came first. Tonight he had files to review.

Tomorrow night would be soon enough. He'd check it out in case the killer had chosen it as a spot to search for his prey.

Besides, a strip show would be the perfect distraction to keep him from lusting after Clarissa.

Clarissa checked on Eloise and found her resting, and Ronnie had retreated to his room with a six-pack of PBR.

She'd taken his keys and hidden them, deciding a drunken tear at home was better than him being on the road in his condition, full of anger and male testosterone.

Unable to sleep for worry, she retrieved her computer from her car and booted it up, checking her calendar for the next day. She made notes to cancel two appointments so she could be free to offer grief counseling for the Cantons and Tracy's friends and to confer with Vincent and the sheriff.

Headlights blared up the drive, and she checked the window. The deputy's car. He parked and climbed out, and she opened the door and met him on the front porch. His serious expression sent alarm through her.

"Hi, Tim. Any news?"

He gave a clipped nod. "I thought there was something odd about that feebie. You should take a look at this." He shoved a printed file toward her.

Her throat closed as she read the contents.

Ten-year-old Vincent Valtrez was found near death on the edge of the Black Forest. Valtrez was in shock and had suffered numerous physical injuries.

Authorities reported that the boy claimed he thought his father had murdered his mother, but authorities found no evidence of a murder.

Although the child sustained a blow to his head, doctors say there should be no permanent brain damage, but he did suffer acute memory loss and couldn't tell authorities how he'd survived the Black Forest.

Legendary tales about the dangers in the forest abound, but three police officers ventured inside the terrifying woods to search for the boy's parents.

No one has seen or heard from them since. And no bodies were recovered.

The boy was sent to a foster home.

Clarissa swallowed back tears as she studied the picture—Vincent, dark-haired and somber, with eyes that had seen too much, dry and expressionless as the social worker escorted him from the hospital.

That photo and the pain in his eyes had haunted her as a child. Hoping to help, she'd sneaked over to the foster home and offered to talk to the spirits, to ask if his mother had passed. But he'd exploded in anger, called her crazy, and told her not to ever bother him again.

And she hadn't. Hearing him call her Crazy Clarissa like the other kids had done had cut her to the bone.

She glanced up at Tim and saw him watching her. "I knew all this, Tim. Remember I told you I grew up with him."

"What else do you know about him?"

She handed him the article. "Not much. I haven't seen him in years."

"He claimed his father killed his mother. Did it occur to you that he might have killed them?"

She sucked in a breath. Of course, she'd heard that

rumor. "He was a rough kid," she said. "And his father
was cruel and beat him, Tim. But I don't think he would
have hurt his mother." And if he'd killed his father, she
couldn't have blamed him.

His eyes narrowed, and a frisson of fear slivered
through Clarissa. "Stay away from him, Clarissa. For all
we know, he may be a cold-blooded killer."

Vincent and Waller stopped by the real estate agent's
office on the way back to the station, but a sign on the
door said the man was out of town on business.

Was this so-called trip a ruse to hide his real agenda?

Back at the cabin he'd rented, he spread the files on
Billie Jo Rivers and Jamie Lackey on the desk and examined the notes Sheriff Waller had made.

The photos disturbed him. There was something odd,
gray and grainy, like the silhouette of a person's body,
blurring the scene that he couldn't quite distinguish.

He reviewed the details of each death, searching for
connections. Billie Jo had been close to her mother; her
father was deceased. Her fiancé, Curtis Riggs, had an
alibi for the night she died; apparently he drove a big rig
and had been in North Carolina at the time of her death.
He confirmed that she was terrified of drowning and that
she would not have gone to the creek alone, especially
at night. She had no enemies, was well liked, and volun-
teered at the local Baptist church.

No one would want her dead.

Except that she had died a suspicious death.

A random killing, or were the deaths connected?

He skimmed the notes on Jamie Lackey. Jamie's father, the town drunk, claimed he hadn't seen his daugh-

ter in days, that she moved into town to be on her own. The sheriff had questioned her roommate, a girl named Wanda Gibbons, who worked at the Dollar Store. She'd been distraught over her friend's death.

Perhaps the father and Jamie had had a run-in, and he'd been angry with her because she'd defied him and moved out. Maybe the man had killed his daughter and her case wasn't related to the other two. Or maybe he had murdered her and now was killing others to cover up the crime and make it appear to be a serial killer. Although why use different MOs? And if the man was a drunk as Waller had noted, he probably wasn't smart enough to concoct such a devious plan.

Now for Tracy Canton. Waller and Clarissa had both vouched for Tracy's brother, and he had seemed genuinely upset.

Vincent spent the next hour checking Tracy's computer, searching her e-mails, looking for sites she might have visited, chat rooms she'd signed on to. Nothing struck him as suspicious. She didn't have a MySpace account, had never been on Facebook. She also hadn't joined any online dating services, and most of her e-mails were related to the online classes she'd taken from UT and the faculty at the school where she taught.

No love notes, hate notes, not even the hint of someone who disliked her.

And no communication or connections to the other girls.

He examined the girl's pocket calendar but found no notations for clubs or meetings that warranted suspicion.

He rocked back in the oak chair. Three local girls, supposedly with no enemies. All dead by different causes.

And so far, the only connection appeared to be that they were all single.

Yet Clarissa insisted their deaths were related.

He cursed, then stood, shucked off his clothes, dressed in running shorts and tennis shoes, and headed outside.

Heat seeped from the paved drive that wound through the knot of cabins standing on the side of the mountain near Redtail Creek. A central lodge housed individual rooms for rent and served a hot breakfast, but he'd chosen the cabin for privacy.

Darkness cloaked the dense thicket of trees that blanketed the ridge, but Vincent possessed keen night vision, and the deep recesses of the mountain ridges beckoned him. He sprinted into the folds, discovered a hunting trail, and jogged through the woods, the swish of tree branches brushing his arms and the twigs snapping below his feet a welcome reprieve, as if he'd finally come home.

An odd thought when he'd wanted to leave this place forever.

The silence of night met with the distant howl of a coyote, and Vincent sensed a mountain lion nearby, pacing, watching, hungry. Knowing any sudden moves might trigger a predator to attack, he kept his pace steady, the pounding of his shoes creating a calming staccato rhythm in the midst of the animals scurrying through the forest in search of food or cover.

Had Billie Jo Rivers, Jamie Lackey, or Tracy Canton tried to escape from their attacker? If so, why weren't there defensive wounds? Some kind of tangible evidence?

Something other than Clarissa's communication with the dead.

And where had the killer obtained the black rock he'd

left at each crime scene? Was the cave where Vincent's father had killed his mother nearby?

Or was there another cave of black rock in these mountains?

Adrenaline racing through his blood, he spent the next two hours searching the area. He found an old abandoned mineshaft and explored the opening, but the structure seemed unstable, so he opted not to explore it further. A cave to the north also drew his interest, and for a moment, memories transported him back in time. He could hear his father whispering his name. Urging him to go deeper. To surrender to his dark side.

To kill.

He flexed his fingers, remembered the torture he endured if he didn't comply with his father's orders, then the surge of power he'd felt when he'd choked the life out of an animal.

The grief and guilt he'd experienced after.

His father laughing, rewarding him, forcing him to take the kill home to show his mother. The pain in her eyes when she'd seen the brutal slaughter.

He'd wanted desperately to please her, to be strong, to resist his father, but he had failed.

Now he had to fight the urge to be like him . . .

But again he lost the battle. Slowly the forest blurred, the colors faded, the darkness pervaded. And he spiraled downward to the ground, falling into the black holes that drained his life and soul.

Where time lapsed and he woke with no memory.

~

Sadie Sue LaCoy was too seductive not to fuck. Too voluptuous beneath that flowing red cape not to push her to the floor and demand she pleasure him with that red-hot mouth.

Pan had touched her back, knew her fears. Knew she liked to play and be played with.

He'd do that before he killed her.

After all, he hadn't possessed a real live human's body in hundreds of years. Might as well take advantage of the perks of being a man. One of them was to take from a woman.

He would have her before he let the snakes at her.

He'd done his research, too. She had a son. Maybe she'd trade her soul for a chance to live for her kid's sake. Then he could use her to entice Valtrez. The Dark Lord had been wavering lately, having moments of nearly succumbing to his evil side. Entering the black holes made him vulnerable, brought him closer to relinquishing his soul.

Valtrez never had been able to resist a sexy woman. It was part of the charm/curse of the Dark Lords.

The Dark Lords were born demons, part beast inside, were insatiable, their lust for sex driving them just as their lust for blood did.

Pan would use both to destroy any good left within Vincent.

CHAPTER NINE

Four days until the rising

Hours later, Vincent finally emerged from the dark abyss. He rolled over, realized he was lying inside a cave, the damp coolness of the interior a haven against the infernal heat that seeped from the ground through the soles of his feet. The sound of water trickling over rock filled the ominous silence, soft and soothing compared to the panting of his own ragged breath.

He stood and wiped at the sweat rolling down his face, then turned in a wide arc to study the inside of the cave, but gray stone lined the walls, not the black rock he was in search of.

He flexed his hands, then glanced down and saw they were bloody.

Dammit. What had happened?

He dragged out a handkerchief and wiped off the blood, wracking his mind to recall the past few hours. He had no idea how long he'd been in the cave or how he'd gotten inside, but a faint stream of sunlight streaked the walls, and he realized it was almost morning.

He inspected the cave, but there were no signs anyone had been staying inside, so he jogged back toward the cabin. Broken images surfaced, of being locked in a small closet with no food or water for days, of being taken into the woods and left alone, forced to learn to survive off the land.

His heart racing, he picked up his pace, running faster and faster until he was near exhaustion and ready to collapse. He wanted to purge his soul of the evil that flowed through his veins, but it was impossible.

He was a lost soul. Had lost his soul the day he had driven a stake into his father's cold, unbeating heart.

Clarissa tossed and turned, the screams of the dead tormenting her and driving her from the Cantons' couch. Not just Tracy's voice or the other two girls', but dozens of voices from years gone by.

"I'm trying to help you," she whispered as she stumbled outside on the porch, heaving for fresh air. "I just need more time."

But the voices continued to bombard her, as did the sound of rustling leaves from the woods, cackling laughter, and screams as brittle bones crumbled, the wind scattering them like white ashes across the parched land.

"You can't stop them," a shrill voice cried.

"The devil is here," another cried.

"The evil is too strong."

"I was murdered, too. In the old mine."

"A demon took me in my cellar," another voice shouted.

"He's coming for you."

Clarissa covered her ears with her hands to drown them out. Yet the stench of fear invaded her pores, and she began to shake uncontrollably.

Shadows filled the woods behind the house, the glint of glowing eyes shimmering through the spiny leaves as if the demons roamed aimlessly, watching her torment and waiting to strike.

Her grandmother had warned her to be careful of Vincent. Tim had warned her, too. But Vincent was the only one who'd entered the Black Forest and survived.

What if he was the key to stopping this demon and the evil in the town?

~

By the time Vincent reached the cabin, dawn streaked the sky. He was physically drained and exhausted, but still his body felt tense, raw, needy. The ache of an insatiable man who needed another kind of release. The kind only a woman could offer.

He stripped off his sweat-stained clothes, turned on the shower water, and stepped inside. The soles of his feet burned from slapping against the fiery ground, tension tightened his body, knotting his shoulders and legs.

He threw his head back, letting the water pulse over him, willing it to wash away the darkness that lived inside him.

He'd thought running would alleviate his anxiety, but the smell of trees, mud, rotting foliage had only drawn him deeper into the bowels of the past.

Needing a reprieve, he banned the images of the victims, of his mother's charred body. He should have gone to that club, met up with a woman, and pounded out his tension between her legs.

He closed his eyes, slid his hand down to his cock. His balls felt heavy, swollen, craved release. Slick from water and soap, he began to knead his cock, working out the tension coiled inside him. His breath puffed out in hungry, angry pants as he stroked his shaft, each touch driven by primal desires spurred by some nameless woman.

He tried to picture the face of the one he'd fucked back home, remember the way she'd climbed on all fours, spread her ass for him and the way he'd rammed inside her.

Instead Clarissa's heart-shaped face and big cat-like eyes obliterated the image. Knowing he couldn't, *wouldn't* have her, he allowed himself a momentary fantasy, imagined her stark naked on her knees in front of him, her breasts swaying, nipples extended where he'd twisted them to hard peaks with his fingers, her pussy damp and aching for him. But she'd resist when he tried to lift her and impale her with his cock, whispering that she wanted to eat him first.

Lips parting, she licked his rigid fullness, flicking her tongue up and down his length, circling her tongue around the tip of his penis until he couldn't stand it any longer.

Still fighting his release, he gripped her head and moaned, trying to control her movements, but she enveloped him between those rose-red lips and sucked, long, deep, throaty strokes that milked and squeezed him. His hips jerked forward as she cupped his balls in her hands and massaged them, and he rammed himself deeper into her mouth, the force of her ministrations driving him over the edge. Wild, gut-wrenching sensations of pleasure and pain pummeled him, and he roared, spurting his warm cum down her throat, titillated as she swallowed it.

He cursed and leaned against the wall, spent.

It was the closest he'd ever get to having Clarissa.

But it was not enough.

~

Clarissa finally lay back down on the sofa, her head pounding from the voices, her mind swirling with thoughts of Vincent. With the possibility that he might be Eerie's only hope of salvation.

But she jerked awake an hour later, her hair damp with perspiration, her breasts heavy and aching, moisture pooling between her thighs. Odd, but she'd expected nightmares again, and the dead to visit.

Instead, another image haunted her. An image of her with Vincent Valtrez, her in submission. Her kneeling at his feet, rolling her tongue around the head of his giant cock, taking it deep inside her mouth and sucking him, feeling the warm splash of his cum slide down her throat as he plunged deeper into her mouth.

Breathing heavily, she sat up, straightened her clothing, glanced around to make sure she was alone. She could still feel the agent's thick length inside her mouth, his hands drawing her head closer. Her body yearned to have him between her legs, pumping in and out of her, filling her.

Heaven help her. She never had sex dreams.

So why had she dreamed about *him?*

And why did she suddenly sense that her dream had

been a shared fantasy, that she had somehow mentally connected to the man?

That had never happened to her before.

Had he dreamt about her?

Impossible. She connected only with the dead . . .

Yet earlier, when she'd touched Tracy's photo, she'd had a vision of her death.

Her gift must be evolving.

She stood and stretched, trying to shake off the lingering tension in her body and any thoughts of a relationship with Vincent. But her body still ached with hunger.

She had to forget the dream. She couldn't give in to temptation and throw herself at Vincent.

He would only hurt her.

He had too much baggage. A past filled with violence, just like the job he'd chosen.

All she could hope for was that he'd stop the killer in town. Then she'd say good-bye and forget about him.

⌐

Sadie Sue spread her legs wider, closed her eyes, and let the man screw her. It was the first time he'd paid for her, and she'd been surprised when he'd bound her arms and legs to the bedposts.

Funny the secrets she could tell about the people in this town.

He squeezed her tits, pinching her nipples so hard she cried out. Laughter bubbled from him, and he bounced up and down, the bedsprings squeaking as the scent of his sweat filled the air.

He moaned, his vile breath bathing her face as he leaned over to suck her neck. She twisted, playing along with his bondage fantasy, and his teeth sank into her skin.

She cried out, but he bit her again, then made a loud keening sound as he shot his cum into her.

She opened her eyes, and fear gripped her at the darkness clouding the room. The shadows spun sickeningly as his face twisted into that of a black monster.

She had to be imagining things.

But she blinked to clear her vision, and the ominous shadow remained, this time its orange eyes beaming down on her in a faceless black mask.

She tried to scream and struggled to escape, but the sound died in her throat and her limbs refused to cooperate. She was not only tied to the bedposts, but frozen in place. Had he drugged her somehow?

With a menacing growl, he raised a black hand, and suddenly a dozen snakes rained down on her, hissing and spitting.

She hated snakes, was deathly afraid of them, especially rattlers.

Yet she couldn't move, couldn't fight or escape. Fear ripped at her insides as the snakes circled her, slithering between her legs, up her arms, down her bare thighs.

The scream in her throat gurgled and came out raw, a plea for the monster to save her.

But the poison slowly seeped through her, burning her veins, causing her body to seize and convulse with pain.

"Please, I'll do anything . . ." she pleaded. "Just get them off of me . . . don't let me die . . ."

The maddening roar of darkness beckoned nearby. Heaven or hell—where would she go?

"Anything?" he hissed.

"Yes," she whispered. "Anything."

His sinister laugh chilled her to the bone, and her body jerked as death began to claim her.

"Trade me your soul," he murmured in a menacing voice that sounded inhuman. "Be my slave, and I'll breathe life back into you. Then you will live forever."

Her son's tiny face flashed in her mind just as the well of death consumed her. She'd promised to take care of him, protect him. What would happen to him if she was gone?

"Your soul?" he asked.

A snake darted his tongue out and licked at her ear; another brushed her cheek, its scaly skin scraping her tender flesh. Little Petey's face flashed in her head again. She couldn't leave him . . .

"Yes, please, whatever you want. Take my soul, and I'll do anything for you."

Clarissa shivered as a scream reverberated in her head. "Help me! Save me!"

Startled, she hugged her arms around herself and closed her eyes, struggling to see the girl's face.

But the images blurred, and instead, she saw a faceless black monster.

The demon . . .

Then a bed of snakes as they covered the girl's body. A timber rattlesnake, then another and another . . .

God . . . this creature, whatever it was, was sadistic and without mercy.

Nausea clawed at Clarissa's throat and stomach, but she fought it and ran for the phone. She had to call Vincent and the sheriff. Tell them there had been another victim.

And let them know that the killer they hunted wasn't human. He was a demon monster with a black, soulless face.

Laughter burst from Pan's lungs as he waved his hand and made the snakes disappear. Only a whisper of his demonic breath into Sadie Sue's lungs and her body surged back to life. The woman was his—a victory on his part, a soul for his collection that would aid in his journey to a higher level in the underworld.

All she needed to do now was make her first kill, and she would be Satan's servant forever.

Had Clarissa heard Sadie Sue's screams? Were the other voices he'd sent taunting her?

Another smile curved his mouth.

She had to be growing weak now, her sanity teetering on the brink of destruction.

Yes, soon she would be his, as well. He could almost taste the joy of victory and the sweetness of her demise.

CHAPTER TEN

Vincent's cell phone rang just as he finished the ham and biscuits he'd ordered in the lodge. Designed for hunters and vacationers, the oak-paneled walls held deer heads, along with stuffed trout, farm tools, hunting rifles, and photos of various hunters and fishermen showing off their prizes.

He'd requested a copy of the registry for the last six months to search for frequent visitors, out-of-towners, a name that might appear more than once or stand out. Maybe he'd find the killer here. He might be staying in the cabin next to him or in the lodge, sipping coffee this morning and enjoying the view, smug and thinking the police had no clue as to his identity.

His phone jangled again, and he checked the number, noted it was the sheriff, and connected the call while he gestured for his bill.

"Valtrez, it's Waller."

"Yeah?"

"Clarissa called and thinks there's been another murder."

Hell. He cursed, then tossed some cash on the table to cover the tab, slurped down another sip of coffee, and scraped his chair back from the table.

"Does she have a name?"

Waller sighed. "No, just that the girl screamed for help and she saw rattlesnakes."

He crossed to the lobby, a massive space with a two-sided stone fireplace in the center.

"I know you wanted to question the family and friends of the other victims, too, so I called and they're coming in at eight."

"I'll be right there."

The waitress, a twentysomething brunette with a tattoo of a butterfly on her ankle, winked at him as she rushed by with fresh coffee to fill the bar beside the registration desk. "Hurry back, sugar."

He offered her a slight smile, for a fleeting second contemplating taking her to bed. Last night's hand job had left him less than satisfied, wanting more. He needed to assuage that ache, because the woman in his fantasy the night before wouldn't end up in his bed.

Clarissa was too damn complicated, whereas the brunette had a fuck 'em and leave 'em kind of look, as if she'd been around. The kind of woman he used on a regular basis to quench his insatiable thirst for fleshy raw sex.

But he had pressing business to take care of, so he strode outside without setting a date.

Normally, even in summer, the mountain ridges offered shade and cooler temperatures, but today the blinding sun beat down on him, blasting him with heat so oppressive it was hard to breathe.

Gravel crunched beneath his boots as he walked to

his Land Rover and climbed in. He activated the GPS system and headed down the mountain into town, his gaze tracking the winding road into the forest. A doe paused to stare in his direction, and his gaze caught the animal's, its eyes huge with innocence, yet a heartbeat later a hunter's shot sounded in the air, and the deer scampered away in search of safety.

Neither man nor animal was safe in these mountains.

Deputy Bluster tossed the printed article about Valtrez on Waller's desk. "Take a look at that. See who you've invited into our town."

Sheriff Waller glanced up from his desk with a scowl and took a sip of his coffee. "What the hell is this about?"

"Just read it, Waller."

The older man's jowls shook as he worked his mouth from side to side, but he lowered his gaze and read the printout. "You think I didn't know this?"

"You did, and you asked him here anyway?" Shock strained Bluster's face. "For all we know, he killed his parents. And who's to say he isn't the one killing these women?"

Waller took another sip of coffee, then leveled a calm look at Bluster. "He was only ten when his parents disappeared, and the truth is, if he had killed his daddy, I wouldn't have blamed him. That man was one mean SOB."

"All the more reason to suspect he'd be just like him."

Waller poked his tongue in his cheek. "Valtrez has an

impeccable record as a closer. Besides, he was in Nashville when I phoned and requested his help."

Bluster crossed his arms. He'd expected more of a reaction. "So you're defending him?"

"You don't understand. That's the reason I requested Valtrez in the first place. He went into the Black Forest and survived. He's seen things that we don't know how to deal with. And I've lived through too many of these damn eclipse years to play around." Waller scowled. "Now, stay out of his way, Bluster, and let him do his job."

Furious, Bluster stormed out the door. Waller was going to keep the guy around.

Bluster would have to be on guard. Not draw suspicion from the feebie.

He'd covered himself too well to let Valtrez find out the truth about him.

Blocking memories of forced hunting trips, of running from the pack of killer dogs on his scent, Vincent braked as he drove down the ridge, feeling the blistering heat seeping through his vehicle all the way to his bones. Five minutes later, he parked and strode inside. Waller had a pot of coffee brewed, so he poured another cup, needing the jump start of caffeine to make up for the sleepless night.

Waller greeted him in the front reception area. "Billie Jo's mama is in my office," Waller said. "And I pulled the phone records for each victim. Nothing suspicious, no similarities or common friends."

"How about Bennett's?"

"I checked those, too. No phone calls from Tracy Canton."

Vincent frowned and started toward the office.

"Wait a minute, Valtrez."

Vincent halted. "What is it?"

Waller waved the printout at him. "Bluster came in with this. I thought you should know he found it."

Vincent clenched his hands into fists. "Does this mean you want me off the case?"

Waller shook his head. "No. We need your help."

Vincent stared at him for a long minute, wondering at what Waller wasn't saying. But Waller turned and headed to his office.

Vincent followed him into the sparsely furnished room, bracing himself for an emotional scene. Beverly Rivers looked haggard and frail, her skin a pasty green.

Vincent took a seat across from her. "Mrs. Rivers, do you know anyone who would have hurt your daughter?"

"No." She wadded a tissue in her gnarled hand. "We've lived here all our lives and have lots of friends. And we were getting ready to plan Billie Jo's wedding."

She twisted her hands together until the tissue disintegrated into shreds. "It's the damn moon again. Another year of the eclipse. Bad stuff always happens then. I just never thought it would touch my family."

The anger and sorrow in her voice resurrected Vincent's anguish over his mother's death.

Vincent had seen photos of his parents when they'd married, had heard his mother talk about how Vincent's father had charmed her, how their love was as vibrant as a summer storm. But then he'd changed.

It had been a year of the eclipse then, too . . .

Vincent hadn't understood the significance. Now he wondered . . .

Was that the trigger that had caused his father to change? To mentally and physically be so cruel that he'd take his own wife's life?

Exhaling, he turned back to the case at hand.

The next hour and a half passed, strained, as he questioned Billie Jo's fiancé, as well as Jamie's father and her roommate, Wanda, who claimed Jamie had gone to Six Feet Under to meet some friends for a drink. But according to the waitress Waller had spoken with, Jamie had never showed.

Vincent made a mental note to stop by the establishment and question the bartender, see if he remembered a stranger in the bar or someone who might have looked suspicious.

As soon as Wanda and Mrs. Rivers left, Deputy Bluster stormed in, hands on his hips. "I told you I already questioned these people. Why do you have to put them through this again?"

"Because it's my job," Vincent snapped. "When a tragedy first occurs, sometimes the victim's family and friends are in shock and can't focus enough to recall details. After a few days, they begin to look back and remember little things, sometimes something important that offers a lead."

Irritated, Vincent strode back to the front room for more coffee, leaving Bluster to cool his heels. The bell on the door jangled, and Vincent glanced up as the door screeched open. Clarissa entered, a green tank top hugging her voluptuous breasts, a long, gauzy skirt floating around her ankles and drawing his eyes to her toes. Red-hot like the center of a burning coal.

Shit.

He'd never had a foot fetish, but for some reason he imagined licking those toes.

Sick bastard, that's what he was. He didn't even like the woman—how could he lust after her?

His need had nothing to do with *her,* he told himself.

He was simply a sexual animal who couldn't be satisfied.

Not with any one woman.

Desire rippled through Clarissa at the blatant hunger in Vincent's eyes.

But she couldn't explore a fantasy with him, not when they were standing in the middle of the police station with her mind crowded with pleas from the dead.

Not when they had another girl's body to recover.

Heat flamed in his eyes again, though, the hard set to his jaw sending a frisson of need through her.

She tensed. Tim was right—Vincent was dangerous to her. But not physically. On a sexual level. He made her imagine doing things she'd never fantasized about before.

Like being on her hands and knees and loving him. Even now, with anxiety over the evil in the town needling her, she felt drawn to him, knew that if he ever took her to bed she'd let him do whatever he wanted to with her.

Deputy Bluster stormed into the room, muttering under his breath, but paused when he noticed Clarissa. His expression immediately changed into a smile. "Morning, Clarissa."

She struggled for composure. "Hi, Tim."

Vincent's expression hardened, but he stepped aside, and Tim moved nearer as if to claim his territory.

Vincent poured himself a cup of coffee, then filled a second one and handed it to her. "You called the sheriff about another missing girl?"

She nodded, surprised at his gesture. "Yes. He used snakes this time."

Vincent's jaw tightened. "You don't have a name or face?"

She shook her head, mentally straining for a clear picture of the girl's face, but everything was vague. "Not yet. But I hope she'll talk to me again."

"How about Mrs. Canton? I thought you were bringing her in."

"She wasn't feeling well." Clarissa sipped the coffee, grateful for something to do with her hands. "I suggested she try to eat something, said we'd stop by later."

Waller loped in, pulled at his chin, the craggy lines of his face more pronounced this morning, as if the case had already added ten years. "Clarissa, you know anything else about the girl?"

"I'm afraid not. Have you heard anything?"

He rubbed a hand across his cell phone where it was belted to his waist. "No bodies have turned up, but I just got a call from Trina Lamar. She babysits little Petey, Sadie Sue LaCoy's little boy. She said Sadie Sue didn't come home last night at all."

Tim sighed. "You know she works at the Bare-It-All. She probably got hooked up with a john and just hasn't shown up yet."

"Maybe." Sheriff Waller shrugged. "But Trina's worried and upset. Petey is crying for his mama, and Trina says that Sadie Sue is always home by five. She's obsessive about being there in the mornings when the baby wakes up."

Vincent brushed Clarissa's arm, a gentle touch that took her off guard.

She expected him to argue, but instead he cleared his throat. "Let's go check it out. Then I want to talk to Mrs. Canton."

Their gazes locked, the heat between them simmering as his dark eyes pierced hers. She read his distrust, suspicion, hesitation. For a brief second, something else flickered in his eyes, a moment of truth, as if he accepted, maybe even suspected that she might be right.

Or had she imagined it because she wanted him to believe in her more than she'd wanted anyone's approval in a long time?

~

Daisy Wilson had crawled in bed as soon as she'd arrived home this morning at seven a.m. She'd been working the swing shift for so long that she'd adjusted to the hours and slept during the day, but the heat in the house woke her midmorning.

Or maybe it was the noise.

She jerked her eyes open and reached to tear off her sleep mask, but before she could rip it off, a breath fanned her cheek.

J.J.? Had he slipped inside without her hearing him come in? Was he here to surprise her? Tell her he'd stopped drinking, that he wanted to be with her more than he wanted the bottle? Or that he wouldn't ask her to play out his twisted fantasies?

The scent of something rancid teased her.

When J.J. was drunk, he liked to get rough. The very reason she'd broken it off with him.

She tried to scream. But two large hands pressed her down into the mattress. She tried to fight, but her body was paralyzed.

What had he done to her? Why couldn't she move her arms and legs? Had he drugged her in her sleep?

Please, J.J., she whispered. But no sound emerged from her mouth. Only the sound of him moving. Suddenly she realized he was undressing her. She tried to see his face, but the room was so dark, all she could make out was shadows. A hulking, large black shadow.

Panic seized her. Was it J.J., or someone else?

Hot air seared her skin, air that she realized was his breath as he moved down her body, pulling at her clothes until she lay completely naked.

A sob caught in her throat, and tears spilled down her eyes. He was going to rape her, then kill her.

But instead of climbing on top of her, he tore off a long strip of plastic wrap and wound it around her feet.

Oh, God . . .

He bound them tightly, then worked upward, winding the wrap around her legs, then around her midriff and breasts, stretching it so tautly that it cut off her circulation. He bound her arms to her sides and wound the plastic wrap around them, gluing them to her body like a mummy, then lifted her head and began to wind it up her throat.

A scream echoed in her mind. God help her. Please. She'd always been terrified of being suffocated.

The room spun. She felt light-headed and nauseated. Then a numbness seeped through her, robbing her of feeling. Snippets of her life flashed in the darkness. A time when she was little and played dolls with her sister. The day she'd buried her mama. Her brother's wedding last year, when she'd been a bridesmaid. The babies at the hospital that she tended to daily.

The fact that she wanted one of her own and hadn't had a chance to have one.

He secured the plastic wrap totally around her mouth, then her nose and eyes, and pure terror shot through her. She gasped for air, struggling to make her lungs work, but she couldn't move, couldn't breathe . . .

"Give me your soul and I'll let you live," he murmured against her ear.

What?

"Your soul," he whispered.

Then a sliver of light shattered the darkness. Her mother's hand reaching for her.

"Don't give in to him," her mother whispered. "He's evil, Daisy. He'll make you evil, as well." Her mother began to sing a hymn about redeeming grace that Daisy remembered from childhood, the very song she had sung at her mother's funeral. "There'll be no sorrow in heaven . . ."

Daisy's chest heaved for a breath, but it was futile. Her mother's hand brushed Daisy's head, soft and beckoning, comforting. Daisy stopped fighting and latched on to her voice.

"Come with me—heaven is beautiful."

She reached for her mother, let the darkness swallow her completely, knowing that the light waited for her on the other side.

That her mother would help her enter it. And then the pain would be over.

CHAPTER ELEVEN

Vincent followed Clarissa and the sheriff outside, leaving the deputy to man the station.

"Valtrez, check Sadie Sue's house. I'm going to look around town for her," Waller said.

Vincent gestured toward his Land Rover, and Clarissa climbed in, knotting her hands in her lap.

"You'll have to give me directions to where she lives."

"Go through town and turn left on Greenbriar Road," Clarissa said. "She has a trailer about a mile up on the left."

He shifted into gear, wound through the square, the sun nearly blinding him on the curve around the bluff as they left town. Clarissa pointed out a dirt road, and he veered onto it, gravel spewing from his wheels.

"Tell me about Sadie Sue," Vincent said. "Are you sure she wouldn't just take off and abandon her kid?"

Clarissa winced. "I don't think so. She had it rough growing up, and her mother threw her out when she became pregnant. But she loves that baby. She'd never just leave him." She chewed her bottom lip, then glanced out the window. "You may not approve of how she makes her living, but she's stripping to give her little boy a better life."

Vincent tried to ignore the worry in her voice, just as he tried not to notice the way the sun streaked her auburn hair and made it shimmer, and the fine bones of her hands as she stroked her arms.

Vincent spotted the run-down trailer sitting on the hill and turned into the drive. What little grass had survived the heat in the weed-infested yard was brown, and several tree stumps and broken limbs were scattered around the ground from a storm. A Chevy with peeling paint and a dented fender that probably hadn't run in years was parked in back, weeds overtaking it. A wading pool filled with water and pine needles, a cheap plastic ball, and a worn stroller sat near the sagging porch.

Without speaking, he parked and they climbed out, the sun beating down on his neck as they waded through the weeds to the steps. Clarissa knocked, and a baby's shrill cry echoed from inside, making him tense.

Children didn't like him, and he didn't belong in their innocent world.

The door swung open, and a haggard-looking older woman with Coke bottle glasses stared up at them, the crying baby propped on her ample hip. She smelled like strained peas and sweat and wore the evidence on her baggy housedress.

"Miss Trina," Clarissa said. "This is Agent Vincent Valtrez from the FBI."

Trina jiggled the baby, but the more she bounced him, the more he screamed and waved his chunky fists.

"Did you find Sadie Sue?" the woman asked.

"No," Clarissa answered. "But the sheriff is combing the town looking for her."

"Can we come in?" Vincent asked.

"Sure." She gestured toward the entry, and he followed Clarissa inside the cluttered room. The smell of baby formula, dirty diapers, and musty clothing permeated the air. The den was filled with tattered furniture, a TV set with a rabbit-eared antenna, and a playpen full of plastic toys.

"I just can't seem to quiet Petey." Miss Trina ran a hand through her tangled hair as she swept aside a stack of laundry piled on the sofa, then gestured for them to sit down. Instead of sitting, though, Clarissa cooed at the baby, clapped her hands softly, and reached for him.

"Come here, sugar. I'm sure Miss Trina's worn out, and you need some fresh arms."

Clarissa patted him gently, her voice so soft that it soothed the baby's screams. Like a woman born with natural mothering instincts, she claimed the rocking chair and hummed a lullaby as she rocked the baby in her arms.

The door screeched open, and Trina rushed to greet Sadie Sue. "Sadie Sue, oh, my word. We've been worried sick about you."

Vincent sized up the young woman immediately. Thick, glossy red hair, big tits showcased by a low-cut black top, and heels that made a man fantasize about screwing her wearing nothing but the stilettos.

"I'm sorry," she said in a rush. "I had car trouble, but Hadley Crane stopped by and jumped me off."

He bet the man had jumped her. "Who's Hadley Crane?"

"He's the gravedigger at the cemetery," Clarissa said.

"He has some emotional problems," Miss Trina added.

"Oh, but he's harmless," Sadie Sue said with a wicked grin. She glanced at Clarissa and frowned. "What are you doing here?"

"I was worried about you," Clarissa said.

Sadie Sue rolled her eyes. "You're just as crazy as your mama and granny. I don't want you near my son." She grabbed the baby from Clarissa and clutched him to her chest.

Hurt strained Clarissa's face, rousing Vincent's protective instincts, but he refrained from comment.

Clarissa's premonition had been wrong this time. Sadie Sue hadn't been missing, hadn't been attacked by venomous snakes. She had simply been screwing some john.

And just when Vincent was beginning to believe her.

The redhead offered him a tentative smile, and Miss Trina introduced him, her expression changing to interest as she looked him up and down. "I heard there was an agent in town. Didn't know he looked like you, darlin'."

Clarissa's shoulders snapped back as she stood and walked toward the door. "We're glad you're all right, Sadie Sue. But next time you might call, especially since three women have died around here in the past few weeks. The sheriff is out hunting for you."

Her face blanched. "I . . . I'm sorry. I guess I didn't think . . ."

"Forget it. But do call next time." Clarissa walked through the door and down the steps to the car.

Vincent headed to the door behind her, but Sadie Sue caught his arm. "I'm really sorry, Agent Valtrez. If you want to stop by the Bare-It-All tonight, I'll give you a free lap dance to make up for your time."

He pulled away, heat scalding his neck as he descended the rickety steps and crossed the drive to the car. Sadie Sue was damned attractive and had just offered him an out for his sexual needs. Maybe he'd take her up on her offer.

After all, he needed something to distract him from Clarissa.

Seeing her with the child had disturbed him. He didn't want to like her, but he couldn't help but admire those protective motherly instincts she had for another woman's baby.

What would she do if a child of her own were attacked?

The same thing his mother had done—protect him with her life.

Yes, Clarissa was the type of woman who would want a family, who needed one to be complete. Another reason he couldn't touch her.

But he could sate his hunger with Sadie Sue tonight at the Bare-It-All. A double whammy—he'd question the bartenders and workers for anyone suspicious, a predator hunting down women.

The sooner he caught this killer, the sooner he could leave this hellhole of a town and forget about Clarissa and his past.

Because the longer he stayed here, the stronger his memories were becoming. The more he thought his father's spirit was still close by. That evil thrived in this town and wanted to own him, just as it had his father.

And the only way to escape the darkness was to leave this place forever.

≈

Clarissa clenched the door handle, swung it open, and climbed in the car, steam oozing from her pores. How dare Sadie Sue leave her son all night without calling, letting everyone worry. How dare she accuse Clarissa of being crazy.

And how dare she blatantly come on to Vincent in front of her child and Miss Trina.

Not that Clarissa cared if the man got it on with Sadie Sue, but he was here on business. And Sadie Sue was a slut.

Vincent slid into the driver's seat, started the Land Rover, and headed down the graveled drive without speaking.

She'd been so certain that Sadie Sue had died.

He probably thought she was crazy with her visions of snakes. But the images had been so real, she could still see the rattlesnake's cold scales, the creature slithering across the woman's skin. She could still hear her shrill, desperate cry for help.

Had her vision been of another girl dying instead of Sadie Sue?

"What's wrong, Clarissa? Aren't you glad that Sadie Sue is safe?"

She bit her lip. "Yes, of course."

"What do you know about this guy Hadley Crane?"

Clarissa shrugged. "He's a little odd, keeps to himself. I think he might have suffered a head injury when he was young. As a teenager his mother sent him away for a few months. Rumors were that he had a breakdown." She paused. "Of course, I don't always listen to rumors."

His gaze caught hers. "Meaning there were rumors about me?"

"Yeah, but there were ones about me, too."

He nodded. "Kids can be cruel."

Again she felt that connection with him as she had as a child.

Then the moment passed, and he was back to business. "You sense any bad vibes from Crane?"

"You mean, do I think he's dangerous?"

"Yes."

She contemplated her answer. "Not really. I've heard he takes medication to control his mood swings, but I don't think he's bright enough to orchestrate these murders without leaving evidence behind."

He nodded and lapsed into silence.

But she was curious about where Vincent had been during the years after he'd left Eerie. "What made you decide to join the FBI?"

His fingers tightened around the steering wheel. "I like to track killers."

"You were in the military before?"

"Yeah, after juvy."

She laid her hand on his arm. "I'm sorry. I heard the foster homes didn't work out."

He shrugged off her hand and concern. "Couldn't blame them for not wanting a kid like me."

"You deserved better," Clarissa said.

His jaw tightened as he maneuvered a winding curve and veered onto the road that led to Eloise's house.

"Let's drop it and concentrate on finding out what

happened to these girls. That is what you want, isn't it?"

Confusion muddled her brain, yet the whisper of the dead girls' pleas for help reverberated in her head, and she nodded. "Yes."

The remainder of the ride passed in strained silence. He'd made it clear he wasn't interested in her personally.

She had to accept it and forget that she was attracted to him.

All that mattered was that he stop this killer.

Her grandmother had said that the demon could possess a body.

But whose had he taken?

CHAPTER TWELVE

Mrs. Canton, can you think of anyone who would want to hurt Tracy?" Vincent asked.

Although the temperature in the small unair-conditioned house had climbed to at least a hundred, she cradled a cup of hot tea in her hands as if they needed warming. "No, everyone loved Tracy. She was a sweet-heart."

Clarissa hovered close to Eloise as if she thought the woman might need protection from Vincent. The real-ization irked him, although he didn't understand the rea-son. "Was Tracy dating anyone?"

"Not that I know of." She blew on the steam rising from the mug. "Although a while back, she went out with that boy Lamont Franklin. He's a bartender over at Six Feet Under." She pursed her lips in disapproval. "I never did like him much. He and his mama were pure heathens, didn't believe in going to church."

"Did Tracy have a journal or diary?"

She shook her head. "No, not since she was a little girl."

They talked for a few more minutes, but the woman had nothing more to offer. She loved her daughter, thought she was perfect, and repeatedly expressed disbelief that anyone would hurt her. Finally he thanked her, and he and Clarissa left.

"Where is this place, Six Feet Under?"

"Beside the graveyard on the edge of town."

Why was he not surprised? The diner was named Hell's Kitchen; they had a bar overlooking a cemetery.

"Let's stop by and see if that real estate developer is back in town. He owned Tracy's apartment complex. Then we'll head to the bar."

She nodded and gave him directions, and a few minutes later they stopped at the man's office in the square.

"Simon Thorone," the man said as he shook Vincent's hand. "What can I do for you?"

Thorone was in his thirties, five-eleven, medium built, neat hair, wore a sport coat and tie, and his briefcase overflowed with paperwork, files, and blueprints. Seemed legitimate. Nothing stood out as suspicious.

Vincent explained about the investigation and listed the dates of the victims' deaths. "Where were you on each of these dates?"

Thorone consulted his PDA and showed it to Vincent. "I've been out of town for two weeks. Here's my schedule."

"You have others who can verify you were with them?"

"A boardroom full," Thorone said. He whirled around to his computer, printed out the list, and handed it to Vincent. "You can contact the names on this list and they'll confirm what I just said."

Vincent nodded and took the list. The man's confidence either was a show or he was telling the truth.

"What did you think?" Clarissa asked as they climbed in the car and headed to the bar.

Vincent shrugged. "I'll verify his story."

"I don't think he did it," Clarissa said. "I didn't sense anything evil about him. Except that he might be making a mint off some of his property."

Vincent didn't bother to comment as he made the turn to the bar and parked. The wooden building was a renovated garage, and inside the furnishings were rustic, mostly wooden chairs and picnic-style tables. A few patrons were scattered throughout. Hushed whispers and stares followed them as he made his way to the counter. A short Native American woman with a single braid that hung to her hips greeted him.

He flashed his ID. "I'm looking for Lamont Franklin."

She gestured toward the steps. "He's working the rooftop bar."

Vincent strode upstairs, a hand at Clarissa's back as she preceded him. The sun had faded, and amazingly, a light breeze ruffled the treetops. Two truckers sat at a table sipping beer and eating burgers, while a young couple shared French fries and tapped their feet to the country tune wailing through the sound system.

Lamont Franklin was midtwenties, around five-eight, and thin, with a tattoo of a snake on his upper arm. His shaggy brown hair brushed his collar, and his beady eyes raked over Clarissa as she approached, as if she was a tall drink of water that he wanted to sip badly.

"What can I get you?"

Vincent propped his hip against the counter. "Some information."

Lamont scowled. "Gotta order if you want answers."

Vincent narrowed his eyes. "Scotch, straight up."

Clarissa smiled. "I'll have a glass of merlot."

Lamont grinned at Clarissa. "How about food? We make a mean venison burger."

Vincent ordered one, while Clarissa chose a chicken sandwich and fries. Then they claimed a table facing the cemetery beneath a giant oak. Several patrons had carved initials into it, announcing they were couples. Vincent almost laughed at the ridiculousness. Love and happily-ever-after did not exist, not in his world.

They sipped their drinks silently, and when Lamont brought their food, Clarissa introduced him. "Lamont, this is Special Agent Vincent Valtrez. He's investigating the deaths in the area."

Lamont shifted on the balls of his feet. "Yeah?"

Vincent sipped the scotch. "Tell me about you and Tracy Canton."

His face contorted. "Tracy? God, I heard about her murder. That was awful."

"Where were you the night she died?" Vincent asked.

"Working till two. Ask Nina downstairs. We closed together."

"What happened between you and Tracy?"

He shrugged nonchalantly. "We went out a couple of times, but her old lady trashed me so much Tracy dumped me."

"So you were serious about her?" Clarissa asked.

He hung the cloth over his shoulder. "Could have been. But hey, she ain't the only chick around."

"Bet you were pissed when she broke it off," Vincent said.

Lamont frowned at him as if recognizing the underlying accusation. "Not enough to kill her, man. No chick is worth that."

"So you're not a violent kind of guy?"

He twisted his mouth sideways. "Well, I wouldn't run from a fight, but I don't go around starting them, either."

"Do you know anyone who'd want to hurt her?" Vincent asked.

"No."

"Did she date anyone after you?"

He folded his arms across his chest. "Actually, I saw her with that deputy a couple of times."

Clarissa's eyes widened in surprise. Suspicion roused its ugly head inside Vincent. Bluster hadn't mentioned he'd been involved with one of the victims. Maybe the reason he didn't want Vincent asking questions.

"What was Tracy most afraid of?" Clarissa cut in.

Vincent shot her a warning look, willing her to let him conduct the interrogation, but she ignored him.

"I don't know, but she passed out at the sight of blood. I cut my hand one time on a glass, and she dropped like a rock." One of the truckers waved that he wanted a refill, and Lamont motioned that he had to get back to work.

Vincent drained his scotch. "Let us know if you think of anything else."

Lamont nodded, then hurried away, and Vincent dug in to his food.

"Lamont knew her greatest fear, but I don't think he

hurt her," she said as she plucked a French fry from her plate.

"One of your *feelings*?"

"Sort of," Clarissa said quietly. "He just didn't seem that broken up about her. And I've heard he dates a lot." She paused. "But I still think the killer struck again."

He clenched his jaw. "Look, Clarissa, I know you're trying to help here."

"But you don't believe me."

"I'm not sure what to believe at this point."

She sighed. "I know this sounds crazy. My grandmother told me that a new leader is rising to take over the underworld. And that other demons have surfaced to steal souls to please him. I think that's what's happening now."

His gaze met hers, dark and filled with doubts.

But she forged ahead. "She also said that he might have possessed a human's body. So he could be here among us."

He grunted, and she quieted. The killer was some kind of human monster, someone who was cruel and violent like his father had been, someone in town, someone they trusted. But who?

A demon?

Even though he'd seen his father throw fire with his hands, he couldn't quite believe it. Because believing his father was a demon, not just a human monster, meant that he was one, too.

He contemplated the possibility while they finished eating, then paid the bill. Clarissa caught his arm as they settled in his SUV, and heat scalded him, sending his senses tingling with arousal. "What are you thinking, Vincent?"

That she shouldn't touch him. That his resistance toward her was waning.

"I'm going to confirm Bo Bennett's alibi, then stop at the Bare-It-All to question the bartender and waitresses."

She pursed her lips. "You're going to Sadie Sue, aren't you?"

So what if he was? Maybe he'd sate himself with her tonight so he could finally get some sleep without being plagued with fantasies about fucking Clarissa. "What better way for a sicko to hunt for women than a place like that?"

"Tracy, Jamie, and Billie Jo didn't go to that bar. He wouldn't have met them there."

"But some of the girls might know something. Maybe they've had experience with a stranger or someone who's violent toward women. Someone they saw as a threat. Even a man who bragged about killing."

Clarissa's vision blurred with images of the ones who'd passed as she glanced across the cemetery by the bar before they pulled away. While they ate, she'd struggled to drown out the tortured cries, but the skeletal bodies had floated across the parched grass with outstretched brittle fingers and sightless eyes.

Billie Jo's, Jamie's, and now Tracy's spirits were wavering, clinging to the realm between the dark and light, yet not ready to cross into the light. Yet she'd also noticed a black aura floating around them—Satan had sent his soldiers to steal them over to his side.

She couldn't let him win this war.

Lost in thought, she spent the drive back to the police station with her nerves on edge. She contemplated telling Vincent about the aura, but she'd also noticed it around him on that rooftop, and she'd held her tongue. He wasn't ready to believe in demons. And maybe she wouldn't accept the possibility so easily if she hadn't seen ghosts all her life.

He parked beside her car just as the deputy pulled up and climbed out.

"Thanks for the ride," Clarissa said. "Let me know if you get any leads."

Vincent nodded and stepped from the car, then turned to confront Tim.

"Why didn't you mention that you'd dated Tracy Canton?" Vincent asked.

Bluster's eyes turned to glaciers. "I only went out with her twice, four months ago. Didn't think it was relevant."

"Or maybe you withheld information because you didn't want to be treated as a suspect." Vincent inched closer to him. "The girls around here would certainly trust you if you showed up at their door. Wouldn't hesitate to accept a ride from you or to invite you inside their homes."

"You're barking up the wrong tree, Valtrez." Bluster reared back as if he might hit Vincent, but Clarissa caught his arm.

"Don't, Tim." She turned to Vincent. "Maybe you'd better go, Vincent."

"If you're hiding anything else, Bluster, I'll find out."

"You'd better watch your back, Valtrez," Bluster shouted as Vincent climbed in his car. Clarissa held Tim back, trying to calm him as Vincent drove away.

But she wondered why Tim hadn't mentioned he'd dated Tracy. If that was the reason he didn't want Vincent around. And if he'd hidden his relationship with her, what else could he be hiding?

Vincent ignored Bluster's warning as he drove away. He wasn't afraid of the shithead deputy.

And if he found out he was killing these girls, he'd take care of him personally.

But he hated leaving the man with Clarissa. Like the other girls in town, she obviously trusted the guy.

Which would make it easy for him to catch her off guard and attack.

Curious and on edge, he phoned McLaughlin.

"How's it going?" McLaughlin asked.

"Hard to say. It looks like it might be a serial-killer case. No suspects yet, though." Hell, he couldn't exactly tell McLaughlin about Clarissa's suspicions of demons. "I want you to run a background check on the deputy. His name is Tim Bluster. See if you can dig up anything."

"Anything *specific* you're looking for?"

"Not really. But he made it plain that he doesn't want me here. And he dated one of the victims."

"I'll do it and get back to you."

"I have a list I want you to follow up on, the alibi for a real estate developer in town. He claims he was in Atlanta on business."

"Fax it over." McLaughlin hung up, and Vincent drove to the wrecker service. He parked and went inside the small front office, scanning the place for Bo Bennett.

If he wasn't their UNSUB, Vincent wanted to cross him off the list and move on. The clock was ticking.

A twentysomething big-haired blonde snapped her gum and grinned up at him.

"What can I do you for, Mister?"

He identified himself. "I need to verify Bennett's alibi." He highlighted the girls' deaths, then showed her the photos.

"My God, that's awful."

"Yeah, so tell me about you and Bennett. He says he was with you each of the nights in question."

She glanced down at the dates, then batted eyelids doused with light blue shadow. "That's right."

Bennett appeared from the back room, wiping his hands on a grease cloth. The bleached blonde sidled up beside him. "Bo moved in with me a few weeks ago, and he's been with me every night since."

"You wouldn't lie for him?" Vincent asked.

She pursed hot pink lips. "No need to. Bo did his time. Y'all need to leave him alone now so he can get his life together."

"Yeah," Bo said, yanking the girl next to him with a beefy hand scarred so badly it was nearly disfigured. "Me and Rocky here are getting hitched next month. There's no way I'd be hanging out with other chicks now."

Vincent grunted and left, then phoned Waller. "Did you ever hear back about the Canton girl's car? Was it tampered with?"

"Nope, no signs of foul play."

Vincent hung up, frustrated. If Bennett and the real estate guy weren't the UNSUB, then who the hell was?

—➤

Clarissa claimed her car and drove home, her nerves on edge, the voices of the dead girls pleading for help bombarding her.

The humidity sucked the breath from her lungs, and she powered down her window, but the metallic scent of blood and vile odor of evil laced the air, and she immediately closed it again, as if that gesture could keep the demon from touching her.

But that was impossible. He'd killed her friends.

A dozen different voices haunted her, ones she'd heard before, new ones, all crying that she should help them. Was this how her mother had felt before she took her life? Tormented and helpless?

The headlights of her car shimmied across the asphalt as she turned up the winding road to her cabin, but her heart slammed against her ribs when she drew closer. The halo of a body swinging from the Devil's Tree made her clench the steering wheel with a white-knuckled grip.

The tree the devil had planted. The one she'd seen the ghost's image on so often. The one that had held her mother.

Trembling, she parked, unease chasing goosebumps across her arms as she climbed out. The image was there again tonight. But not her mother's.

And not a ghost's.

A woman she recognized—Daisy Wilson.

Her naked body had been wrapped in plastic from head to toe, then she'd been strung up from the tree and left naked and vulnerable for the vultures to feed on.

⟶

Pan laughed at the sound of rejoicing from the bowels of the underworld. He'd called upon the lost spirits to torment Clarissa, claiming she'd offer them salvation, and they were storming her with their pleas.

Zion was now preparing for his coronation, ecstatic that Pan had brought him Sadie Sue's soul. Even more so because she would be the perfect temptation for Vincent.

Pan had issued the orders as he'd released her from her rebirth. She would seduce Vincent, turn him into a ball of sexual need that would drive him deeper into the black holes that clawed at him daily.

Clarissa had found her surprise tonight.

The girl he'd suffocated.

Above the tall, spindly trees, the full moon was already beginning to wane. He had precious little time to fill his order. Six more souls . . .

Frustration and rage heated his blood. He should have won over Billie Jo Rivers, Jamie Lackey, and Tracy Canton by now, but the medium had given them the strength to fight him.

Still, Pan beckoned them not to cross into the light, to join him, and they hung in limbo. There was still time to beat Clarissa and destroy her hold on them, but he had to work quickly.

Meanwhile, he had to keep hunting for more souls. Needed them for his own redemption.

Slipping out into the night, he reveled in the body he possessed. To think that he walked among the humans, and they had no clue as to his identity, sent a surge of joy though him.

It had been hundreds of years since he'd felt joy.

Tonight he'd find another girl. One touch and he would know her greatest fear.

Then he'd use it to kill her as he had the others.

And Clarissa would hear her screams as he sucked the life from her.

CHAPTER THIRTEEN

Vincent noted the details of the Bare-It-All club as he parked, the posters on the door featuring outlines of two naked blond dolls wrapped seductively around one another drawing his eyes.

A billboard on the main highway coming into Eerie advertised the pit stop for truckers, yet the wooden structure sat surrounded by woods, tucked away on a side mountain road that offered its patrons privacy from other passing cars. Statues of grizzly bears flanked the club's front door, and as he entered, he saw a wrap-around bar to the left, and to the right a runway stage lit by soft lighting that bounced off the near-naked woman gyrating on stage.

Wooden tables situated around the stage held patrons drinking beer and booze, shouting at the blonde, waving dollars and catcalling her to come their way. Tassels twirled from her nipples as she spun around, the thong between her ass showcasing a butt that swayed and twitched seductively.

Business first, though—then he might enjoy the show.

A topless cocktail waitress wearing a strip of red lace for panties greeted him with a tray of cigars, but he declined and headed toward the bar.

She gestured toward the tables. "You can see the show better over there."

"I know. Maybe later."

She shrugged, and he claimed a barstool. The bartender, a big burly guy wearing a wifebeater shirt and sporting a gold tooth, pushed a coaster toward him. "What'll you have, Mister?"

"Scotch, straight up."

Vincent waited until he handed him the drink, then asked his name.

"Marvin," the man said. "You new in town or passing through?"

"Visiting," he said, then identified himself. "I'm investigating Tracy Canton's murder."

Marvin shook his head and grunted a sound of disgust. "Heard about it. You got any idea who did it?"

"No. That's why I'm here. You notice any strangers in town, anyone who looks suspicious?"

"We have guys stopping through all the time. Come and go so fast I don't get their names."

"How about locals?"

The bartender shrugged. "Sure. Most every man in town's been in a few times. Not that their girls or wives know of it."

"That include Deputy Bluster?"

An odd expression twisted the man's features before he looked away. "Why don't you ask him?"

He had his answer. "Anyone stick out as violent?"

His deep-set eyes flickered sideways for a second, and Vincent noticed the jagged scar on his left cheek. "Sometimes one of the guys has a little too much sauce, things get out of hand. Nothing me and Shooter can't handle."

"Shooter?"

He flicked his thumb toward the three-hundred-pounder with the no-neck standing guard in the shadows by the door. "He takes care of things."

"Guess I'd better talk to Shooter."

Marvin nodded, and Vincent grabbed his scotch and headed toward the man. Shooter's shoulders snapped rigid as Vincent approached, and his hand automatically went to the pistol at his waist.

Vincent threw up one hand in warning. "Easy, Shooter. I just want to talk."

"I'm not a talker," the man growled.

Vincent flashed his ID. "It's about Tracy Canton's murder. You know anyone who'd want to hurt her?"

His expression remained bland. "Didn't know the girl myself."

"How about customers who enjoy roughing up the girls? Anyone come to mind?"

Shooter shifted, glanced at the door as two young guys wearing cowboy hats loped in. "No."

"Think hard," Vincent said, irritated with the defensive attitudes. Then again, hadn't the deputy warned him that the locals wouldn't talk to him willingly? "Any names ring a bell? Hadley Crane or Tim Bluster?"

Shooter leaned closer. "Crane's creepy, all right. Likes to wear a damn black cape like he's some vampire, but never heard any of the girls complain that he was violent." He clicked his teeth. "The girls like Bluster, no problem there. Word is the doctor's son, J. J. Pirkle, likes rough sex. I don't ask specifics."

Vincent finished his drink. "Thanks."

He crossed to one of the tables by the runway and took a seat. The waitress appeared again, and he ordered another drink, then probed her for information, as well, but she confirmed what he'd already been told.

The blonde onstage gathered her tips and paraded through the velvet curtain. The music changed to a sultry tune, and Sadie Sue danced in, wearing a red-feathered costume that she slowly stripped off and swung around her head, then tossed into the crowd, earning a cheer. Her breasts were draped with nothing but a red boa, and a sequined thong showcased her long legs and sexy ass. She gyrated and danced, playing up to the men as they stuffed dollar bills into the G-string. When she spotted him, her tongue flicked out to lick her lips in silent invitation.

He gripped his drink and watched her climb the pole, humping it seductively as she flung her head back, and she winked at him as he watched her. He offered her a smile, and she slowly wove the boa off and stroked it between her legs as if it was a man's hands.

Men groaned and clapped; one even reached for her, but she cleverly sidestepped his hands, spun around, and slid around the pole.

Before the dance ended, she winked at Vincent again, then blew him a kiss. He tossed down his drink and ordered another, just as the waitress leaned over and relayed that Sadie Sue wanted to talk to him.

She showed him through a hall housing several private rooms, each draped in a beaded curtain that hid little of the view of girls giving private lap dances.

Maybe Sadie Sue could tell him more about the men in the club.

A second later, he parked himself on the velvet-cushioned bench and Sadie Sue, naked as when she'd left the stage, danced in. Her tits swung forward, nipples brushing his mouth as she straddled him.

He'd had lap dances before, knew the rules, and planted his hands firmly on the cushions, knowing he couldn't touch. She danced up and down him, trailing her hands over his shoulders, down his face, using her boa to stroke his cheek as she ground against him.

"Tell me about the guys who come here," he said, gritting his teeth to maintain control. "Anyone dangerous?"

"They all are," she said with a laugh.

"I'm looking for Tracy Canton's killer. Any names come to mind?"

"Shh, honey," she whispered, then ran her tongue around the tip of his ear. "Just sit back and enjoy."

He barely controlled a moan as she stroked his length through his pants.

"Lick me," she whispered in a deep voice. "Take my nipple into your mouth and suck it."

His breath hissed between his teeth. The primal male in him couldn't deny her or himself. Her nipple brushed his lips, teasing, taunting, and he opened his mouth and bit the tip. She threw her head back and moaned, and he sucked her long and deep, the blood pooling in his loins. Sensing his need, she rubbed him harder, then freed him from his jeans. He groaned, unable to help himself as she gyrated her hips and teased the tip of his sex with her clit.

"Condom," he whispered hoarsely.

She shook her head, and he moved his hands to grip her arms. "I never have sex without one."

He wanted to flip her around, but she lifted herself off his lap and knelt, one hand grabbing his cock and massaging it. Then she wet her lips again with her tongue and met his gaze.

His blood ran cold at the evil glistening in her smile. And her eyes flickered with yellow flecks, then turned a glazed red.

Reality snapped him from his sexually induced haze. Her eyes looked exactly as his father's had when he'd turned violent in that cave of black rock.

Clarissa was right. Demons did exist. One had possessed Sadie Sue as it had his father.

He sucked in a breath, grabbed her, and pushed her away. "Who got to you, Sadie Sue?"

She jerked back, fire flaming from her eyes. "You can't stop now, Vincent. You want me too much."

"I said who are you?"

She traced a finger over his dick. "I'm the devil's child, just like you," she said with a laugh. "The girl who can satisfy you. The girl you want."

Vincent stood, crammed his dick back in his jeans, and zipped them. She grabbed his arm and tried to pull him back to her, but his cell phone rang, and he reached for it, shoving her away. Her eyes were glowing brighter now, a sickening shade of yellow and orange.

Pulse clamoring, he connected the call. "Valtrez."

"Vincent . . ."

Clarissa's voice sounded tiny, far away, streaked with terror.

His heart hammered. "What's wrong?"

"A girl . . ." she whispered. "She's dead. At my house."

Adrenaline pumped through him, and he turned to see Sadie Sue watching, her naked body still glistening with sweat, her words ringing in his ears.

I'm the devil's child, just like you.

He had to get to Clarissa. Make sure she was safe.

Because she was right about everything. Evil thrived in the town, and after seeing the change in Sadie Sue's eyes, he knew that evil wasn't human.

Clarissa trembled as she hung up the phone and stared at Daisy's body swinging from the Devil's Tree.

The dead's voices plagued her, never quieting in her head.

Yet this girl's cry never came.

Because she'd moved on?

A sob wrenched her throat. Daisy Wilson was a nurse at the local hospital. Clarissa had met her on a consulting case. After that, they'd become friends. As close a friend as Clarissa had.

Who would have killed her in such a brutal manner? Daisy helped others, saved lives. She worked on the maternity ward, for heaven's sake. She took care of babies . . .

And why had Clarissa seen images of snakes, when it appeared Daisy had been suffocated by plastic wrap or strangled by the rope?

Daisy's wide, sightless eyes stared into space, her tangled brown hair like a spider web around her pale, gaunt face where the plastic wrap had distorted her nose and features. Moonlight highlighted the red and purple bruises on her neck, and other bruises marked her chest and torso, as if the man had held her down with his knees.

Protective instincts begged Clarissa to wrap a blanket around her, not to let the police or strangers see her brutalized this way. But common sense warned her not to tamper with a crime scene.

Whoever committed this vile act had to pay.

Tree frogs croaked around her, and she suddenly glanced around for Wulf, her pulse racing. Had he attacked the man who'd done this? Or was he hurt?

Panic made her pulse race. Was the killer still nearby?

She scanned the area but saw nothing, only ghosts floating in the shadows, begging for help. A siren wailed closer, and she faintly realized that Vincent must have called the sheriff.

Lights blazed up the drive, flashing across Daisy's body, and tears caught in her throat. What good were her psychic powers if she couldn't stop this madman from killing others?

The vehicle screeched to a stop, and she realized it was Vincent's Land Rover. He jumped out and jogged toward her.

"Clarissa, are you okay?"

She nodded, then fell against him, trembling and shaking, the tears she'd managed to keep at bay overflowing and spilling down her face as a choked sob ripped from her chest. On some level she smelled another woman's perfume, but she didn't care.

She needed him to hold her and make her forget the horror in her yard and the constant barrage of the dead crying out to her.

Vincent cradled Clarissa against him, stiffening as the anguished sobs shuddered through her, and she trembled in his arms. Shock and pain reverberated in her sobs, and even the asshole that he was, he couldn't help but murmur stupid assurances that everything would be all right.

The fact that she was so strong and gutsy yet was clinging to him indicated the depth of her emotions, and he stroked her back, pressing her head into his chest, uncaring that her tears soaked his shirt.

"I'm sorry," he said in a low voice. "Sorry he did this here."

"She was my friend," Clarissa whispered, then glanced up into his eyes. "Her name was Daisy Wilson. She was a nurse."

Fury tightened his jaw at the sound of the pain in her voice. "I'm sorry, Clarissa."

Had the killer chosen these girls to torment Clarissa?

The idea sent pure hot rage and fear streaking through him. If so, why?

The sheriff's car screeched up the drive, siren wailing, blue lights flashing. Waller and his deputy jumped out and ran toward them, but Bluster's look turned feral when he saw Clarissa in Vincent's arms.

Vincent made no apologies as the men approached, but slowly Clarissa pulled away, brushed at her tears, valiantly attempting to compose herself.

"Shit," Sheriff Waller said. "Little Daisy Wilson. She was a nice girl."

"You okay?" the deputy asked Clarissa.

She nodded and sucked in a sharp breath. "I found her here when I got home tonight. It looks like the killer suffocated her with the plastic, then strung her up."

Another shudder tore through her, and Vincent stroked her back. "Why don't you sit on the porch. Let us secure the crime scene."

"Crime unit is on the way," Waller added with a concerned nod.

She clutched the edges of his shirt. "Please, Vincent, you have to find out who did this. We have to stop him before any more girls die."

"We will," he promised as he led her up to the porch. He threw a look over his shoulder, aiming at the deputy. "I'll search inside. Bluster, check the back—let's make sure this guy's not still lurking around."

Bluster growled that he didn't like taking orders from Vincent, but Waller gestured for him to do as Vincent instructed, and Bluster removed his gun and flashlight and eased around the house to the back yard.

Terror streaked Clarissa's eyes, as if she hadn't considered the possibility that the killer was still on the premises. But Vincent had to make certain. He might have waited around, might be waiting to strike Clarissa next.

"My dog . . ." she whimpered as he guided her to the porch.

"I'll find him, but let me secure the house."

She collapsed into the rocking chair on her porch, folding her arms, stroking them as if she was chilled.

Vincent gripped his weapon and flashlight, then slowly opened the door and eased inside. A quick visual assessment—living room and kitchen combination to the right, dining room to the left. Stairs in the middle, which led to the second floor. He checked the living room and kitchen, then inched up the steps.

The first room to the right he pegged as Clarissa's. A four-poster antique bed draped in a white chenille spread dominated the room, and he checked her closet and bathroom, where he noticed a clawfoot bathtub with bottles of scented bubble bath. Must be why she always smelled so damn sweet, like strawberries and vanilla.

Two other bedrooms with antique furniture revealed nothing, so he exhaled in relief and strode back down the steps. When he exited onto the porch, Bluster was climbing the steps. "Nothing out back. He's probably long gone."

"He hasn't gone far," Clarissa said in a strained voice. "He's still watching us. I can feel his presence here now. And he'll kill again."

The crime-scene unit arrived, and Waller yelled for Bluster. He glared at Vincent but, before descending the step, muttered. "Son of a bitch left her in the Devil's Tree."

Clarissa nodded, then lifted her tear-stained face and stared at the girl's body.

"The Devil's Tree?" Vincent asked.

"That's what the people around here call it," Clarissa whispered. "Like Hell's Hollow, grass won't grow around it. And in winter when it snows, the snow melts off the moment it touches a branch."

Vincent frowned, and she continued. "People think the devil planted it when he walked on this land. They thought my grandmother and mother were in cahoots with him, but they were wrong. My family has fought him for generations."

"Why did he leave her there?" Vincent asked.

"To torment me," Clarissa said in a faraway voice. "My mother hanged herself in that same tree."

Vincent's throat closed. He had no idea what to say. Clarissa had had a painful past but had never shared it with him.

Because he'd been a selfish bastard caught up in his own grief and anguish.

His heart squeezed. She was hurting and needed a shoulder, and he wanted to be that shoulder for her.

Unable to resist, he pulled her into his arms.

"My grandmother was right," Clarissa said against his chest. "There are demons here. And one of them killed my friend and left her here to send me a message."

Vincent's heart pounded. "What kind of message?"

"That he's coming after me."

⌐

Hadley loved the year of the eclipse. The year of inevitable death. The air was steeped with the smell of fear, the residents were more guarded, the trees rattled with the whistle of the dying screaming their last breaths.

He had to dig another grave. Yes, another girl would need to be buried.

Upstairs, his mother screeched. "Hadley, you sorry piece of trash, did you take your medication?"

He crushed the pills with his bare hands and dumped them in the potted plant in the den. "Yes, Mama, now go back to bed. I have to go to work."

He didn't wait for her to reply. Didn't want her cane clicking as she toddled down to check his eyes. In them, she'd see the truth. That he hadn't taken the pills in weeks. That he liked the strangers who visited him in his head. Liked the conversations they had. Enjoyed the war between them.

Especially the sick sadistic fantasies and the courage they gave him.

He lumbered out the door, yanking on his work hat as he walked down the road toward the graveyard. Heat bathed his neck, the stench of a dead animal floating through the trees. The Black Forest lay just a few miles away. Sometimes, from his open window at night, he could hear the roar of the inhuman creatures that dwelled within the forbidden land.

Those nights he dreamt about joining them, just as he dreamt about lying with the dead.

The animals. Large. Small. The humans.

Tracy Canton. Jamie Lackey. Billie Jo Rivers. He could see their faces as the mortician meticulously colored the gray pallor of their lifeless skin with thick makeup to make them look more human again.

Their naked bodies as he dressed them and placed them in the satin-lined coffin. The ground that he opened for their final resting place.

The pleasure he took as he shoveled the dirt on top of them. Their loved ones crying upon their graves as they hummed their final good-byes.

CHAPTER FOURTEEN

The next two hours became a blur for Clarissa, as if she was watching someone else's life. She found Wulf cowering in the laundry room, uncharacteristically whimpering and shaking.

What had happened to traumatize him? The dog was as sturdy as an ox and normally would fight anyone who posed a threat.

She brought him outside to the porch, gave him some water and a blanket, and petted him as Vincent conferred with the sheriff and crime-scene investigators.

"Did you see what happened, buddy?" she whispered. "Did Daisy's killer do something to you?"

A pitiful howl rumbled from him, as if he'd been terrorized, and she realized the truth. Although most animals reacted to spirits, Wulf usually handled those encounters calmly. Which meant that whatever he had come in contact with had been of another world, and completely evil.

A helplessness crept over her as dark as the storm

clouds hovering in the sky. How could she stop the demon from ending more lives?

The crime-scene investigator had photographed the scene and Daisy's body, and the medical examiner had arrived along with an ambulance to transport her to the morgue.

Finally the sheriff and Vincent climbed the steps. Wulf growled, baring his teeth at Vincent, but Clarissa laid a hand on his head and gave him a command to be quiet.

"These are the good guys, Wulf."

The dog sniffed each man, then settled by her side, his eyes still watching, guarded.

Sheriff Waller leaned against the post and scrubbed his arm across his forehead, wiping away sweat. "We'll need you to come to the station and make an official statement tomorrow, Clarissa."

She nodded. "What did the medical examiner say? What time did she die?"

"We won't know the exact time until he completes the autopsy, and that will take a while. We have to send her to the state medical examiner's office. But you were right. It appears she was suffocated someplace else, then brought here."

She knew there were probably questions she should ask, but she couldn't think straight. Poor Daisy. She didn't have any family to call.

Vincent shifted. "We found a piece of black rock in her hand, just like with the other girls."

She nodded, not surprised.

"You want to come into town, stay in the inn?" Sheriff Waller asked. "I can drive you, girl."

Clarissa stroked Wulf's fur as he edged up closer to her. "No, I'll be fine."

"I'll stay with her," Vincent offered in a gruff voice.

The deputy appeared at the foot of the steps. "Not necessary, Valtrez. I'll play bodyguard."

Waller shook his head. "I need you to do rounds tonight."

Vincent relayed what he'd learned about J. J. Pirkle at the Bare-It-All.

Waller tugged at his pants. "I'll go have a talk with Pirkle."

Waller glanced at Clarissa. "You okay with Valtrez tonight?"

Her heart thrummed in her chest, but she nodded. The deputy growled an obscenity but followed the sheriff to the car, while the crime unit climbed in their van and followed the ambulance as it rolled away.

"You look exhausted, Clarissa. Why don't you try to get some rest?" Vincent said.

She patted Wulf's head, then pushed up to her feet. "I don't know if I can sleep. I keep seeing Daisy hanging in the tree, her face distorted by the plastic wrap."

Her mother's image surfaced as well, but she couldn't talk about that painful time in her life or the nightmares that haunted her, her fear that she'd end up the same.

"Forensics didn't find much," Vincent offered. "This guy knows what he's doing and doesn't leave a trace."

"Because he's not human," she said, slipping back into that dazed state of shock.

A muscle ticked in Vincent's jaw. "You may be right."

She spun toward him. "You believe me now?"

He stared at her for a long moment, his dark eyes revealing nothing.

"Vincent?"

His breath hissed out between clenched teeth. "Let's just say that I saw something tonight that makes me wonder."

She grabbed his arms, forcing him to look at her. "What did you see?" He averted his gaze, but she refused to let him blow her off. "Tell me. We have to work together if we're going to prevent him from killing more girls."

"Sadie Sue."

Jealousy flickered through her. "You were with her?"

He shrugged, jaw tight. "I went there for information."

"Did you get what you wanted?"

Her gaze held his, the underlying meaning hanging between them.

"The bouncer told me that J. J. Pirkle likes to get rough with girls. Waller's going to talk to him."

"That's not what I meant," she said, then hated herself for asking. Did she really want to know if he'd slept with Sadie Sue or one of the other girls? His sex life was none of her business.

He arched his brow. "She gave me a lap dance, if that's what you're asking."

Irrational jealousy plucked at her. "I'm sure you enjoyed it."

He narrowed his eyes. "It was nothing personal, Clarissa."

"Nothing personal? No, I guess it wouldn't be with you. But it is with me." She released him and headed inside, heat scalding her cheeks, embarrassed that she cared what he did when he obviously didn't care about her.

Except she felt the chemistry between them. Felt it when her fingers had clutched his arms. Felt it in the way his eyes raked over her. In the way he'd just murmured her name.

The screen door screeched open as he followed her in. "What the hell was that about?"

Anger, the shock of the night, frustration . . . a dozen emotions bombarded her. "These girls' deaths *are* personal to me. So is the heat between us, Vincent. But you pretend not to feel anything, not to notice it when we're together." Her gaze latched on to his powerful, sternly set face, and her senses spiraled out of control. She wanted to touch him so badly she ached.

But touching him would be foolish, because she couldn't stand it if he pushed her away again.

Vincent snapped. The night had been hell for both of them, yet in spite of the fact that another girl had died, or maybe because of it, he wanted her more than he'd ever wanted a woman.

He'd tried to ignore the heat between them, but the attraction simmered like a raging fire, intensifying each time he saw her or heard her sultry voice. And when he'd held her earlier . . .

He dragged her into his arms, had to hold her again. Had to taste her just one time.

Once would have to be enough.

His lips fused with hers, savagely, almost punishing, and he nipped at her lips, plunged his tongue into the recesses of her mouth, and kissed her thoroughly. He hated that he wanted her, hated that he hadn't walked away.

Hated that he couldn't have her because he knew he'd want more.

Hated even more that she was right about the heat between them, just as he sensed she was right about the evil in the town.

He was part of that evil, carried it inside him all the time.

Bad blood, bad blood . . . he was just like his father, born a demon.

She parted her lips for him and moaned in invitation, then clasped his face between her hands as if she didn't want to let go, and he shunned the voice ordering him to stop. With a groan torn from deep in his gut, he explored her, tasted the sweetness of her desire, the frenzied depth of her need as she urged him on.

His heart hammered against his ribs, and he trailed his tongue down her neck, savoring the saltiness of her skin as she clung to his arms. Heat suffused him, and blood pooled in his cock as it hardened and begged to be inside her.

He wanted her on her knees naked and opening for him. Wanted to take her in the most primal way, outside on the porch against the wall with the crickets chirping and tree frogs croaking in the distance.

What in the hell was he thinking?

A woman had just been murdered and strung up in the tree in her yard.

He tore himself away, pushed at her hands as she clawed for him to hold her again.

"Please, Vincent, I want you tonight."

"You don't want me, Clarissa. You've just suffered a

terrible shock, finding your friend in your yard. You're running on adrenaline and fear."

She grabbed his hand, placed it over her left breast. Her chest heaved for air, her nipples stiff peaks that he wanted to wrap his lips around and feed on.

"Stop it, Clarissa." He yanked his hand away, a brutal edge to his voice.

Her eyes were half closed, her lips parted, bruised from his mouth, and she reached down and stroked his erection. "You want me, Vincent. I can feel it."

She had that right. But he couldn't continue this game, couldn't lose control and take her now or he'd crave her even more.

It was too dangerous for her, and for him. Wanting, needing someone would make him vulnerable. And if he let down his guard, allowed himself to *feel*, then turned into his father as he feared he one day would, he'd hurt anyone who cared about him.

Then the evil would win.

"It's late, Clarissa," he growled. "Go to bed and get some rest."

"What are you going to do?" Anger flared in her eyes. "Go back to Sadie Sue? Let her finish what we started?"

The idea of having Sadie Sue after Clarissa's kiss held no appeal. "I'm not going to fuck Sadie Sue," he said crudely. "What I started to tell you earlier was that I think you're right about the evil here."

"That there are supernatural forces at work?"

"Yes."

She bit her lip. "What happened to make you change your mind?"

"Sadie Sue's eyes turned this strange yellowish-red

tonight, as if they glowed in the dark." He hesitated, might as well tell her about his father. That would surely scare her off. "And I remembered things about my past, about the night my father murdered my mother."

Her eyes softened in sympathy. "What happened, Vincent?"

"He burned her at the stake, Clarissa." His voice cracked, and he cleared his throat, emotions churning in his chest. "In a cave of black rock in the Black Forest. I still don't know how I got out of there afterward."

"Maybe you repressed those memories because you saw demons in the woods."

He shrugged.

"It sounds as if Sadie Sue sold her soul to the devil," Clarissa murmured.

"I know," he said between gritted teeth. "So did my father. He turned into a monster that night. When I saw Sadie Sue's eyes, I remembered my father's looked the same way."

He gripped her arms with such force she winced. "I inherited his blood, Clarissa. So if you know what's good for you, you'll keep your distance from me."

CHAPTER FIFTEEN

Clarissa couldn't stop trembling. So part of the rumors were true. Vincent had witnessed his father killing his mother.

Was Vincent's father inhuman? A demon?

Was Vincent?

No . . . he wouldn't hurt her.

Would he?

Vincent straightened. "Lock the door. I'm going to question Hadley Crane. See where he was tonight."

She nodded, although fear crawled through her. If they were dealing with demons, a locked door couldn't keep them out.

She'd been frightened of the spirits when the dead had first visited her as a child. And she'd been terrified and distraught the night her mother had died.

But she'd never had such a cold chill sweep though her, such deep-rooted terror crowding her chest as she did now.

Vincent closed the door behind him, and she sagged against the wall.

Her grandmother's warning echoed in her ears. Was that the reason her grandmother had warned her to stay away from the Valtrez family? Had she known that Vincent's father was demonic?

No wonder Vincent had been secretive, had repressed memories—he'd been tortured by what he'd seen his father do.

Walking on wobbly legs, she climbed the steps to the attic. A full-length mirror occupied one corner, several older pieces of furniture were crammed into another, and assorted dishes and knickknacks filled a shelf to the right. The trunk was covered in hatboxes, but she laid them aside and brought out the candles she used when she wanted to summon her grandmother. The attic was dark, so she placed the crystals, then the candles in a circle, knelt and lit them, then closed her eyes and recited the chant her grandmother had taught her years ago.

> *"To the present*
> *From the past,*
> *Bring this spirit*
> *To speak at last."*

Seconds later, the sound of tinkling filled the humid air, particles of light flickered against the shadows, then a shimmering white glow appeared—her grandmother.

"You called me, dear?"

Clarissa nodded. "Grandmother, you were right about evil rising." She explained about the snakes, hearing Sadie Sue scream, then Vincent's recollection. "Tell me, am I crazy? Did something happen to Sadie Sue?"

"Yes," her grandmother said gravely. "According to the legend, when a person trades his soul to defy death, he becomes one of the Walking Dead."

"You mean Sadie Sue died and came back to life?"

"Yes. But to become a true servant for Satan and gain immortality, the Walking Dead must take another's life."

She shuddered, knowing Vincent was in danger. "So Sadie Sue has to kill someone to gain immortality."

Her grandmother nodded, then continued, "Legend has it that Satan's followers will leave pieces of black rock in their wake to symbolize their purpose. The legend can be traced back to Greek mythology. It was believed that Hades' palace was built of black rock.

"Locals claim that such a palace can be found deep in the midst of the Black Forest. But beware of entering it without protection, for the evil within swallows humans alive."

"And Vincent?" Clarissa asked. "Was his father a demon?"

A heartbeat stretched between them before her grandmother answered. "Yes. He was demonborn, and now the other demons will come after him."

Clarissa clenched her hands together. Would the demons win Vincent, or would he be strong enough to fight them off?

Vincent had to find this killer and leave Eerie before he lost control. Before he took Clarissa into his bed.

Before his father won.

The temptations here were too strong. He smelled

the evil in the air, felt his father pulling at him to follow in his footsteps.

Felt Clarissa drawing him the opposite way. Making him want things he couldn't have.

Hardening himself, he parked at the Cranes' house, a trailer on the side of the mountain that had seen its better days. At one point, the family had added a front porch, but weather had aged the wood and it was sagging and rotting.

He kicked dirt off his boots as he climbed the creaking stairs, noting the overgrown yard, the rusted lawn mower that obviously hadn't been used in months, the broken plastic chair in the yard.

Clarissa speculated that this demon could possess another body—had he borrowed Sadie Sue's?

No . . . according to the profile, their killer was probably a man.

He knocked, tapping his boot as he waited. Shuffling came from inside, then the door screeched open, and a stooped, elderly woman wearing a faded housecoat and bifocals peered up at him. "Yeah?"

He flashed his ID. "Mrs. Crane, my name is Special Agent Valtrez. I'd like to ask you some questions."

She worked her mouth sideways. "What about?"

"About your son, Hadley. Is he here now?"

"Yeah." She gestured over her shoulder, her snuff-stained teeth black as she spoke. "In the bath. Came home all dirty just like he always does."

Vincent nodded. "May I come in?"

"I reckon." She stepped aside and waved him in, and he stepped over magazines and catalogues piled on the floor. The room was dark, yet pictures of Jesus and religious plaques covered the walls. A Bible sat on the rickety coffee table along with a half-full coffee mug.

She hobbled toward the hall and pounded on the bathroom door. "Hadley, you got someone here wants to talk to you."

"What?"

"Some agent from the government! Get your ass out here."

"I'm coming!" he shouted.

"Mrs. Crane, where was your son tonight?"

"Working, I guess." She hobbled to the rocking chair and collapsed into it, her arthritic hands gripping the wooden arms. "He had to dig another grave. All them girls dying, he's been busy."

"Have you noticed him acting strange lately?"

She wrinkled her nose. "As a matter of fact, yeah. I asked him if he was taking his pills, and he got mad. Said he was, but I ain't so sure."

"Has Hadley ever shown violent tendencies?"

She shrugged and drew an afghan over her bony legs. "He's got a temper but ain't never laid a hand on me." A laugh escaped her. " 'Course he knows if he did, I'd beat the snot out of him."

The bathroom door opened and Hadley lumbered out, wearing baggy jeans and a plaid shirt. He was an awkward, gangly guy, almost six feet, with calloused hands and a big head. His eyes were a little too close together, and he tilted his head at an odd angle.

Vincent tried to imagine how a woman would see him—as mentally challenged and needy, or dangerous?

Vincent introduced himself. "Crane, where were you tonight?"

His eyes shifted back and forth as if he couldn't focus. "Tending the cemetery like usual."

"What time did you arrive and leave?"

He checked his watch. "Don't know what time I went." He dug his hands in the pockets of his faded jeans. "And I just got home and took a bath. Mama don't like me bringing in the graveyard dirt."

"Can anyone verify that you were at work?" Vincent asked.

Crane shrugged. "Don't know. Angus was there part of the time."

"Angus?"

The rocker creaked as Crane's mother shifted. "Shut up talking about your daddy. You know he's been dead for years."

"I know, but I talk to him," Crane said in a heated tone. "And he tells me he's proud of me. Not like you."

Vincent fisted his hands by his side. Crane obviously had psychological problems.

And he didn't seem smart enough to pull off these murders without anyone seeing him.

So who was their UNSUB?

Fear for Clarissa rose in his gut. He had to get back to her. If she was right and the killer had left Daisy's body in the Devil's Tree as a warning, he didn't want to leave her alone too long.

If the killer returned for her, Vincent wanted to be there so he could destroy him.

Wrath had its vengeance. Pan's anger toward Clarissa King turned his hands and eyes into weapons.

He snapped the tree branches off the tree above him with a flick of his hand and chuckled as they popped and crackled, disintegrating into dust. Another wave of his fingertips and pine needles and twigs whipped across the forest, hurtling through the air as if a tornado had picked them up in its eye.

Human blood pumping through his veins tonight, he flung a squirrel and then a rabbit into the air and watched them splatter onto the rocks, guts spilling out as their bodies exploded.

He'd lost Daisy's soul to her mother, and she'd crossed to the light, but he still maintained a faint hold on the others.

All because of Clarissa.

She was stronger than he'd thought, stronger than her mother. She was supposed to crack, yet she was holding the girls back from giving in to him.

Worse, she was bringing out the good in Vincent.

He'd seen Vincent and Clarissa together on the porch from where he watched in the shadows of the oaks. Yes, Valtrez was part animal, his natural instincts surfacing as he'd ground his cock against the woman.

But succumbing to Clarissa could prove to be his fatal weakness as a Dark Lord.

For she held the key to destroying the dark entity inside him. Or at least controlling it.

Pan needed Valtrez out of control. Needed him savoring the feel of death on his hands, the taste of blood as his own father had taught him when he'd sucked it from a mutilated animal. Needed him craving the evil as much as he craved the flesh of a woman.

He had to destroy Clarissa before Valtrez had her.

Tonight had been a start. The dead woman in the tree. The reminder of her mother's insanity.

Taunting her with the fact that she hadn't been able to save either woman.

Just as she couldn't save Valtrez.

He knew the way to get to him, too. Torture him with reminders of his past. Twist time from his mind and guide him back to the blackouts.

And to his destiny as a master of the darkness.

CHAPTER SIXTEEN

Three days until the rising

Vincent stared at the predawn sky, noting the way the sun forced its way through the tops of the ridges in shades of red, gold, and orange, just like Sadie Sue's eyes. The temperature had climbed near a hundred degrees, the heat like an oppressive blanket covering the land.

But the light hurt his eyes. He preferred the night, thrived in the darkness.

Just like the monster who'd strangled Daisy Wilson and hanged her in the Devil's Tree.

He could still see her body dangling helplessly above the dry, parched ground, the bugs nipping at her decaying flesh, her sightless eyes empty of life and full of terror.

Upstairs, he heard a moan, then a cry, and instincts sent him flying up the steps. Had the killer returned to attack Clarissa? Was he trying to strangle her now?

Was that her greatest fear? Had it been Daisy's?

The stairs squeaked as his boots pounded them, and he drew his gun as he rounded the corner. Holding his breath, he peered inside her bedroom, pausing to listen for an intruder as he searched the interior.

Sheers draped the window, flapping as the ceiling fan twirled above, and a faint sliver of morning sunlight streaked her bed. Clarissa cried out again, twisting the sheets in her hands as she rolled to her side. Then she pummeled her pillow as if she was battling an attacker.

He saw no one in the room, though, no one but the silent monsters in her dreams. His pulse clamored, his chest tight. If he had any sense at all, he'd leave her to fight the ghosts on her own.

But the pain in her cry shredded his common sense. It had been too long of a night. Compassion mixed with desire and drove him to her bed with the bone-frenzied need to soothe her cries.

Wulf growled, and Vincent knelt and stroked his head. "Shh. I'm here to protect her, too." The dog tilted his head and stared at Vincent, and a silent understanding passed between them, as if the dog might be half human.

"Clarissa." He gently laid his hand on her shoulder. "Wake up. You're having a nightmare."

Instead she sobbed and kicked at the bedcovers, knocking them to the floor.

"Clarissa . . ." Slowly he lowered himself onto the knotted sheets and murmured her name again. He didn't know how to help her, how to be soft and gentle, didn't even know if he had it in him, but he stroked her hair from her tear-stained cheeks. "Shh, it's all right. You're safe now."

"Save the girls," she whispered. "They're lost, hanging in limbo. Have to save them."

Clarissa was so unselfish. Even though she knew this demon might come after her, she was still worried about others. The realization stirred something deep inside Vincent, knotting his stomach, and he stretched out beside her and pulled her into his arms. She felt so warm and soft that the ice in his heart melted.

"We will save them," he murmured. "And I'll protect you, too."

She opened her eyes and looked up into his, her expression tormented.

"You were having a nightmare," he said in a gruff voice.

"No," she said softly. "The dead came to me. So many of them. I can't help them all . . ."

He clenched his jaw, understanding her feeling of helplessness.

"Daisy never saw his face," Clarissa whispered. "She never had a chance. But Daisy has faith. She refused to relinquish her soul. She crossed into the light."

He had no idea what to say, couldn't mutter false promises of hope when he didn't yet know exactly what they were up against.

A well of sadness filled her eyes, then she curled up next to him and drifted back to sleep. He stared at the ceiling, holding her as he listened to her breathe, guarding her in case the killer returned, staving off the demons that chased her in her sleep and the ghosts that haunted her day and night.

Bastard that he was, he'd promised to protect her.

That meant protecting her from the monster that lived within him, as well.

Unbidden, though, his urges emerged.

His body wanted her. His hand ached to slide beneath her gown and stroke her flesh. His sex craved her wet heat.

And he wasn't certain he possessed enough willpower to keep from taking her if she invited him into her bed again.

⤙⤚

When Clarissa awakened again, sunlight streaked the room and Vincent was gone, leaving her alone and aching for his arms.

A mixture of horror and dread consumed her. During the night, the spirits had emerged through the shocked fog of their sudden deaths, their helpless pleas wrenching Clarissa's heart.

Yet each time she'd felt Vincent's arms around her, her resolve to remain strong deepened. And so did the bond between them. She only hoped that together they could fight the evil spreading across the town.

She hurried downstairs and found Vincent on the back porch with a mug of coffee, his body rigid as he stared into the dense woods. The mountains seemed eerily quiet this morning, like the calm before a terrible storm.

"Vincent?"

"I questioned Hadley Crane last night. Something's not adding up with him."

Clarissa pressed her hand to her throat. "You think he's the killer?"

He exhaled. "I don't know. He said he was at work after three. I talked to the coroner while you were sleeping, and Daisy Wilson died before noon. When I phoned Crane to check his alibi, his mother said he took off this morning like he does every morning. She hasn't heard from him since. She thinks he goes into the woods."

"I still don't think he's methodical enough to pull off these crimes," Clarissa asked.

He nodded. "I agree. And there's not enough for a search warrant, either." Vincent's jaw tightened. "The air is different now," he said in an oddly low voice. "I smell blood in the forest. Death."

A painful breath lodged against her breastbone. "You think the killer struck again?"

"It's not a human's blood," Vincent said. "But animals, yes. And more than one."

She leaned against the porch rail for support.

His heels clicked as he pivoted toward her, the pain and emptiness in his eyes making her heart clench. Dark beard stubble shaded his jaw, and the memory of his arms around her sent a tingle of need through her.

His gaze fell to her breasts, and her nipples hardened beneath her thin cotton gown. With the sun pouring down on her, he could probably see through the transparent material. She should walk away, run, but she couldn't tear herself from him. She wanted him to look, to touch, to feel.

His jaw tensed, the hunger that fired his eyes so primal that her mouth watered and moisture pooled between her thighs.

"Get dressed, Clarissa."

Remembering his arms holding her during her nightmares, his strong body pressed close to hers, the heady odor of his skin, she reached for him, wanting Vincent to hold her again. Wanting him to touch her with his hands the way he had with those eyes.

"I warned you to stay away from me, Clarissa."

"I'm not afraid of you, Vincent."

"You should be. I told you I'm dangerous, just like my father was."

But his gaze lingered on her breasts, his breathing growing labored. She touched his hand, and hunger flared in his eyes. Clarissa momentarily forgot about the danger. She wanted him desperately, had wanted him since the first minute she'd seen him at the police station. And last night, lying next to him, having him hold her had taken their relationship to a different level. She'd sensed a tender side of him that lay buried beneath the rubble of his pain, buried so deeply she doubted he knew it existed.

Aching to ease his suffering, she reached for him. He threw up his hands and backed away from her. "Don't."

"Why not? You want me. I want you. And in the midst of all this death and evil, making love with you is the only thing that makes sense to me right now."

"I don't make love to anyone," he said gruffly. With a scowl, he stalked down the steps.

"Where are you going?"

"To hunt for that cave of black rock. I think it's the place where the killer takes his victims."

She hurried down the steps and grabbed his arm. "Let me go with you."

He jerked away from her touch. "No. It's too dangerous."

Then he disappeared into the wooded mountains, leaving her alone and aching for his return.

The metallic taste of blood nearly overpowered Vincent as he jogged into the wooded mountains, although the taste of Clarissa's lips from that heated kiss warmed him, helping to stifle his urge for a kill and replacing it with raw desire for her.

Hell. His body throbbed incessantly, driving him insane. It was almost as if sex fed his body, was the only thing that kept him alive, that kept him from killing.

Disgust filled him. He wanted her. No doubt about that. In fact, even as he'd backed away, all he'd been able to do was stare at her breasts. Her nipples had stiffened and made his head swim with desire. Beneath that see-through gown lay the softest, sweetest heat. His primal instincts told him it begged for his cock.

Dammit, he could practically taste her damp juices on his tongue.

Shocking that she could talk to the dead but hadn't run from him like she should. She probably thought she could save his soul like she did the spirits hanging in limbo.

Wanting her was becoming an obsession, the need shattering his concentration. The next time she asked him, he might accept her offer. Get her out of his system once and for all.

Show her what a heartless bastard he was beneath. A bastard like his father.

Other memories followed. His father whipping him with a leather strap. Teaching him how to hunt, to sniff out the prey. How to gut an animal with a pocketknife and drink blood from its wounds.

The razor blade cuts on his back where he'd tortured him in the name of proving he was a man. The way his father had thrown out his hands and tossed fire into the woods. The animals scurrying for safety.

Too late. Their bones crunched between his father's brutal hands.

He paused and flexed his fingers in front of him, studying them. Could he start fires with his hands?

He closed his eyes to concentrate, then opened them and flung them outward, but no fire erupted. Yet a tree in front of him cracked and splintered. He tried again and rocks went crumbling. Another thrust and two small trees exploded.

He did possess a supernatural power, not as a fire-starter, but he could make things explode. He shook with the realization. Could no longer deny that he had demon blood running through his veins.

Suddenly the air swirled around him, hot and filled with the scent of blood. He spotted a rabbit that had been ripped apart, its insides strewn across a rock. The work of an animal or sadistic man?

Or maybe a demon, like his father.

Another few yards down, he found several dead squirrels and rabbits, their bodies also shattered, guts strewn on the parched ground. The stench of larger animals filled the humid air, robbing his breath.

Following the blood trail, he spent the day tracking other kills, each time his stomach clenching at the brutality.

An old mine drew his eyes, and he checked it out but found no one inside. Just bats, their eyes piercing the darkness.

Ominous gray clouds cluttered the sky, the heat oppressive and accentuating the vile stench of death. Slowly the blackness crept over him, sucking him into its abyss. He tried to fight the sadistic, seductive lure, but the pull was too strong.

He was going to black out. Lose time.

Lapse into one of the black holes.

He staggered, clawed for control, tried to fight it. His head swam, and the trees twirled and blurred, the jagged stone of the mountains reaching for him like giant monster's arms.

The heavy pull of evil begged him to succumb, his father's voice echoing off the hills. He closed his eyes, time slipping away as the darkness engulfed him.

Then he heard the whisper of a voice, low and lethal, telling him that Clarissa might be dead before he returned.

And that her blood would be on his hands.

～

Cary Gimmerson tried to scream as she looked down at the steep ridges below, but her vocal cords refused to work. How had she wound up in the mountains on this ridge?

Slowly, through the fog of her confused mind, the past hour rolled back. She'd brought her dog to the park for a walk and he'd run off, then she'd chased him and gotten lost.

Then what? She'd fallen . . . collapsed . . . someone had struck her from behind?

When she'd roused to consciousness, the sun had completely blinded her. But a man's voice had soothed her, and he'd lifted her in his arms and carried her up the hill, up the ridge.

Then everything turned hazy. Her heart raced with fear.

She'd tried to cry for help but couldn't move.

Struggling to free herself from his spell, she squinted through the blinding sun.

Then his face slid into focus. No, not a face.

A hulking black monster with yellow eyes.

She tried to move, to scream again, but her limbs were paralyzed, and terror seized her.

She was going to die alone on the mountain, and no one would hear her cries.

CHAPTER SEVENTEEN

Vincent walked at the right hand of darkness, the black-faced demon he accompanied leading the way through the mountains.

Where was he going? To the graveyard, where he would count his kills?

The vile smell of another human's fear swirled around him, and he saw the source. The woman the black shadow held in his clutches.

She couldn't be more than twenty years old. Wavy blond hair. Amber eyes. Lips parted in terror as if a scream had died in her throat.

Frozen at the edge of the precipice as if in bondage, but she was free of any visible ropes or bindings.

She was literally frozen, he realized. Frozen in fear.

"She is afraid of heights," the demon said in a hazy whisper that sounded like sandpaper, less than human.

Yet here they stood at the top of one of the tallest ridges in the Smokies, overlooking a canyon that fell to the ground miles away. Excitement slithered through his blood at the images that played out in his mind. The woman falling over the edge, spiraling out of control, hands and arms flailing for a lifeline yet grasping empty air. Would they hear her scream as she fell? Or would it fade in the endless chasm between her and the waiting ground?

Would she feel the splat of her body, blood splattering in a million directions? Would she hear her own bones crunch, jagged ends knifing into her organs, before she drew her final breath?

The demon lifted his shapeless black hand, held it suspended for time that seemed to stand still. She moved her mouth, her throat muscles working to form a cry for help, for mercy, but no sound emerged, only air whistling through her teeth.

Bleeding through his enthralled state, the truth registered.

This was the demon he chased. One touch and the demon knew the woman's deepest fear, then used it to kill her.

Vincent should destroy him. Instead, he'd followed along to watch.

Even as he ordered himself to move, to stop the demon and vanquish him, his limbs refused to function, as if he, too, had been hypnotized by the demon's spell.

He was trapped in the blackness. Powerless to stop the scene before him as the faceless monster created a surge of wind that caught the woman and spun her above the ground, then flung her over the ledge.

He tried to shout for the demon to stop, but his voice choked, emotions pummeling him as the girl fell to her death.

Her hair floated around her as she spiraled through the air. Finally the scream came, distant and hollow, boomeranging off the mountain walls, mingling with the sound of the demon's laughter.

Vincent bellowed in rage, his body trembling with the force. He'd seen death before, had caused it himself. But the young girl wasn't a criminal . . . she was just a child.

Self-hate made him nauseous as he flexed his hands. He halfway expected to see fire shooting from his fingers, but none came. Only guilt and self-condemnation . . .

And the realization that he was weak. Had lost to the demon.

And with his supplication, his powers would grow, his hands more dangerous, his mind a sieve to mastermind plots to take lives and offer the helpless souls to Satan.

No . . . The scream ripped from him. He couldn't relent.

Mindless with pain, the black hole swirled around him. He saw the future, saw himself walking through the graveyard of lost souls, looking at the burial plots for the ones whose lives he would steal. Hearing their screams as they realized they'd traded their souls for a hell that would never end.

Fire seared his skin and fingers, yet a cold gray blanket of despair washed over him as he stopped to stare at his next conquest. The woman who would assure his place as a master of the darkness.

The name etched on the granite tombstone was Clarissa's.

Stunned, he finally jerked himself free from the demon's trance.

⌐━━━

Terror spiked Clarissa's heart rate as she searched the foothills and mountains. Where was Vincent? Was he all right?

Had the demon gone after him?

Was he coming for her next?

Her grandmother's predictions disturbed her even more, as did the stories about the Black Forest. What other kinds of creatures lived within those miles of rolling hills?

Who had this demon disguised himself as?

A scream tore down from the mountain, resounding off the jagged ridges, and a chill clutched her as the dead girls' skeletal faces floated in front of her, their haunted eyes etched with horror.

"He has another . . ."

"He's killed again . . ."

"Why didn't you stop him?"

A feeling of helplessness made her legs buckle, and she ran outside, then screamed into the mountains, anger and frustration ringing through her cries.

"Why hide your face and kill innocent girls? Why don't you show yourself to me, you coward?"

A cold wind rustled the trees, whistling through the leaves, the sound shrill. Yet a low, haunting voice rode on its tail.

"Don't worry, I'm coming for you, Clarissa." Laughter rumbled from the hills. "Soon you will be mine."

❧

Vincent stirred from the depths of the black hole, clawing his way back to reality. Had he just dreamed about the demon, or had he really walked along beside him?

The whisper of death brushed his neck, and he opened his eyes, the muted gray shades of light and shadows flickering through the trees, igniting fingers of tension coiling inside him. Above him a black hawk soared, and somewhere in the distance a coyote wailed while the vicious sound of gnashing teeth—a predator tearing into his meal—sliced the silence.

He rubbed his temple where it throbbed, then glanced around and found himself lying at the edge of the precipice where he'd stood and watched the girl fall to her death.

Nausea gripped him, but he swallowed the bile, holding his breath as he forced himself to look down into the canyon.

Hell and damnation. His head swam as he zeroed in on a body.

He hadn't been dreaming.

He had truly walked with the black-faced demon, and he hadn't prevented the kill.

Which made him just as responsible.

Balling his hands into fists, he raced down the mountain. His boots skidded over rock, and he pushed branches aside, ignoring the ones that slapped his face and tore at his back. He had to get to the girl. Find out if she was the one he'd seen die at the demon's hands.

Then he had to call the sheriff and report the death. But what could he say?

That a black-faced, shadowlike demon killed the woman? That he pushed her over the edge without touching her? That he was working for the devil?

That Vincent had witnessed the murder and had done nothing to save her?

Guilt and self-hate nearly immobilized him, but he jogged faster, weaving between the trees, grimacing at the dead animals along the path. Had the demon killed them, or had he?

Fury balled in his gut, and he flung his hands out,

literally snapping branches from the trees to clear his path and sending small rocks flying.

Cold fear made his heart pound. He'd seen Clarissa's name on her tombstone. The killer was coming after her.

He'd die before he'd let the demon have her.

———⟨⟩———

Denial stabbed at Clarissa's nerves as she ran back inside, making her cold and achy. She banished the cries of the dead, begging them to leave her alone. And Vincent was fine. He was tough and could take care of himself.

Meanwhile, she had to get dressed for Tracy's funeral.

But there would be more lost spirits at the graveyard, more voices crying out to her . . .

She swallowed back a sob. She had to be strong, couldn't break down like her mother.

Sucking in her courage, she climbed in the shower, closed her eyes, and let the water warm her.

The demon wouldn't get her. Vincent would protect her, as he'd protected her from his father years ago.

He wasn't evil.

Still shaken, she dried off, blew dry her hair, and dressed in a long turquoise skirt and white blouse for Tracy's funeral. But the heat plastered her clothes to her skin as she headed to her car and drove to the chapel.

Trying to drown out the cries of all who lay buried in the cemetery, she entered the church, her heart clenching as she spotted Ronnie and Eloise Canton huddled together on the front pew. Friends filled the rows, the sound of the organ drummed an old gospel song. She slid onto a rear seat, searching the faces.

Deputy Bluster sat near the front, but she didn't see Vincent or Sheriff Waller. Bo Bennett loped in and claimed a back pew, and the bartender from Six Feet Under took a seat near the middle.

Hadley Crane stood in the back in that gray pinstripe he always wore for funerals, his movements jerky as his gaze shifted across the crowded church.

The preacher began his eulogy, and Clarissa knotted her hands together, struggling to focus, but the cries of Tracy's friends and family blended with the spirits', making her head swim and throb.

She massaged her temple, time blurring as the funeral continued. Finally the last prayer was said, and the pallbearers carried Tracy's casket down the aisle. The somber crowd rose to follow, sniffles echoing all around. A few offered their condolences at the church, while others strolled outside, braving the heat to join the family at the graveside services.

Skeletal ghosts roamed the grounds, rising from the dirt, floating above the tombstones, and screaming, their agonized screeches assaulting Clarissa.

She walked down the path, noting the way some graves were well tended while others lay neglected, flowerless, with weeds marring the surface. Mourners gathered outside the tent situated by the burial plot while the family and closest friends filled in the metal chairs beneath it, and dozens of flower arrangements and wreaths surrounded the tent. Clarissa stood to the side to make herself available for the Cantons, but supportive friends surrounded them.

The reverend murmured another prayer, yet Tracy's spirit lingered beside the freshly turned earth, her pale face somber as she watched her family grieving. Then her gaze met Clarissa's, and Clarissa silently relayed assurances that they would find her killer.

Hadley appeared near Clarissa, and she tensed.

"Death is not the end," Hadley murmured to her.

Clarissa inhaled sharply.

"You know it, Clarissa. You're not afraid of it, are you?"

A shudder rippled up her spine, then Hadley left to join the pallbearers.

Tim Bluster stepped up beside her. "Are you okay, Clarissa?"

She twisted her hands together, unsure how to answer. She hadn't thought Hadley dangerous before, but his cryptic comment raised her doubts. He definitely sounded menacing and deranged.

Still, she hated to point the finger without knowing more. "I'm fine," she said. "Just sad for the Cantons."

Sheriff Waller strode up to her and gestured at his phone.

"That was Valtrez. He just found another victim in the mountains."

Clarissa clenched her hands, desperation mushrooming inside her.

⟶

Pan reveled in the tortured expression on Clarissa's face. She was beginning to break, the cries of the dead wearing on her. He could see the strain on her face, the pain in her eyes, the fear in the way she shivered as she tried desperately to hold herself together.

The sweet taste of victory burned his tongue. Another kill, another soul teetering on the edge, on the verge of succumbing. Yes, the Gimmerson girl was weak. So young that she had silently begged for another chance at life. And of course, he had offered it to her.

He was winning Vincent, as well. Forcing him into the black hole and making him walk by his side to the kill had been genius.

Tonight Sadie Sue would fill his sexual needs and bring him another step closer to his fall.

And while she was working her charms on Vincent, Pan would continue to torture Clarissa.

Torture her until she hanged herself like her mother.

When Vincent realized she had died as an offering to his father, he would face Zion.

Then the two would reconnect and battle.

And evil would thrive as it was meant to do.

CHAPTER EIGHTEEN

Not wanting to contaminate the crime scene, Vincent forced his hands by his sides. Although he doubted forensics would find trace evidence.

Unless the girl had torn skin or blood from the body the demon had possessed.

But if he told the sheriff he'd seen a demon, Waller would think he was crazy. And he couldn't identify a human face, just a black shadow.

Frustration knotted his insides. The girl lay facedown, was barely recognizable. Her bones had crunched and shattered, her face was distorted, her nose smashed, cheekbones jutting through skin, arms and legs twisted at odd angles.

Had she suffered a heart attack before she'd hit the ground? He hoped so, or she would have felt horrendous pain. For a second the canyon swirled around him, trees racing past, time suspended, and he felt himself slipping back into that black hole where he enjoyed the pain.

No . . . He latched on to the last vestiges of his morality and fought to resist the pull.

The screech of a siren alerted him to the sheriff's arrival. Vincent fisted his hands by his sides as he and the deputy pushed through the trees to the clearing.

"Holy mother of God." Waller's complexion turned a pasty green, and he halted and swiped at his forehead with the back of his arm.

The deputy took one look at the body, then glanced at the ridge above and whistled. "Hell of a fall." He twisted to stare at Vincent with narrowed eyes. "How exactly did you find her?"

Vincent dredged up every ounce of his restraint to maintain a detached face. "I was searching the mountains and discovered several dead animals in the woods—looks like they'd been mutilated. Then I heard shuffling, and screams. By the time I ran through the woods, she had plunged below."

The edge to Bluster's voice hardened. "Thought you were guarding Clarissa?"

He gave Bluster a hard stare. "I was. But the black rock each victim held came from a cave somewhere in these hills. I thought the killer might be taking his victims there."

Waller inched closer to the dead girl's body, then checked around her. A second later, he lifted what was left of her right hand and cursed again. "There it is, the black rock."

"Do you know who she is?" Vincent asked.

Waller leaned closer, turned the woman's head so he could study the shattered face. "Think it's Cary Gimmerson, but . . . hell, there's not enough there to recognize."

Vincent nodded. "The ME can verify her ID through her dental records. If not, we'll use DNA."

"That'll take time," Bluster said. "But I'll check for missing persons reports."

"The crime-scene team on the way?" Vincent asked.

"Should be here any minute," Waller said. "So should the ME."

"You got your camera?" Vincent asked. "Let's take some pictures." Although he wasn't sure what good it would do, they had to follow protocol.

"I'll get it." Bluster hurried back to the car.

A minute later, he returned, and shortly after, the crime-scene unit and medical examiner arrived, each as shaken by the shattered body as the sheriff.

Only Bluster hadn't been sickened. He'd seemed impressed by the distance of the fall.

Vincent clenched his hands. He had walked beside the demon and knew the killer wasn't human. If only he could have seen the human's face the demon had borrowed.

"If there was a scuffle, we should find evidence to prove it, footprints, maybe signs of a fight." Waller walked over to one of the crime-scene guys and relayed the information, and one of the techs began the hike to the top of the ridge.

Tension knotted Vincent's shoulders. He had to get back to Clarissa, make sure she was safe and that the demon hadn't come for her.

＊

The sun had set as Clarissa drove home from the funeral, the sky a dismal smoky gray, clouds casting a fog over the land. Still haunted by the cries of the dead, she turned onto the isolated road that led to her house, but the mountains seemed to swallow her, the heat sucking the air from her lungs. She cranked up the air conditioner, but the hairs on the back of her neck bristled, and she sensed someone following her.

Or that she wasn't alone in the car.

She glanced sideways, expecting to see a spirit, but the seat remained empty. Still, a breath tickled her neck.

Maybe one of the ghosts had followed her from the graveyard . . .

She tapped her nails on the steering wheel. "If you're there, tell me who you are."

Just the hiss of a breath again, and a vile heat scalded her skin.

She pressed the accelerator, speeding up and taking the curvy road too fast. Her car skimmed the guardrail, causing sparks to spew against the darkness; then a rush of cold air skated across her arm. A second later, a girl suddenly moved in front of the car.

Blond hair hung limp and tangled around a face that had been smashed to pieces. Dear God, it was Cary Gimmerson.

Bones jutted through skin; her features were twisted, blood oozing from her head and running down her face, her teeth jagged and broken. A scream tore from the woman's bloody lips, boomeranging across the mountain in a cry of anguish that sounded like an animal being eaten alive.

Clarissa swerved to avoid hitting her, and the tires screeched, wheels skidding as the car flew into the rail, bounced off, and landed on two wheels. She jerked the wheel to compensate, but the car hit the side of the mountain and spun out of control, sliding and twirling until it finally slammed into the rail and ended up hanging nose first over the ridge.

Waller gave Vincent a ride back to Clarissa's to get his car and he headed back to his cabin. Clarissa had left a note saying she'd gone to Tracy Canton's funeral.

She should be all right surrounded by the crowd.

He hadn't showered since the day before, had slept in his clothes at her place, and after tracking through the woods and scouring the crime scene of the murdered woman, bugs had glued themselves to his salty skin, and he smelled like sweat and vile odors that needed to be cleansed.

Although no amount of bathing could wash away the guilt permeating his soul for standing at the right hand of the demon and doing nothing to save the girl. Guilt and a thirst for vengeance gripped him in their clutches.

Somehow the demon had hypnotized him and prevented him from reacting.

The images of the mutilated animals taunted him, as well. He stared at his hands, at the imprint of the angel amulet. His hands were lethal.

What if he had ripped apart those animals with his hands during the time he'd blacked out? What if this demon had the power to possess him, to lure him into the darkness forever as it had his father?

Bile filled his throat as he parked and headed inside the cabin. He removed his gun and placed it inside the nightstand, ripped off his clothes and boxers, and turned on the hot water.

But even when he scrubbed himself until his skin was raw, his teeth felt gritty with the woman's death.

The animal in him was so strong—could he repress the urge to kill forever?

Shaking water from his hair, he wrapped a towel around his waist, but the sound of a door squeaking open jarred him. Caution kicking in, he eased toward the door, wishing like hell he'd brought his weapon into the bathroom with him. Then again, would a bullet destroy a demon?

And would the demon need to use the door?

Heart hammering, he glanced in the doorway, the scent of an overpowering, exotic perfume suffusing him.

Not Clarissa. Her fragrance was natural and subtle. Sweetly seductive.

This one was more blatant.

Sadie Sue.

He watched in the shadows, wondering why in the hell she'd come. Then she zeroed in on his half-naked body and rasped a startled response. "Oh, my."

He ground his knuckles against his thighs. "What are you doing here?"

"I came to see you, sugar."

His pulse kicked up a notch, but he remained in place. "Why? You know something about the murders in town?"

She shook her head, then lifted one hand and released the clasp holding her hair at the nape of her neck so that it fell like a mane around her shoulders. With a low whisper of his name, she slowly walked toward him. Another step and pure animal need bolted through him.

Her breasts spilled over her sequined top, a scrap of fabric so fitting and transparent that her nipples strained the fabric. And her shorts—shit.

They hugged her voluptuous ass so tightly they molded to her clit and rode so high they showcased her crotch as she hiked one foot onto the bed. His cock jumped, aching to be between her legs.

He remembered her eyes changing color, though, and struggled to control his libido. This woman was not one he needed to tangle with.

"I don't have time for games, Sadie Sue," he said sharply. "Get out of here."

"I smell your lust, Vincent. You want me . . ." A grayness swept over the room, the moon barely discernible through the cloud cover, yet suddenly her eyes glowed, penetrating, piercing, enthralling.

He tried to jerk his gaze away, but the draw was too strong, as if she'd somehow cast a spell over him.

Time fled again, as if the devil's hands had swallowed him in another black hole, one that was drowning him in its churning waters.

As the dark hole diffused his rational conscience, his body became a hungry animal, feeling, craving, needing to be sated.

He hadn't been fucked in so long, his balls were full and throbbing, swollen with the need for release. Her warm, willing scent enveloped him, the smell of woman and animal mingling. His eyes narrowed, and a violent hunger for her flesh seized him as she tossed the scraps of her clothing to the dull brown carpet.

He could crush her with his fists, devour her blood as he had an animal's. Gorge on her until he was sated. Then snap her neck in two with his bare hands.

"You need me now," she said in a purrlike voice that sent a sharp pain of longing through his groin. "But you have to earn your pleasure, Vincent."

Fear coursed through him, the memory of his father saying those same words ripping open wounds he thought had bled out forever.

On some deep level, another voice whispered to him that this was wrong, that he had to fight her, that succumbing to her would only draw him deeper into the devil's arms, but he was powerless to do anything but watch her and let her take control.

"You like to be whipped, don't you, Vincent? Whipped for being a bad boy?"

Though her voice sounded sultry and seductive, a hideous smile lit her orange eyes, and she suddenly shoved him down on the bed. With a tug, she jerked the towel from him, exposing his heavy sex and the scars on his body.

She rolled him over. "You have to be punished."

He shook his head in denial, but memories of fighting his father's beatings as a child roared through his head, and he lay immobile.

She wound a piece of rope around her hands, then lifted one of his arms and tied his wrist to the bedpost. In seconds, she'd secured his other wrist and ankles. Fear burned his throat, but his cock swelled and hardened as she cracked the whip and flung it against his back. Pain ripped through him, the sharp sting causing blood to rush to his head, and he choked back a cry of agony and arousal as she continued to whip him.

Finally, she untied him and rolled him over. He thrust his hips up, silently begging her to fuck him now. Instead, she retied him and cracked the whip across his chest.

Sickened by his own weak cravings, he closed his eyes and pictured his reward when the beating ended.

Clarissa wiped at the blood on her forehead and tore at the air bag. The car shifted slightly, rocking forward with a shrill screech, and she held her breath, terrified her car would career over the mountain ridge and dive into the canyon.

Another screech sent terror streaking through her. She had to get out of the car. She fumbled with the door handle, latched her other hand around her purse strap, and shoved open the door. The car rocked again, teetering on the edge, metal scraping the rail, which had buckled with the impact. Praying it didn't give way, she shoved open the door and jumped onto the embankment.

Her ankle twisted, and she grasped for something to support her as she stumbled across the pavement. Remembering the girl in her path, she shuddered. Her face and body had been crushed by something.

Clarissa searched the road and the railing but didn't see Cary anywhere.

The truth dawned, making her heart clench. The girl was already dead; her spirit had been reaching out to Clarissa. But her spirit had faded now.

Had she been murdered like the others? Had she crossed into the light, or to the dark side?

Sweat beaded on her neck and blood trickled down the side of her face, but she swiped at it and collapsed onto a grassy patch, then scrambled in her purse for her cell phone.

Dragging in a breath, she punched in Vincent's number and let it ring, but no one answered. Frustrated, she realized she hadn't thought to call the sheriff's office, so she punched in his number. Tim answered on the second ring.

"I've had an accident," she said. "Can you send a tow truck?"

"Are you hurt, Clarissa? Do you need an ambulance?"

"No, I'm okay. But I need help with my car."

"I'll call Bennett on my way over."

"You don't need to come, Tim."

He grunted into the phone. "No, I'll be there."

She hung up and breathed in deeply, searching the darkness for the spirit to reappear, but the shadows revealed nothing.

Feeling edgy, she paced the side of the road, time ticking by in slow motion as she waited for Tim and the tow service. The road was virtually deserted, the heat stifling.

But screams of the dead assaulted her, echoing from the hills, the whisper of a demon against her neck. She spun in circles, searching the darkness, covering her ears to drown out the cries, but they refused to leave her alone.

By the time Bo drove up in his wrecker, she was near panic, her neck and hands sweating.

Bo's scarred face contorted into a frown as he scrutinized the scene. "You okay, Clarissa?"

She nodded, although being alone with him made her nervous. "Just shaken up. Afraid my car didn't fare so well."

"I'll take care of it. Don't worry." He examined the vehicle and clicked his teeth. "You're lucky. Another inch or two and you would have plunged over."

A shiver chased up her spine. "I know."

His beady eyes settled on her. "What happened?"

She couldn't tell Bo about the spirit. "I was upset after leaving Tracy's funeral, and I took the curve too fast and lost control."

"It's easy to happen." His tattoo glinted in the faint light spilling from his parking lights. "They say around town that you see things. Ghosts. Is that true?"

She folded her arms, hugging herself. "Yes."

He took a step closer. "You see Tracy today?"

She hesitated and bit on her lip. "As a matter of fact, I did. She and Billie Jo and Jamie are having trouble moving on."

Unease tickled her spine, but Tim's cruiser arrived, saving her from elaborating. He parked and climbed out, a worried look on his face.

"You're sure you don't need a doctor, Clarissa?" Tim asked.

She nodded. "Yes, I just want to go home."

"I'll take care of the car and give you a lift," Bo offered.

Tim cleared his throat. "I'll give her a ride. I need to talk to her anyway." He angled his head at Bo. "Where were you earlier, Bennett?"

Bo's jaw snapped tight. "Dammit, Tim. Why do you keep asking? My girl already told you I've been staying with her."

"Just answer the question," Tim insisted.

Bo cursed. "At the trucking service working on a Ford. You can call my office and my receptionist will verify that."

Tim nodded, and Clarissa followed him to his cruiser, still shaken by the close call.

"What happened?" he asked.

She hesitated. "Do you really want to know?"

He pressed his hand over hers. "Yes. Talk to me, Clarissa."

She sighed and leaned her head against the seat. "I'm sure you've heard that I relate to spirits."

He nodded, looking unfazed, so she continued and explained about Cary Gimmerson's spirit in the road.

Tim rubbed a hand across the back of his neck with a nod. "You're right, she's dead. We just finished at the crime scene."

Clarissa twined her fingers together. "What happened?"

"She was pushed over a ridge. Shattered her face and crushed most of the bones in her body. They're transporting her to the state medical examiner's office for the autopsy."

"Did you find a piece of black rock with the girl?"

He nodded.

"Where's Vincent?"

He arched a brow. "Said he was coming to see you."

Tim kept one hand on the wheel but laid the other one over hers again. "Listen, Clarissa. I realize you trust this guy, and that Waller asked him here to investigate, but he acted strange today."

"What do you mean?" Clarissa asked.

He clenched his jaw. "For one thing, he found the dead girl. And he acted like he was holding something back."

She didn't want to confide the things he'd admitted about his past. Somehow it felt like she'd be betraying Vincent if she did. "I'm not afraid of him," she said. "Listen, Tim, he's had a troubled life, but he's a good agent."

"He's dangerous. And I don't want to see you get hurt," he said gruffly.

His concern touched her. Tim was a friend, but she couldn't see him as anything else. "I'll be careful, I promise."

He nodded, then cranked the engine and dropped her at the rental car place. She signed out a small sedan, then drove back to her cabin, weary and wondering where Vincent was.

The image of Daisy Wilson's body dangling from the Devil's Tree remained imprinted in her mind as she parked in her drive. Again she sensed that a vile force had followed her, and she checked over her shoulder but didn't see anything around.

The sounds of the forest beyond blended with her erratic breathing as she unlocked her door and went inside.

She froze, her heart racing. The air smelled different, a vile scent heating the rooms.

Someone was in her house.

Suddenly, fingers scraped across her back and tiptoed across her neck.

She screamed, then turned and raced outside to the car.

Hands shaking, she jumped in and started the engine, frantic to escape.

But she glanced up at her front porch, and her breath lodged in her chest. An eerie, faceless black shadow filled her doorway, hulking and inhuman.

The demon had come for her, just as he'd said.

CHAPTER NINETEEN

Panicked, Clarissa spun the car around and raced down the road toward Vincent's cabin.

The hills that had welcomed her as home all her life now stretched with endless miles of places for demons to hide and evil to thrive.

She and Vincent had to stop it from spreading and consuming the town.

Anxiety plucked at her as she veered down the graveled road. She spotted his Land Rover by his cabin and parked next to him, then swiped her sweaty palms across her skirt as she ran to the cabin door.

Trembling, she knocked on the door. No answer. She knocked again, then called Vincent's name, but he still didn't respond, so she wrapped her fingers around the doorknob and tried it. The door swung open, but a movement caught her eye. A woman.

A faint light spilling from the distant lodge fell across the bed. Clarissa's throat closed.

Sadie Sue was naked, her breasts swaying as she walked toward Vincent.

Pain splintered through her. He had turned her away, yet now he was going to make love to this other woman.

Sadie Sue glanced over her shoulder at Clarissa and smiled, a wicked smile that sent a chill up her spine.

Steeling herself against the pain, Clarissa's gaze met the other woman's and fear cut off her breath. Sadie Sue's eyes had turned bright yellow and glinted as if shooting fire.

Clarissa stepped inside the room, then glanced down at Vincent to gauge his reaction. He lay beneath the woman, unmoving, sweat and droplets of blood dotting his bare chest, his wrists and arms tied to the posts. His eyes looked odd, glazed as if he'd been hypnotized by the devil.

Could she save him, or was she too late?

~

The sound of a woman's voice penetrated the dark chamber holding Vincent prisoner. Somewhere in the far recesses of his mind, recognition dawned.

Clarissa.

Shame and humiliation washed over him.

"So she's what you want, Vincent," Clarissa said, bitterness lacing her tone.

"Get out of here." Sadie Sue screeched an inhuman sound. "He's mine now, and nothing you can do can change it."

A wild rush of hunger snaked through Vincent. Sadie Sue cracked the whip, the sound cold and violent. Then she ran a finger over his cock . . .

"Go ahead and enjoy it," Clarissa cried.

Sickened by his own vile needs, Vincent choked back

bile. Succumbing to Sadie Sue would mean relinquishing his soul to the very ones he fought, and he'd become his father.

Summoning every ounce of resistance he possessed, he focused on escaping her clutches, then snapped the ropes in two and flung Sadie Sue off of him. "Get out of here," he growled.

She toppled onto the floor, stunned and flailing her hands in fury, but lunged back up in attack. "You can't do that, you beast. You belong to me now."

"No!" With a growl, he sent her away from him again, this time so hard she fell against the wall. Body wound tight with sexual need and fury, he flung his hands out and shattered the lamp next to her, sending glass scattering. He'd never hit a woman before, but he was tempted now.

She screamed and vaulted toward Clarissa, who'd backed up against the door. "He's mine—I have to have him to please the master. If you'd leave him alone, he'd come to me."

Clarissa tried to escape, but Sadie Sue was a madwoman and threw Clarissa against the wall.

Fury raged through Vincent as Clarissa slid to the floor with a moan.

Vincent clutched Sadie Sue's arm and dragged her toward the door. "Touch her again and you'll find out what pain really is."

She kicked and screamed, her shrill voice echoing off the walls as he threw her outside. Determined to get rid of her, he flung his hands, and wood splintered and exploded around her. Then he bared his teeth.

He must have finally frightened her, because she pushed herself up and ran to her car.

A heartbeat later, her car engine fired up and she screeched down the mountain. When he stepped back inside, he was sweating and shaking.

Clarissa dragged herself up, stunned, rubbing the back of her head.

Horror and regret suffused him. She'd seen the animal he'd become, the way he'd let Sadie Sue use him.

Through the haze, her face registered. A bruise marred her forehead and another marked her chest. Sadie Sue hadn't caused those.

What in the hell had happened to her?

Suddenly oblivious to his nakedness, he strode toward her. "Why did you come here, Clarissa?"

Her breath rattled out. "I saw another spirit tonight; Tim said you'd found her."

He zeroed in on the cut on her hand, then her bruised forehead. Emotions warred in his chest, and he reached out and tipped her chin up with his thumb. "Jesus. What happened?"

"I wrecked my car to avoid hitting the girl."

"I thought you said she was dead."

"She was, but I didn't realize it until I'd crashed." She wet her lips, but her gaze fell to the shattered glass on the floor, and he realized how much of himself he'd revealed tonight.

Hell, better she see the real Valtrez man. And he wouldn't apologize for threatening Sadie Sue. If she hurt Clarissa again, he'd snap her neck in two with his bare hands and take pleasure in her screams.

"I called you, but you didn't answer." Her eyes darkened. "Obviously you were busy."

Words of regret hovered on the tip of his tongue, then died on his lips. "I'm not going to apologize for what

I am," he said in a gruff voice. "I have needs that you would never understand."

Just as he'd touched her bruise, she reached out and traced a finger over the slash on his chest. Her gaze locked with his, and the softness returned to her eyes, filling the hollow, empty hole inside him with something bittersweet and more painful than the beating he'd just taken. Emotions he didn't want crowded his chest.

"You don't need Sadie Sue, Vincent." She pressed her lips gently to his wound, and a bolt of heat and longing unlike anything he'd ever experienced shot through him. The intensity of his hunger for her fueled his rage.

Dammit. He didn't want to want her, or to need her, but he did. The darkness inside him warred with the last sliver of conscience he possessed. He knew how to drive her away.

He grabbed her hand, gripped her wrist painfully, and forced her to look into his eyes, to see him for what he was. "All I need is a warm cunt, Clarissa, not love or softness."

Her breath caught. "No, you need more. I feel it in your touch, in the way your chest trembled beneath my hand. I see it in your haunted eyes."

He shoved her toward the window, gripped her face, and forced her to look outside. "See how dark it is with those clouds covering the moon? That's me inside—my heart is black, empty, Clarissa."

"I don't believe that." She took Vincent's hands in hers and flipped them over and traced a finger over his scar. "There's good in you, too, Vincent."

She kissed his scar, then cupped his face in her hands and traced her tongue around his mouth.

He pressed her body into the wall. "I can't control

that darkness, Clarissa. You're lying to yourself if you think differently."

"You're not all darkness," she whispered breathily. "That's why you chose to be an agent, why you protect innocents."

He kneed her legs apart, rubbed his foot up her calf seductively. "I track down killers because their darkness feeds my soul, because I understand the sickos. You can't save me, Clarissa, no one can."

Instead of bolting, though, she flicked her tongue along his chest. His skin sizzled where her lips touched the scarred flesh.

"You'd let a whore have you," she said softly, "let her whip you because you like to be abused? Or because you think you deserve it? Because you couldn't save your mother?"

He clenched his fists by his sides, hating her words yet aching to tunnel his hands through her hair and throw her down on the floor and take her. To ease the pain that gripped him in a chokehold. "I asked for it," he said in a gruff voice. "I told her to give me pain."

Her gaze met his, searching, probing, finding her way deep inside to the void he didn't want her to see. "Because it's all you've ever known," she said softly. "I can show you how different it can be. How beautiful love-making is when you care about someone."

He hated that softness about her.

He didn't want her comfort. Didn't need anything from her but to be left alone.

Or the release that he hadn't gotten with Sadie Sue.

Her gaze latched with his. Then she licked a droplet of sweat from his chest and he flinched, knowing that the release from being with Sadie Sue wouldn't have sated him anyway because, dammit, Clarissa was in his head. He wanted her body, not Sadie Sue's. And not just for tonight.

He craved her as if she was the seed of life, as if she could obliterate the darkness and guide him back to the light.

"Don't try to shrink me, Clarissa. I am what I am. A heartless son of a bitch who needs to be fucked every day." Determined to convince her that she should run from him, he cupped her breasts again, this time even more boldly. Her nipple stiffened between his fingers, and he twisted it so hard she gasped. "If you still think you can fill my needs, here are my rules." He lowered his head, his lips a fraction of an inch from her ear. "I take a woman only once, Clarissa. And always from behind."

God, he wanted her. Wanted to feel her in his hands. Hear her moaning his name as he came inside her. Feel her skin slick with his sweat, her flesh quivering with pleasure he'd given her.

He flicked his tongue along her neck, pressed his stiff cock between her legs, and shoved her hands upward, splaying them on the wall, trapping her, taunting her, wanting her even though he knew it was wrong.

"Then take me, Vincent," Clarissa whispered. "Any way you want me. I'm yours. I've always been yours."

A silent war raged within him. She should be afraid of him. Should have gone running into the night at his crudeness.

Instead, she twisted, stroking his shaft with her center, tormenting him to follow through on his craving.

Take her like the animal you are, a voice whispered in his head. *Show no mercy.*

"Go ahead, Vincent," she said, rubbing her hips to

stroke him. The movement lodged his throbbing cock between her legs. "I'm not afraid. I want you. I'll spread my legs and welcome you inside me."

Her sultry offer made his body go even more rock hard with desire and raw hunger. He craved the scent of her cum on his tongue, ached to feel her naked skin against his own, to feel her writhing as his slick cock slid into her wet chamber.

Yet he couldn't allow himself the pleasure of a slow fuck.

Sensations spiked his need, and he ripped off her tank top and tore off her bra.

Then, he lowered his head and bit her nipples. She cried out, clutched at him, but he grabbed her hands and shoved them away again, holding them prisoner so she couldn't touch him.

Greedily, he licked and sucked her turgid nipples until she moaned and her knees buckled. The scent of her longing filled the air, the sound of her heart pounding echoed in his ears and drove him onward until he heard nothing but the voice inside his head telling him to love her fast and hard, to make her his completely.

He ripped off her skirt and panties then, spread her pussy lips with his fingers, groaning with arousal at the feel of her wet, slick folds. Then he fused his mouth to her, licking and sucking her clit, thrusting his tongue inside her as he would soon do his cock.

"God, Vincent . . ."

A moan tore from her, and his sucking noises echoed in the sultry air as she rocked against his mouth.

He released her hands, cupped her ass with one hand, and thrust two fingers deep inside her. She clawed her hands through his hair, cried his name on a ragged breath; then he sipped her juices as she quivered and spasmed with her orgasm. He drank deeply, sucking and lapping her up, quenching his thirst with her sweetness, a thirst that only she could slake.

His body hammering with need, he rolled on a condom, then spun her around, pressing her face against the wall. Growling in anticipation, he thrust his length into her damp chamber. Slick with her release and still quivering, she groaned his name again as he filled her. He pushed her hands above her head, grinding himself into her, her pants of excitement sending waves of sensations rocketing through him.

The darkness swept over him again, clawing, trying to suck him into its abyss, and he closed his eyes, battling the need to relent to the ugliness, to make their coupling more violent as another need churned through him.

He wanted to see her face. Wanted to look into her eyes, see the excitement building as he pumped inside her, wanted to feel her breath on his cheek as he claimed her mouth and tenderly kissed her.

His climax rippled like a tidal wave through him, hot and bold, mind-numbing in its intensity.

He poured himself inside her, thrusting so hard their bodies slapped the wall and the windowpane rattled. Heat suffused his skin, imprinting her scent on him forever.

He had never wanted to see a woman's face when he screwed her. Never craved the taste of her cum or ached for her again before he was even finished.

Terrified of the sudden savage need in him, he tore himself away from her.

With a curse, he yanked on his pants and zipped them, then grabbed her clothes and shoved them toward her. She was shaking, clutching the wall as if she might fall if she released it, her body damp with his sweat, her breathing an erratic rhythm that mimicked his own.

Sadie Sue's torn clothes and whip lay on the floor in the midst of the broken glass, reinforcing the reality that he was vile, that he had no right to have taken Clarissa like an animal. That she deserved better.

"Go home," he said gruffly.

She slowly turned around, trembling, her eyes glassy with passion. "Vincent, let's talk," she whispered.

He shook his head. Her bruised skin and swollen lips mocked him.

"I said *go*."

His barked command must have finally frightened her, because she dragged on her skirt and tank top, then walked toward the door. "I'll go for now. But it's not over between us. I played by your rules because I wanted you to see that we're good together. That you deserve to be loved."

"It is over," he snapped. "It has to be."

She shook her head, then tunneled her fingers through her hair and glanced down at her underwear, which lay in shreds on the floor. "All right, then I guess I'll deal with the demon that was in my house earlier alone."

She started to stalk away, but he grabbed her. "What are you talking about?"

"When I got home tonight, someone was in my house. I saw his black silhouette, a faceless demon. That's why I came here to you."

"Not another one of your ghosts?"

"No." She shivered. "This was different. Not a spirit reaching out, but death coming for me."

She reached for her purse. "But don't worry. I won't bother you again, Vincent."

His chest heaved as she walked outside into the humid

night. He wanted nothing more than to disappear into the woods, to run for hours, to forget that he'd ever had her.

To kill and mutilate as his father had taught him to do and purge the longing from him. Painful to have both inside, this constant war tearing at him. The bad came easy; the good was more difficult.

But a killer, a demon was out here and had come for Clarissa. The same one he'd seen in the woods . . .

Emotions squeezed his chest, and he touched his pocket, where he kept the angel amulet. She had stood up for him when he was young. Had the nerve to tangle with his father. And even now, she'd given herself to him without asking anything for herself.

He couldn't let any harm come to her.

He had to follow her, stay with her. Had to do his job. Protect her and find a way to slay this demon.

But he wouldn't touch her again. He couldn't, or he would lose himself completely.

Clarissa gasped for a breath as she hurried outside into the humid air. She was a fool to throw herself at Vincent like that. She was barely holding on to the thin, tattered strands of her own sanity—how did she think she could save him?

And how could he be intimate with her and throw her out as if there was nothing between them but sex?

Because he'd been abused and no one had ever loved him.

Thunder rumbled above, hinting at an impending storm and a reprieve from the oppressive heat. The earth was dry and hot, dying, starved for water as if the devil had lit a wildfire beneath the ground and drained it of life.

But she had never felt more alive.

Yet at the same time she felt drained, as well. Starved for more of Vincent.

She hated herself for it.

Her skin tingled from his fingertips, her nipples throbbing for his mouth, her womb clenching as if he was still inside her, her entire body quaking with the intensity of their lovemaking.

He hadn't made love to her, he would say.

Whatever he called their coupling, she wanted him again.

Because she had made love to him.

And once was not nearly enough.

But his warning pounded in her ears as she climbed in the rental car and drove toward her house—his father had lost control and killed his mother.

She had to protect herself. Guard her emotions or he would steal not only her body, but her heart and soul.

She could survive a broken heart, but her soul he couldn't have. If she surrendered it, the spirits who depended on her would lose their way. Then they, too, would be left vulnerable and lapse into the darkness instead of the light.

She couldn't let that happen.

Pan rejoiced in his conquests. The young girl from the ridge had taken his hand tonight and relinquished her soul.

She was his now, another victory on the notch of his bedpost into the upper realm. When she made a kill, she'd be his forever.

And Vincent was teetering . . .

Winning a Dark Lord would ensure he earned that extra lifetime he'd yearned for since the early days of his demise.

A demise that had been painful, an existence that had meant burning in eternity forevermore on the lowest plane of the underworld. This short stint on earth had reminded him of what it was like to be free of the pain.

To be human.

He wouldn't go back, no matter whom he had to torment or kill.

Time was ticking. Three days until Zion arose from the grave for the coronation.

Destroying Clarissa was the only answer. He had to stop her from sleeping with Vincent again. The Dark Lord's sexual prowess lended to his vulnerability, and she had the key to absolve his dark side to the point of nonexistence.

He had to escalate his attack on her. Yes, tonight he'd show himself to her in demonic form again.

She had to fold sometime. And soon.

And when she did, he'd be watching. Then he'd offer her salvation.

A chance to join Vincent forever as he claimed his post at his father's side and led the demons.

And if she didn't, he'd find a way to get Vincent to kill her as his father had his mother.

But first he'd lead her to the mines, where so many of Eerie's people had died. There the dead never rested.

And when he trapped her there, they would torment her forever.

CHAPTER TWENTY

Fear for Clarissa sent Vincent's heartbeat into a spin. He grabbed his weapon, rushed out to his car to follow her, and sped down the mountain.

He should call the sheriff, request that Deputy Bluster drive to Clarissa's and watch her tonight. She'd be safer with him than she would with Vincent.

Or would she?

Bluster was human, couldn't go up against a supernatural demon.

Would Vincent be able to defeat one if necessary?

A week ago, he would have denied believing in their existence.

But today he'd seen the monster cause an innocent girl's brutal death by pushing her off the mountain ridge without even touching her.

A light of recognition dawned.

It was all tied to him and his father, he realized. The

evil, the eclipse, the black rock, maybe even these girls' murders . . .

What if his father had found a way to return from the grave? Maybe the cave with the black rock served as some type of portal for Satan's warriors.

Bad blood, bad blood . . .

He parked in front of Clarissa's house, then strode up to the door. She opened it before he even knocked. A menacing growl echoed from inside, but this time Wulf stared at him but stood back.

Clarissa lowered one hand to rest on the top of the huge animal's head, her voice low but commanding. "Good boy. He's not the enemy."

"Are you certain about that?" he asked.

"Yes." She paused, her mouth set in an angry slash. "But you made it clear that you have no feelings for me, Vincent. So we'll finish this investigation and we can both go our separate ways."

He gave a clipped nod. "Is the demon here now? Did you sense him?"

"No." She ran a hand through her hair, raking it back, and his gaze zeroed in on the bruise on her forehead.

He removed the amulet from his pocket. "I want you to put this on."

She frowned. "I don't understand."

"The amulet was my mother's. The bloodstone stands for courage, and the angel is for protection."

Her expression softened. "I can't accept a gift like that, Vincent."

He lifted her hair and slipped the chain around her neck. "Please, Clarissa. I'd feel better if you wore it. It might help keep you safe from the demon."

She traced a finger over the golden wings and looked

up at him, emotions glittering in her eyes. "The wings look like the scar on your hand."

He nodded. "They are. My mother lost it in the fire when my father killed her. I couldn't save her, but I reached into the flames and retrieved it."

"Thank you, Vincent."

He wanted to hold her again, but he couldn't make false promises. "Go to bed now. You look exhausted."

Sadness and confusion flickered in her luminous eyes, but she turned and climbed the steps to her bedroom, ordering the dog to follow her as if she accepted his statement. He heard the water kick on, knew she was taking a shower. His body throbbed with the need to join her, to be inside her again, but he forced himself to step outside on the porch instead.

The night sounds of the forest engulfed him. Then came the screams of the girl as she'd fallen over the ridge. The image of his father's hand touching the black rock, fire glowing from its edges.

And his mother's pain-filled cries as the fire consumed her.

As soon as he destroyed this killer and made certain Clarissa was safe, he'd leave this damn area. Clarissa would be better off without him.

Still, he phoned the research center and left a message for the doctor to call him to discuss the study. He wanted to know what they'd learned about his blood.

If he was pure evil, or if he had a chance at redemption.

~

Clarissa scrubbed her body, desperate to free herself of Vincent's masculine scent, but it had invaded her pores and lingered on her skin just as his touch lingered in her mind, and the intensity of their lovemaking lingered in her heart. She was connected to this man now; maybe she had been from the beginning.

And nothing could break that connection.

Unless he kills you.

A seed of worry sprouted inside her as she flipped off the water, dried off, and dragged on a cool cotton nightshirt. She hated sleeping in underwear, so she slipped into bed without it, aching to have Vincent's arms around her and his sex between her thighs again—the emptiness inside her was almost unbearable.

She traced a finger over the amulet, hurt and confusion lodging in her chest. She had to accept that he didn't love her.

But why would he have given her something so special if he didn't care about her?

Finally exhaustion plagued her, and she closed her eyes, welcoming sleep. But Cary Gimmerson's spirit came to her—her shattered face, then her blood-soaked hands reaching for Clarissa, pleading for her to save her. Jutting bones, broken and protruding through bruised and battered skin, cracked and popped as the girl's body floated in the shadows of the moss-covered trees.

"He's coming for you next," the voice whispered. The other victims appeared beside her, each one paler, their bodies disintegrating.

The wind picked up, sending dust and bones swirling in a haze around her, and she choked as the ashes invaded her throat and the scent of decay filled her nostrils.

"Who killed us?" Billie Jo wailed.

"I didn't want to die," Daisy cried.

Suddenly, a sea of other ghosts bled into the darkness,

their screams of pain and anguished moans bombarding her.

"Why don't you help us?"

"Someone killed me."

"He cut me open and ripped out my organs."

"Why have you deserted us?"

"She can't help us. She's weak like her mother."

"We're all alone now. She's sleeping with the enemy, in bed with a demon."

A thousand more voices shouted in her head, screaming that she was a failure, that she would betray them, that being with Vincent would sway her into becoming one of the demons.

She twisted and turned, clawing to escape the horrific images and sounds, yet her mother's dead body swinging back and forth from the Devil's Tree taunted her. The *creak, creak* of the branches, the whistle of the trees in the wind, her grandmother's cry when she'd found her.

Daisy's body hung beside it, her wide, sightless eyes staring into space, pleading.

Then Clarissa saw herself. Her hair tangled around her ashen face. Slash marks across her wrists where she'd first tried to end her life. Tear tracks where she'd cried as she begged for death to end her misery.

The rope tightening around her neck, choking her, cutting off the air as she kicked the chair from beneath her and prayed for God to forgive her.

A tortured cry wrenched her from sleep, the wail of a dying animal making her jerk her head up and search the room.

The demon was here; she sensed his presence.

Then she saw the shadow. A black faceless monster hovered at the foot of her bed. A hideous laugh reverberated through the air, and the animal's cry followed, this time more distant. The smell of blood assaulted her, an animal's blood, and she vaulted off the bed.

She recognized that animal's cry. Wulf, her beloved dog, her best friend and confidant.

He was no longer in the room. But his blood soaked the floor.

A scream of anguish jolted Vincent, and he clutched the porch rail with a white-knuckled grip, searching the shadows of the live-oaks bordering Clarissa's property for the source. No, not out here.

Inside.

Another cry boomeranged through the screened doorway, and he spun around and ran into the house.

Heart hammering in his chest, he took the steps two at a time, terrified that he'd find Clarissa dying or in the hands of a demonic monster.

Suddenly, he slammed into Clarissa rounding the corner to the staircase.

She screamed and tried to jerk away, her body quivering as he embraced her.

"Clarissa, it's me, Vincent." He searched her face, yet the hallway was pitch black, and all he could discern was the terror in her wide-set eyes. "What's wrong?"

Her nails dug into his arms as she gulped a sob.

"Are you hurt?"

"No," she cried. "It's Wulf . . ."

"What happened?"

She dragged him back to her bedroom. "In here, he's gone. Blood . . ."

A sliver of moonlight fought through the clouds and

streaked the room, just enough to illuminate the blood. But he didn't have to see it to smell the metallic odor or to know that it had spilled from an animal.

"The demon must have hurt him," she said, her voice breaking. "I was here, sleeping. Wulf was at the foot of the bed, then he was gone . . ."

And Vincent had been downstairs on the porch. He hadn't seen or heard anyone come in.

But he might not, not if a demon could slither through the shadows or orb through time.

Clarissa's knees buckled. "Wulf can't be dead, Vincent, he's the only family I have left."

"We'll find him," Vincent said, although instincts cautioned him that the dog might be dead. He might be chopped to pieces, his body scattered in the woods for the other animals to feast upon.

He urged Clarissa to sit on the edge of the bed. "Stay here. I'll go search for him."

She shook her head, a desperate air to the frenzied movement. "No, I'm going with you." She stood, threw off her gown, and rushed into her closet, grabbing clothes. He sucked in a deep breath at the sight of her naked body, his own instantly growing hard with desire.

But now wasn't the time . . .

What if the killer was watching? Had taken the dog to lure Vincent away so he would leave Clarissa alone and vulnerable?

If he fell into that trap, Clarissa might die. He couldn't let that happen.

She dragged on jeans and a T-shirt, then socks and sneakers. "Come on, we have to hurry. He's bleeding—he might be in real trouble, or worse. Near death."

Panic laced her voice. Still, reservations kicked in. What if they did find her dog ripped apart as he had the other animals?

Or what if this was a ploy to lure them into the demon's trap?

~

Clarissa didn't intend to take no for an answer. She refused to let Vincent search for Wulf alone. Wulf would respond better to her, especially if he were injured and sensed a threat.

"Let me grab some flashlights." She rushed past him, down the steps to the laundry room. Vincent's boots clicked on the wood floor behind her.

"Clarissa, it may be dangerous out there." His dark eyes met hers. "We don't have any idea what we'll find. I discovered other animals mauled and mutilated in the woods. If the same demon that killed them has done something to Wulf, it won't be pretty."

She swallowed back another bout of tears, willing herself to be strong. "Don't you see, Vincent? It's the only way. We have to do this together."

She handed him a flashlight, gripping another in sweat-soaked hands, anxious to leave.

"I don't like you going," he said in a gruff voice. "So stay close to me and follow my lead."

She nodded and gestured to the laundry room. "I saw more blood in there. I think Wulf went out through his doggie door. He was probably chasing the demon."

A hint of fury flickered in Vincent's eyes before he masked it, and she understood his silence. He suspected Wulf had gone off to die alone.

Grief welled inside her, but she forged ahead, determined to find him no matter what his condition.

Vincent led the way as he tracked the trail of blood through the woods, forging deeper and deeper into the heart of the mountain as if he instinctively knew which direction to go, as if he'd become one with the land and smelled the blood and evil.

Clarissa followed close behind, breathing deeply as she increased her pace to keep up with his long stride. The smell of fear felt oppressive, cloying, and her energy began to drain as if some physical force were sucking the life from her.

Heat from the ground seeped through the soles of her shoes, and an eerie quiet blanketed the mountain, the occasional howl of a mountain lion or bear rumbling in the distance. Fear vibrated off the ridges, echoing in her ears, and the stench of blood and maimed animals swirled in a vile stench around her.

Vincent paused, body rigid, a hiss escaping into the tension-filled air.

Clarissa hesitated and held her breath. "What?" she finally asked. "Do you hear Wulf?"

"No, other animals. I smell their blood."

She stepped forward, but Vincent stood, blocking her sight with his big body. "You don't need to see them, Clarissa. It's brutal."

"You think the demon destroyed them?"

"Maybe. Or it's possible that some teenagers are up to satanic rituals."

She didn't believe that and neither did he, but she refrained from comment as he pulled her aside, then guided her to the left through a path heading west, away from the desecrated animals.

A sick feeling pitted Clarissa's stomach, but she said nothing, simply followed Vincent.

As they plowed through the woods, the cries of other lost spirits poured from the stone walls of the mountain, closing around her. Beckoning her to help them. Drawing her deeper into their pain and the realization that something sinister was trying to recruit them to leave the light and join the quest for darkness.

"Look!" Vincent shouted. "The blood trail is leading into that mine."

Clarissa hesitated, shaking all over, willing the voices to be quiet.

"What is it?"

"This is the mine where all the miners lost their lives. I hear their voices screaming in pain."

He squeezed her hand, and she drew in courage. If Wulf was inside, she had to save him. She couldn't let her fears imprison her as her mother's had.

Her heart racing, she pushed past Vincent and raced ahead to the mouth of the cave. Vincent grabbed her hand to stop her. "Let me go in first, make sure the mine is safe."

But Wulf was inside. Clarissa heard his low growl of pain. Recognized his scent. Knew he'd welcome her but that he might not Vincent.

Racked with fear, she jerked away and charged inside. "Wulf! Wulf, where are you?"

She shone the flashlight across the rocky dirt floor, noticed weathered rotting boards jutting from the ceiling as she plunged deeper into the mineshaft, listening.

The spirits gathered from the stone walls, floating and drifting toward her with outstretched skeletal fingers, their cries screeching from the depths of the tunnel to taunt her, crowding her mind with wails of sorrow. "Help."

"We didn't deserve to die."

"Get us out. We're trapped here . . ."

"A demon caused the explosion."

"He killed us, took us from our families."

A sob caught in her throat. How could she possibly help them all?

Wulf's whimper mingled amid the roar of spirits. Then a rumbling sound followed, and rocks and dirt crumbled from above, raining down. Dear God. The mine was collapsing.

She stumbled and dropped her flashlight. It hit a rock and flickered off, plunging her into total darkness. She pivoted to search the ground just as another rumbling exploded behind her. Rocks and dust swirled in a brown and gray cloud as the mineshaft collapsed behind her,

"Clarissa!" Vincent shouted. "Come back, it's too dangerous!"

She yelled his name and started to run back toward the mouth, but rocks pelted her, and she ran the opposite way, dodging falling debris. Like a mudslide, the walls tumbled down around her and the floor shook. A wooden beam slammed against the back of her head, and she stumbled forward, the sharp, jagged rocks tearing at her hands as she pitched to the ground.

She tasted blood and dirt, and pain splintered through her calf just before the endless darkness swallowed her.

Sadie Sue had never been so furious in all her life. She'd always had a temper, just enough to give her the grit to do whatever the hell she had to do to survive.

The reason she'd slapped the living shit out of her drunk daddy when he'd tried to crawl in her bed one night. The reason she'd slept with anyone who'd given her attention as a teen.

The reason she'd kept her baby instead of giving it away to strangers, like Petey's daddy had wanted. The reason she'd taken the dance job and then spread her legs to make ends meet for her and her son.

The reason she'd made the deal with the devil.

Ever since that fatal night when he'd wrapped that snake around her skinny neck and offered her eternal life, she'd felt different, as if blood no longer ran through her veins. She burned with heat and an energy that pulsed through her soul, tormenting her with vile thoughts and telling her to do things she'd never considered before.

Like whipping Vincent Valtrez until she'd licked the blood from his back.

Now she lay like a rag doll while another john screwed her, his grunts bouncing off the cheap hotel room walls as he rutted.

Finally he finished, heaving for air, sweating profusely.

Sickened by him, she laughed.

He snatched a hank of her hair. "What are you laughing at, you bitch?"

She laughed harder, watching as his jowls reddened with rage. "Your puny little dick. No wonder you can't keep a wife."

He slapped her, so hard her ears rang. Laughter died in her throat, and rage replaced it, oozing from her pores. Every time she'd given a blow job to some ugly creep flashed into her mind, followed by the time her daddy had pinned her between the wall and the bed. She'd grabbed his balls and twisted them so hard he yelped in pain, and she thought his head would spin right off.

"Don't mess with me again," she said as she lunged up, shoved him back on the bed, and glowered over him. That strange feeling suffused her, as if she no longer owned her body, and she blinked, then felt her eyes swirling back in her head.

He whimpered in fear. Thrilled by his terror, she gave his balls another vicious twist, then retrieved her clothes while he rolled into a fetal position.

A sliver of moonlight played off her hands as she grabbed the money he'd put on the table.

"That slap will cost you extra," she said with another bitter laugh. Still glowering at him, she took his wallet from his pants where they lay wrinkled on the floor, emptied it of cash, and stormed out.

Reeling with the humiliation of having Valtrez dump her for crazy Clarissa, she contemplated revenge on the woman.

And she would have Vincent one day. In fact, he'd be her servant, worshipping at her feet, licking her ass if she told him to.

This time she'd be the one taking pleasure while she'd leave him hard as a rock.

Yep, Sadie Sue had the devil on her side now, and there was no stopping her.

A few minutes later, she let herself into her house. Trina was sleeping on the couch, snoring softly. Sadie Sue shuddered and walked past, then hurried into little Petey's room.

When she saw her reflection in the window by the crib, her chest constricted. The devil had sunk his claws into her. She could see his fire burning in her eyes.

Little Petey stirred, then looked up at her, the scent of baby powder sweetening the air. Her head spun as vile voices whispered in her head.

"Your baby will only get in the way."

"He'll be better off without you, you whore."

"Let the devil have him."

Her head throbbed, vision blurring, and she reached for Petey.

He screamed as her hands closed around his body, and she pulled him from his crib.

CHAPTER TWENTY-ONE

Vincent's heart thundered in his chest as he ran deeper into the mine after Clarissa.

He almost wished he could see them so he could fend them off for her.

More rocks tumbled around him, pinging off the walls, jerking him back to the present.

Clarissa . . .

Dammit, she was supposed to stay behind him, but he'd screwed up and she'd gotten past. Then he'd spotted bones, stopped to check them out, and the mine had begun to rumble.

What if she got killed in the collapse? He couldn't lose her . . .

Ignoring the panic rippling through him, he shouted her name as rock and rotten wood tumbled down, but she didn't respond. He smelled animal blood, then saw more bones jutting out from inside the cave. A human skeleton. Years old.

Dodging more falling debris, he veered to the right,

pebbles scattering below his boots as he searched the tunnel.

Suddenly another rumble rent the air, the ceiling ahead totally collapsed, and more rock and dirt crashed down. He coughed against the dust and screeched to a dead halt, nearly plowing into the mound.

Cursing, he threw up his hands, but his anger sparked the power in his hands, and he sent a side wall caving in. Realizing he might make things worse, he forced his hands by his sides and inhaled a deep breath.

"Clarissa, make some sound. Let me know you're back there. That you're alive."

He closed his eyes, focused on each sound in the dark mineshaft, but the scattering of more rock and dirt colliding filled the deadly silence. Somewhere in the distance he zeroed in on a dog's pain-filled whimper and knew it was Wulf.

At least the dog had survived. Maybe Wulf would find Clarissa and protect her until Vincent could shovel his way through the mound to reach her.

He unpocketed his cell phone to call the sheriff for a rescue crew, but his phone showed no service.

He didn't have time to hike back to call—Clarissa might be injured or run out of air.

Knowing that the mineshaft was still unsteady, he assessed the sides and roof before he started to yank away rock and wood.

Carefully he moved stones and splintered wooden boards, leaving enough space so they could crawl back through in case there wasn't an opening on the other side.

If not, he'd have to make one himself. Because he would get Clarissa out. He had to.

A whistling sound floated through the mine, then the sound of a sinister laugh echoing from the hills. Vincent froze, recognizing the voice in the recesses of his brain.

His father's laughter. His voice assuring Vincent that one day he would win. That destiny was calling.

An image of his mother's face flashed against the darkness, her screams mingling with his father's vile laughter, and he flung his hands out, tearing away rock and boards with such a fury that his body vibrated from the force.

Sweat soaked his shirt and body as he dug with his bare hands. He coughed again, spitting out dirt as he dropped onto his belly and slithered through the narrow opening. Dirt caved around him, dust and the stench of blood filled his nostrils, and rocks scraped his hands as he dug away more debris.

His lungs ached from trying to conserve air as he levered himself between some wedged stone and dropped to the clearing beyond. It was so dark that even with his heightened senses, he saw nothing but shadows.

He felt for the flashlight he'd tucked into his belt, but he'd lost it in the mess.

"Clarissa!"

No response.

"Clarissa, dammit, answer me! Where are you?"

A low moan emerged from his right, and he slithered forward, clawing his way along the stone until he found her. She lay slumped in a bed of rocks and dirt, limp and barely breathing.

Heart hammering, he reached out to check her for injuries and felt blood trickling down her forehead.

———❦———

Clarissa moaned, covering her ears with her hands to drown out the sorrowful cries reverberating off the walls. The dead who lay trapped beneath the rubble from years before stared up through the ground with horror-stricken eyes as flesh fell from their bones and their skin disintegrated into dust.

She saw and heard it all as if it was happening that moment. The terrified, shocked screams and panic as the mine collapsed. The bloody hands clawing through dirt and rock for freedom before the suffocating darkness and dirt sucked the last breath from their lungs.

Crippled by the dead who held her prisoner to their tortured souls, she barely realized that Vincent had found her.

He patted her cheek gently, and slowly she responded, battling her way back from the dead to the living.

"Clarissa, I feel blood. Are you hurt?" He ran his hands over her arms and legs, over her torso, checking for injuries, his fingers gentle, his voice gruff with concern.

She pressed her hand over his. "I'm okay . . . it's the voices . . . the dead crying out to me." She gulped for a breath. "There are so many here."

He squeezed her hand. "I'm going to find a way out."

She nodded, although she wasn't sure he could see her in the dark.

"Just rest while I explore the cave."

She clutched his hand, suddenly not wanting him to leave her alone. "Some of these mines go on for miles and miles underground. The tunnels connect to underground caves."

"I know. I'll be back. I promise." He squeezed her hand again, and she released him, but a chill invaded her as he scrambled away.

Somewhere in the distance, water trickled over a rock, and Wulf whined. The scent of decay assaulted her, the sound of a small animal skittering along the ground. She shivered, a sob catching in her throat as the spirits returned to haunt her, begging her to save them from where they lay trapped for all time.

She closed her eyes and prayed for the souls, begged God to help them find peace, then whispered for the lost souls to look for the light.

"You have to move on, cross into the light. God is with you," she said softly.

A sliver of light warmed her, yet another bevy of screams bombarded her, and she rolled into a ball and rocked herself back and forth, continuing the prayer as she waited for Vincent's return.

But panic set in like a slow-eating virus. What if they died in here tonight? What if they couldn't escape and she was buried here among the lost souls, forced to listen to their tortured cries through eternity?

Her breathing turned shallow as she faded into a semiconscious state, her head pounding from the torment.

Footsteps and skittering rock tore her from her panicked state, and Vincent's voice came as blessed relief, soothing in the darkness.

"Clarissa, there's a clearing about a half mile up where the mine connects to a series of tunnels and caves. There's an underground spring there. Wulf is resting by the pool."

"That's one of the sacred places," Clarissa whispered. "I've heard about them. He's safe from demons there."

"Let's go, then. We can rest, and I can check your head injury. Then I'll find a way to get help."

She nodded and tried to stand, but her legs wobbled, and she was so weak she clutched at him. He slid an arm beneath her waist and they crouched low, shuffling their way through the mine. Vincent led her as if instincts were his guide, and a streak of light illuminated the clearing, light that seeped from above ground and shot a ray of moonlight across the pool. Cool air offered a reprieve from the heat, and the soft gurgle of the water lapping against the stone walls brought a sense of peace.

The voices of the dead momentarily quieted.

Maybe the ones who'd made it this far had crossed over.

Wulf lay by the edge of the pool, looking weary, but he was alive. "Oh, baby." She knelt and hugged him, checking him for injuries. His paw looked bruised but the pool water had washed away the blood and he seemed okay. She petted him. Had Wulf instinctively come here because he'd known the water would heal him?

"It's beautiful," she whispered as Vincent helped her sit down by the pool edge and Wulf nuzzled up beside her. She'd never seen water so clear and beautiful. Her reflection caught in the shimmering softness, and so did Vincent's.

He looked like a giant primitive Roman god, his expression etched in granite as chiseled as the naturally rough, statuesque walls of the cave.

His expression softened, and he removed a handkerchief from his pocket, knelt and dipped it in the water, then gently pressed it to her cheek. The water felt blessedly cool, soothing, as did his touch. Her breath hitched as he wiped her scratches; then he pressed the cloth against her forehead. The throbbing in her head eased slightly.

"Vincent—"

"Shh, I want to check your injury."

He circled to her back, parting her hair, and examined the wound where the board had slammed into her scalp.

"It's really okay," she said. "Just a bruise."

"It doesn't look like it needs stitches," he replied. "Do you feel dizzy? Light-headed?"

Yes, but not from the head wound. From having him touch her here in this private cavern. The mineshaft had echoed of the dead and pain, but this place felt like a sanctuary. The faint light spilling through the darkness created shards of colors like a rainbow across the gray walls.

But the fear she'd felt earlier, the panic, rose to taunt her, and she pressed her hand to his cheek, need spiraling through her. If—*when*—they left, they had to face the world again, fight the demon.

His throat worked as he swallowed. "Try to relax. I'll go ahead and hunt for a way out."

"Not yet," she whispered. "It's safe here, free from the demons."

She parted her lips on a sigh, then pressed a kiss to his lips. He was so handsome and virile, so protective and strong, that her body ached for him.

"Clarissa, don't," he growled. "I told you my rules."

"We might not make it out of here alive," she said softly. "And if or when we do, we might not survive this demon." She wet her lips, traced a hand down his chest, and began to unbutton his shirt. "I don't want to die without having you one more time."

He caught her hand, jerked away, and turned to face the stone wall. But tension laced his big hard body, and he seemed to be struggling for control. "I said stop it. You don't know what you're doing."

"I know that I can't help myself, that I want your hands on me, Vincent. I want you to make me feel alive again. I need you to fill the emptiness inside me."

He clenched his hands by his sides, but she massaged the tension from his shoulders, then pressed a kiss to his back and pulled his shirt over his shoulders. The scars on his back made her throat convulse, yet tenderness filled her. He had suffered, possessed a dark side, but concern and tenderness underscored his touch as he'd washed the dirt and blood from her cheek.

He wouldn't hurt her. Even now, he was trying to protect her from himself.

And she knew what it was like to have him throbbing inside of her.

She kissed one scar, then another and another. His breath hissed between clenched teeth, and he stood rigid, unbending. She slipped around in front of him and trailed more kisses over his chest, each one tender and erotic. His dark gaze met hers, a battle raging in his eyes.

She took his hand and gently coaxed him to the water. His dark gaze flared with the fierceness of a warrior lover as she removed his shoes and socks.

Quivering with longing, she stripped her clothes and stood naked before him. Naked except for the angel amulet he'd given her.

His erection pushed against his jeans, begging for

freedom. Whispering her desires, she lowered his zipper and shoved his jeans down his legs. He stood ramrod straight, as if he refused to take part, and she smiled, then pushed his boxers down his legs.

With a shiver of anticipation, she pulled him into the crystal clear water with her.

———

Pan cursed the saints—Vincent had run into the mine to save Clarissa.

Maybe here the voices of the lost souls would finally drive her over the edge.

Her goodness was screwing with his plan, resurrecting the sliver of good inside Vincent, the good that his father had savagely beaten out of him. If Valtrez continued to have the woman sexually, she could feed his soul to the point of no return.

But Vincent would have to feed daily on her flesh, and no human woman was that unselfish.

Or could totally please an insatiable beast like Valtrez.

Soon he would lose control and the darkness would overcome him. Then he'd take her in the primitive ways, as his father had taught him.

Was Vincent fucking her now?

He homed in to listen to their voices, lifted his hands to feel their aura, tried to smell Valtrez's scent, yet it evaded him.

Had they discovered one of the sacred places? Was that the reason he'd lost track of them?

He cursed again, needing another kill.

Just as he needed to make certain that Sadie Sue made hers.

He blinked, morphing himself to her, his demonic form floating in the shadows as she stood in her child's room. The babysitter, the baby . . . it didn't matter to him who she chose as her first victim.

Only that she kill.

He blew his breath into her ear, whispered for her to feed the evil growing inside her, to squeeze the life out of the child until his last breath faded into silence.

CHAPTER TWENTY-TWO

The cool water lapped against Vincent's naked body, washing away the last strains of his resistance. He didn't want to feel anything for Clarissa, especially this all-consuming hunger that snaked through him like an out-of-control beast every time she whispered his name or touched him.

And seeing that amulet around her neck, glinting against her naked flesh, had nearly brought him to his knees with emotions.

Emotions he didn't want to feel. The love for his mother. The pain of losing her. The guilt that he hadn't saved her.

The fear that he might not be able to save Clarissa.

Adrenaline fired his need, and the terror that had nearly paralyzed him when the walls had caved still burned through his veins. While he'd dug his way through the rubble to reach her, all he could think about was that she might be dead.

That he didn't want her to die. That he couldn't bear to lose her.

She ducked beneath the pool, then surfaced, bubbles from the natural spring cascading around her naked breasts as they bobbed in the water. Hunger stabbed his groin. She looked so damn tantalizing that he wanted to eat her up.

The walls of the cave created a haven unlike anything he'd ever felt before, a quiet seclusion that erased any rational thoughts and obliterated the reasons he shouldn't take her.

You never fuck a woman more than once.

But somewhere deep in his soul, he'd known that she would drive him across that line, a line he'd never breached before.

The need was too strong, too all-consuming. He had to have her.

Thoughts fled, as did the reality of the danger awaiting them, and he plunged beneath the water, grabbed her by the waist, and fused his mouth to her nipple.

She cried out his name, and he sucked one breast, then the other, running his hands over her hips like a greedy animal, then between her thighs to play with her clit, then inside her. He needed more. Needed to feed from her. Needed all of her.

Her hands became urgent, begging, reaching for him.

He carried her from the pool, spread their clothes on the floor of the cave, and laid her below the sliver of moonlight, which cast a radiant glow over her naked body. He had never in his life seen anything more beautiful. She was the moonlight on a clear night, the sun setting across the aquamarine blue of the ocean, a breath when there was no air left in the world to swallow.

The last good thing a bastard like him should have.

But the one he wanted and would want with his dying breath.

The crystal drops of water that clung to her body begged for his mouth, and he licked them off, drop by drop, savoring the mixture of salt and sweetness on her skin and the smell of her arousal as the precious juncture between her thighs grew moist with need.

He tasted the dewy dampness there, too, and smiled at the way she bucked when his tongue teased her flesh and danced along her folds, taunting her.

"Let me taste you, too, Vincent. Please."

Her wispy voice sounded so sultry that a thousand sensations splintered through his nerve endings all at once. He thought he might explode as she pushed him backward, so he lay beneath her. She claimed his mouth with hers, probing his lips apart with her tongue until he groaned and dragged her on top of him. Her bare breasts brushed his chest, the friction almost unbearable as she stroked her foot up his calf, and plunged her tongue deeper into his mouth.

He'd never imagined a kiss could be so damn sensual, but she played her tongue along his teeth, nipping and sucking at his lips, then his neck, using her body to mimic her tongue as she teased him to the brink of insanity. He raked his hands over her buttocks, squeezing her cheeks, loving her ass with his hands, as he ground his hips upward and imagined being inside her.

With a guttural groan, she tore her mouth from his, then trailed her tongue and kisses along his jaw, down his neck to his nipples. He'd never had a woman suck him the way he had her, but she did, and his body spasmed with erotic sensations that shot straight to his groin and set him on fire.

He tunneled his fingers through her hair and ordered her to stop, but she continued torturing him by sliding south and enclosing her hand around his cock. It bulged with need, the tip of his penis oozing cum that she licked off; then she pushed his legs apart and cupped his balls in her hands. He clenched her hair, wanting her mouth around his shaft.

She licked her lips, then his engorged head, circling her tongue around the tip until pleasure rippled through him. Sighing in contentment, she licked him from head to base, cupping his swollen sex in her hand as she slid her lips over his length and took his cock into her mouth. His penis twitched and ached, throbbing for release, yet he clutched her shoulders, willing himself to hold back.

He wanted, had, to be inside her when he lost himself.

And he would lose himself if he took her again. It was against his rules, against everything he'd taught himself.

Dangerous to him.

Deadly for her.

She lapped him up, though, sucking his length and stroking him at the same time, licking her way around his shaft until he was mindless with pleasure.

Unable to restrain himself any longer, he grabbed her arms and flung her down on the makeshift bedding, then climbed above her. For a heartbeat of a second, he looked into her eyes, and shock sent spasms of erotic sensations through him at the blatant hunger in her eyes. She was strong, courageous, hid nothing from him. So giving that it humbled him.

His chest ached, and his mind screamed at him to stop, but he lowered his mouth and kissed her. He tasted her need, the intensity of her desire, his own cum on her lips, and kneed her legs apart.

Dragging his mouth away from hers, he looked into her eyes once more. She watched him with passion flaring in her eyes, her chest heaving for a breath, sweat beading on her brow, then licked her lips and smiled.

"You taste delicious," she whispered.

Her words shoved him over the edge, and he gripped her hips and thrust inside her. She cried his name as he filled her, and he pushed deeper, lifting her hips to sink himself further, pumping and grinding in and out as she clung to him.

Driven by the animal inside him, he rode her, hard and fast, their bodies slapping together in frenzied heat, his cock aching yet engorged with pleasure. A pleasure that was so exquisite it bordered on pain.

He'd known only pain before. Mindless sex with no connection.

Yet as he pounded inside her, his soul whispered that she was his lifemate. That after her, no other woman would be able to sate him.

He shut out the voice, rammed himself deeper, threw his head back, and relented to the primal man inside him. A low cry ripped from her throat as her body spasmed beneath him. The muscles of her womb clenched him, milking him as he threw his head back, gave in to the sensations, and came inside her.

Something sharp and painful splintered Vincent's chest, emotions he didn't recognize and didn't want.

Emotions a man like him had no right to feel and no right to pursue.

His breath tore from his throat as he levered himself on his hands and forced himself to push away from her. He'd already crossed the line, and he hadn't used a damn condom.

For God's sake—he couldn't bring another demon child into the world.

Clarissa grabbed his arm. "Don't pull away, Vincent. We were meant to be together."

Anger fueled his words. "That's what my mother said about her and my father. And he ended up killing her."

Vincent pried her fingers from his arm, leaving Clarissa bereft at his withdrawal. Only seconds earlier they had been connected in the most intimate way possible.

But their connection hadn't been only on a physical level. Erotic tremors that still quivered through her paled compared to the depth of the emotions overwhelming her.

"Don't do this, Vincent. I love you."

She did. Heart, mind, body, soul.

He angled his head, venom glittering in his eyes. "Love? That wasn't about love, Clarissa. I told you that before."

"But I felt the difference this time, Vincent." She gripped his arms. "And so did you."

"Don't you get it, Clarissa? I can't care about anyone, because that makes me a danger to them."

She couldn't let him walk away from her now. "You came back here because we belong together."

"I came back here to solve these murders. Because of a demon."

"But fighting that demon brought us together."

His look hardened even more. "Is that why you screwed me? Some kind of pity fuck because you think you can save me like my mother tried to save my old man?" He grabbed her arms and shook her. "Face the facts, Clarissa. It didn't work so well for her. My father had evil in his soul, and so do I. He burned my mother at the stake, and if you stay with me, I could turn into him one day and kill you, too."

"You won't do that."

"How do you know?" he shouted. "Did the dead come to Crazy Clarissa again and tell you that you're safe with me?"

His words cut her to the bone. Kids had called her crazy when she was little, and he'd known it.

But she hadn't expected him to say it tonight. She thought he'd accepted who she was.

How could she have been so wrong?

"I have blackouts, too," he said harshly. "Sometimes I lose time, hours, days, where I don't know what I'm doing. I've woken up with blood on my clothes, my hands. I can smell the stench of death all over me, and I know that I've been at it again. That I've gone out to kill."

She started to interrupt, but rage burned in his eyes, silencing her.

"I can't control when I disappear into that black hole or what I do when I'm there." He scrubbed a hand over his neck. "Last night, I was sucked back into the hole, and I walked beside the demon when he pushed that girl over the cliff. I stood by and did nothing while she died." His voice cracked. "That makes me just as responsible for her death as the demon who threw her over the cliff."

He flexed his fingers, waved them, and made rocks crumble. "You know I'm not human. My hands are lethal weapons just like my old man's." He made another small pile of rocks shatter. "He set things on fire with his hands. I make things explode without even touching them."

His choppy breathing rattled in the quiet as he faced her. "Remember all those animals mutilated in the woods? I've done that before, Clarissa. When I was a child, my father taught me how to kill with my bare hands. Cruelly, coldly, without remorse."

His breath hissed out, filled with self-disgust. "That's what I am. Part demon, a Dark Lord like my father. You made me realize that, and I have to accept it. And so do you."

He stalked away from her, grabbed his clothes, and yanked them on.

Hurt stabbed her. She was a fool. How many times did he have to tell her that he didn't want her?

This was the last time.

She tore the amulet from her neck and thrust it into his hand.

His face twisted. "I told you to keep it."

"I don't want it," she said in a strained whisper. "I don't want anything to remind me of you after you leave Eerie."

His jaw tightened as he folded his hand around the amulet, then he turned and headed toward the tunnel. "I'm going to find a way out of here."

She dressed, gave Wulf a command, and followed,

her heart shattering, her resolve setting in. She would help him find this demon so the girls could cross over.

Then she would forget that Vincent ever existed.

Love?

Pain and panic shot through Vincent as Clarissa's words echoed in his head.

Love? No one except his mother had ever used that word around him. He couldn't possibly say it in return. Couldn't feel it, either.

The only emotions he allowed were anger and hatred. They drove him to do his job. Find killers. Save the innocents.

Clarissa was an innocent.

Ironic that she thought she could save him when he had to save *her,* even if it meant saving her from herself and this ridiculous idea that they belonged together.

Vincent understood his destiny. He had to be alone.

Making love to her—no, fucking her—had been a huge mistake, possibly one of the biggest of his life.

She had gotten under his skin. He only hoped that when he lapsed into one of the black holes again, he didn't kill her because of it.

Sadie Sue felt the force of evil gripping her as if she'd been hypnotized by the devil. She had to do his bidding. Had to because she'd sold her soul to him to save her life.

A life she'd wanted so she could raise Petey.

Hazy voices whispered in her head, though, warning

her that her son would be better in heaven, free from the dangers on earth.

Safe from her.

Yes, he'd be better off dead.

All little babies went to heaven. God would take care of him, then. There'd be no sorrow or pain, only peace forever.

Little Petey screamed, and she felt the demon's breath wash over her shoulder. He was watching, waiting for her to put the baby out of his misery.

She began to shake him.

"Sadie Sue!" Trina shouted. "You're going to hurt Petey!"

Sadie Sue shook the baby harder. "Please, God, take him and give him peace. Keep him safe from me."

Petey screamed louder, his tiny fists clenched, his cheeks and face beet red as he wailed harder. Suddenly someone was shaking Sadie Sue, pulling her hands away from the baby.

"Sadie Sue! What are you doing?" the old woman screeched. "Stop it!"

Sadie Sue glared at her, and panic flashed in Trina's eyes. "Lord have mercy . . ."

The dark commands that had plagued Sadie Sue moments earlier faded slightly, and for a brief second, the horror of what she'd nearly done twisted her insides with nausea. She'd traded her soul to save her son, yet she had almost killed him.

Sickened, she thrust Petey into Trina's hands and ran from the room, then outside into the darkness. Tears streaked her face, huge gulping sobs wracking her body. What was she going to do now? The devil owned her, and she had to do his bidding.

But he wanted her to kill little Petey.

No. She wouldn't. She loved her son. She was his mother.

She had to protect him.

But what if the evil trapped her again and she couldn't control it?

CHAPTER TWENTY-THREE

Two days until the rising

Wulf paced over to Clarissa's side and rubbed up against her leg, then barked.

She stooped to pet him. "I'm glad you're better, buddy. Drinking from that pool saved you."

She patted him again, grateful to have his presence as she felt her way along the dark walls and tried to keep up with Vincent.

As they left the safety of the clearing, the sacred place where the voices had quieted, they began to haunt her again, screaming, crying for her to release them from their entrapment.

Ahead, Vincent paused. "This is a dead end."

Clarissa's breath caught. "What do we do now?"

He turned to her, his eyes dark orbs glowing in the tunnel. "Get back and cover your head. I'll create an opening."

A frisson of fear danced up her spine at his tone, but

she did as he ordered. A minute later, he flung his hands, and a rumble began. Rocks falling. Dirt swirling. Pieces of stone flying.

A faint light spilled in, and fresh air seeped toward her. She uncovered her head, brushing off rock and debris, then stood, shocked to see the damage Vincent had inflicted with just a flick of his bare hands.

"Come on. We need to get back and talk to Waller."

But Waller couldn't save the girls now, not from some supernatural force. Even she and Vincent weren't sure how to accomplish that feat.

"Clarissa?"

His voice sounded harsh, and she didn't realize he'd moved up beside her. "Come on. There could be another collapse any minute."

But the voices screamed in her head again. "Don't go."

"Don't leave us."

"Help us. We're trapped."

She barely stifled a cry as a lump formed in her throat. How could she desert those who needed her? But how could she right the wrong that had been done to them?

Vincent grabbed her arm and pulled her forward, pushing her outside into the early-morning darkness.

She glanced back at the cave and saw bony hands stretching their decaying fingers toward her.

Oblivious to her turmoil, Vincent coaxed her onward. Wulf barked and nuzzled up beside her, and she knew he understood. She silently vowed to do what she could to save the lost trapped in the mine, but doubts mingled with the cries, overwhelming her with guilt and remorse. So many lost . . . so many needy . . .

So many girls dead recently.

Their salvation lies in your hands. You have to help them.

Only she didn't know how to rid the town of the evil.

~~~~~

The insufferable heat served as a reminder of the devil playing his hand, that the short reprieve Vincent had experienced with Clarissa inside that cave had been a fleeting lapse in judgment.

They did not live in a vacuum or a sacred place.

They had to return to the real world and the battle that awaited.

He didn't trust himself with Clarissa. The thought of her dying at his hands terrified him.

He glanced over his shoulder, and his stomach clenched at her pale complexion, the dark circles beneath her eyes, the haunted expression that he'd helped put there.

"Are you all right?" he asked gruffly.

For a tension-filled minute she didn't reply, simply stared back at the cave as if the spirits inside were calling to her.

Her tormented look wrenched his gut. She couldn't help them all, and it pained her.

The reason she was too good for him.

He gently touched her arm. "We have a long hike. Can you make it?"

She nodded, but her eyes were glazed and distant. "Yes, just lead the way."

He wanted to drag her in his arms, comfort her, quiet the voices. Place the amulet back around her neck so she would have it for protection.

But caring for her only made her more vulnerable to
him and to the demons who might come after him.

So he turned and began to hike down the mountain.
She followed, her dog at her side, although Vincent
paused to help her down the rockier terrain. By the time
they reached the slope that led back to her house, she
was wavering unsteadily. Between the heat, exhaustion,
and the blow to the head, she had to be suffering. Unable
to stand watching her struggle any longer, he scooped
her into his arms.

She muttered a protest, but he shushed her and carried her the rest of the way to her house. She fell asleep
against his chest, and he cradled her close, carried her
inside, then undressed her and tucked her in bed.

He stood and watched her for a moment, longing to
join her, but the amulet she'd returned to him weighed
against his chest, and he knew he had no right. Stifling
his own needs, he turned and strode down the steps.

He had to be stronger than his father. His mother
would have been better off, safer if she'd never loved
him.

Just as Clarissa would be better off without him.

Hours later, when Clarissa finally awakened, only a
sliver of daylight still remained, bleeding through the
gray sky. Her body ached, and an emptiness swelled inside her.

The voices had haunted her in her sleep.

"You have to help us."

"We need you."

"You'll never be able to stop this demon."

"Join us in the darkness."

"It's your fault we're lost."

"You should die like your mother."

"He's going to keep killing . . ."

"How many more of us have to suffer?"

Trembling from the sound of their anguish, she dragged herself from bed and climbed in the shower. She had to do something, summon the girls and force them to face what had happened, make them see the demon's face so they could catch him.

She scrubbed her hair and body, aware she was sore and tender from her lovemaking with Vincent. Yet her body yearned for him again, ached to share the closeness they'd experienced at the pool's edge. To feel his arms around her, his length inside her.

Where was he now?

"You're going to lose," a voice whispered.

"He'll die, and so will you."

"No!" She shouted at the walls, at the voices, willing them to stop. But they continued to pummel her as she dried off and dressed. Knowing they would haunt her until she did something to help the lost, she hurried down the steps.

Vincent had left a note by the coffee pot. "I went to meet the sheriff. Call me if you need me."

Right now, she needed to talk to the spirits. She'd be closer to them at the graveyard.

She hesitated for a moment, contemplating whether to wait for Vincent's return, but she couldn't keep depending on him. He would leave soon, and she had to stand on her own, just as she'd always done.

Her heart aching, she grabbed the keys to the rental car and drove toward the cemetery. The winding roads and tall ridges rolled around her, the spiny leaves and branches reaching out to grab her, the jutting ridges and overhangs filled with lost spirits, roaming restlessly.

Helpless frustration washed over her. For the first time in her life, she understood the pain her mother had suffered and why she'd chosen to end her life. Forgiveness teetered on the edge of her consciousness, but her mother had also deserted her, and she'd needed her.

How could she possibly help all the ones who called to her? The dead from Hell's Hollow, the lost miners, the girls who'd been killed by the demon . . .

Their voices melded together in her head, and by the time she arrived at the cemetery, dusk was already settling, the sun slipping beyond the treetops and into the canyon. Climbing out on wobbling legs, she wove her way through the endless rows of graves, her skin crawling as the ghosts pushed through the ground to claw at her arms. A shadow lurked at the edge of the graveyard, and she tried to discern who it was. A human or a spirit? Or maybe a demon . . .

She halted by Tracy's grave, then closed her eyes and beckoned the girls to join her. Suddenly, cold air swirled around her, rustling the leaves and her hair, sending a chill down her spine.

When she opened her eyes, Billie Jo, Jamie, and Tracy appeared to her. She searched for Cary Gimmerson but didn't see her. Alarm bells clamored in her head. What if Cary had traded her soul to the evil?

Then the voices of the girls began.

"Help me . . ."

"I didn't deserve to die."

"Who murdered me?"

"You have to tell me," she cried. "I know it's painful,

but you have to think back to your murder, to the last few moments before you died. Tell me what you see."

"Only darkness," Tracy said.

"A black-faced monster," Billie Jo cried.

"Before that. Did he have a human face? Maybe the demon possessed the body of someone in town. Think." She raised her hands in comfort. "If you face the monster and tell me his name, I can catch him. And then you can cross over."

Another whiff of icy air swirled around Clarissa and she stumbled, then touched the edge of a tombstone to steady herself. It was a freshly dug grave waiting for a body.

Cary Gimmerson's?

She glanced down at the tombstone and saw an image of a skeleton reaching for her, trying to drag her into the ground.

But her breath caught as she read the name on the granite marker.

Clarissa King.

Reality dimmed as images bombarded her. Visions of a body being lowered into the grave, her skin peeling off in rotting layers, her bones crumbling and turning to dust.

A thousand voices assaulted her at once, tortured screams of the dying. She crumpled to the ground on her knees, covered her ears with her hands, and rocked herself back and forth, trying to drown them out.

But the pain was unbearable.

A sinister low voice rumbled through the wails, "The only way to end this is to bury yourself here with them. Climb underground and join them."

The demon's voice? Or was she going crazy?

A clawlike hand pressed against her shoulder, pushing her into the dirt, and she curled into it.

Excitement zinged through Hadley as Clarissa curled up by the grave. He'd watched her here before, knew she talked to ghosts. That she carried voices in her head just as he did. That the dead were her friends.

The voice in his head ordered him to end her misery. To help her join the others in their dirt beds.

He had to do as the voice commanded.

He glanced around to make sure he was alone, then slowly crept from the shadows of the giant oaks. She was so lost in her tormented thoughts that he approached her from behind, and she didn't even look up.

Raising his shovel, he brought it down against the back of her head.

She moaned, her body going limp, then lost consciousness. A smile curved his mouth. He'd bury her here with the dead so she could talk to them day and night.

But a car puttered in the distance, and he glanced up and saw it approaching. Shit.

He grabbed Clarissa's arms and began to drag her toward the woods. He'd have to dig a new hole for her. Bury her with the animals he'd put underground.

Then no one would ever find her.

CHAPTER TWENTY-FOUR

Waller glared at Vincent as they gathered in his office along with Deputy Bluster. "Where in the hell have you been, Valtrez? We just got done questioning J. J. Pirkle. He was dating Daisy Wilson, but he's been out of town and arrived home to learn of her death."

"So Pirkle is in the clear?"

"Looks that way," Waller said.

So far, they'd eliminated Bennett, Lamont Franklin, the real estate agent, and J. J. Pirkle. Who was left?

Vincent explained about tracking Clarissa's dog into the woods and the collapsed mine.

"Jesus," Waller mumbled.

"Where's Clarissa now?" Bluster raised his eyebrows in accusation.

"Home resting."

Waller consulted the report on the latest victim. "The girl who went over the ridge is definitely Cary Gimmerson. ME matched her dental records. Said she shattered almost every bone in her body in the fall." He glanced up, pain etched in the deep grooves around his eyes.

"She was twenty-one. According to her sister, her only living survivor, she was terrified of heights."

Vincent nodded. "Just as Clarissa suggested."

"I know you thought the girl was pushed," Waller continued, "but the initial examination shows no evidence to prove it."

Because the killer hadn't physically touched her. The gray areas in the other crime-scene photos took on new meaning. Perhaps they were the spirits of the girls, or demons.

He grimaced. How could he explain that to Waller?

"I talked to Cary's sister," Bluster interjected. "She said she didn't have any old boyfriends who might be pissed-off enough to kill her. Just J.J., and he was out of town."

"We need a damn witness." Waller scratched his head in frustration, and Vincent silently cursed.

He was their damn witness. Yet he wasn't ready to share that fact, or the fact that the killer wasn't human.

The phone rang, and Waller answered it. "Yeah. What? Hell, we'll get on it." When he hung up, the grooves beside his mouth deepened.

"What's wrong?" Vincent asked.

"That was Hadley Crane's mother. She said she found all his pills dumped in a potted plant. And when he left for work earlier, he was talking out of his head, talking about Clarissa and how she communed with the dead."

Vincent's chest tightened as fear gripped him. "I'm going to check on Clarissa."

He jogged to the door, punching in Clarissa's number as he climbed in the SUV. The phone rang and rang, but there was no answer.

Dammit. He'd never felt connected to anyone before, but he felt a connection with Clarissa.

And she was in terrible danger.

Hadley dragged Clarissa deep into the woods. The graveyard would have been better, but he couldn't get caught. And she was close enough here to commune with the lost souls she hadn't been able to save.

He found a spot beneath a live oak and began to dig her hole. Deeper, deeper, he wanted it to be just right like the others.

Didn't want anyone to find her.

She started to stir, but he whacked her again on the back of the head with the shovel, smiling as blood trickled from the wound, dotting her thick coppery hair. She groaned, then lost consciousness again.

The next time she woke up, she'd be staring at the world from her grave underground and holding hands with the spirits.

Vincent sped up the winding graveled drive to Clarissa's, his pulse racing as gray clouds covered the waning moon.

He never should have left her alone. If she died, it was his fault.

Screeching to a stop, he scanned the yard and drive, but Clarissa's rental car was missing.

He tried her cell phone again, but the machine picked up, so he left a message.

Anxiety plucked at him, and he decided to check her house anyway. Maybe she'd left a note.

He jumped out and jogged up the porch steps to the front door, then pounded on it. "Clarissa! Are you here?"

His heart clenched as he waited, but she didn't answer. Panic ate at him, and he turned the doorknob, expecting the house to be locked, but the door screeched open. Instantly alert, he pulled his weapon, although he doubted a gun could stop a demonic killer.

Wulf barked from somewhere in the house, but he didn't see him, so he inched inside and scanned the entryway, then the living room. Slowly he moved through the downstairs, but it was empty. Wulf howled again, and Vincent found him in the laundry room, pacing madly.

Where in the hell was Clarissa?

Wulf whined, and Vincent stroked his head, then jogged up the stairs and headed into her bedroom. But she wasn't there, and he didn't find a note anywhere.

He had to go to the graveyard, find Hadley. If he'd hurt Clarissa, he'd kill him with his bare hands.

He raced back to the car and flew around the mountain to the graveyard. Outside the temperature felt like a hundred, and his palms were greasy with sweat as he gripped the steering wheel and passed the turnoff for Hell's Hollow. The stench of smoke and charred bodies still lingered, as if the horrendous fire had just burned through the neighborhood that day.

Time would never be able to erase the vile odors, just as it couldn't erase the images in his mind from his own past.

He swung a left into the graveyard parking lot, glanced at the church—a sacred place, Clarissa called it. His heart pounded when he spotted Clarissa's rental car. But he checked it and she wasn't inside. He strode through the rows of tombstones, his jaw tightening when he spotted her purse lying by an empty grave, the contents spilled.

The wind whistled through the bare trees, sending the hairs on the back of his neck at full attention. His instincts kicked in, and he scanned the graveyard for Clarissa.

A noise to the left jarred him, then he noticed the ground had been disturbed. Marks from a body being dragged across the yard created indentions in the ground.

His heart thundered as he followed the trail in the woods, wielding his weapon.

More scraping. He hiked on. A mile, then another, until he spotted a shadow in the distance. He hesitated behind a live-oak, assessing the situation.

Clarissa was lying on the ground, blood seeping from her head. Hadley Crane stood above her, sweating and dirty, a shovel in his hand.

Vincent clenched his hand tighter around his gun, then jumped Crane from behind. A barbaric sound careened from Crane, and he bucked backward in an attempt to throw Vincent off his back.

But fury fueled Vincent's strength, and he wrapped his hands around Crane's neck in a chokehold. Crane screeched, but Vincent tightened his fingers, digging them deeper and deeper into Crane's throat. He could hear him wheezing for air. A crack of his windpipe and he'd snap . . .

Clarissa stirred, then dragged herself up and tugged at his arm. "Vincent, stop, please," she whispered, "don't kill him."

But all Vincent could see was the grave Crane had

dug for Clarissa. All he could feel was the black rage eating at his soul.

Clarissa jerked him again. "Please, Vincent, look at me. Stop. Arrest him and turn him over to the cops."

But the monster inside him wanted to forget the law. End Crane's life for trying to hurt Clarissa.

She gently stroked his back, his shoulders, her soft voice whispering against his neck. "You can't do this, or you'll be like him."

Crane gurgled with another scream. His eyes were bulging now, rolling back in his head.

Finally, somewhere in the far recesses of his brain, Clarissa's words registered. He was a Dark Lord. This was a battle he'd have to fight all his life.

He couldn't give in to it.

⌖

Clarissa sagged with relief as Vincent released Hadley. He dropped to the ground in shock, clutching at his throat, wheezing and coughing violently. Vincent grabbed handcuffs from his belt and cuffed Hadley's wrists, then phoned Waller.

"Crane assaulted Clarissa. He's in cuffs now, so send an ambulance to the graveyard."

He hung up and dragged Clarissa into his arms. She curled against him and he stroked her hair, holding her and rocking her, his heart pounding.

If he'd been a few minutes later, she wouldn't have made it. Crane would have buried her alive.

Finally Waller and the ambulance arrived. Hadley screeched and cried like an animal as Waller jerked him up and shoved him toward the squad car. "The voices told me to do it. I had to listen. I had to obey."

The medics rushed to Clarissa and examined her injuries. "You need stitches, miss. And you probably have a concussion. We have to do x-rays."

Clarissa protested going to the hospital, but the medic insisted she needed further testing and observation.

"Let them take care of you, Clarissa," Vincent said. "I want to interrogate Crane."

She grabbed his arm. "I need to take care of Wulf."

"I'll take care of him," Vincent promised.

A dizzy spell assaulted her, and she conceded, then allowed the medics to help her onto the stretcher. She should be relieved Crane was being arrested, but as the ambulance rolled away, a sick feeling pinched her stomach.

If they had found the demon, the girls should move on.

But so would Vincent.

Crane's crazy screeching echoed from the back room as Vincent entered the police station.

He slammed his fist on the table in the interrogation room, his blood still sizzling with rage, from the need to kill.

If the sick, twisted bastard gave him one good reason, he'd strangle the life from him without remorse.

Waller's phone rang and he let himself out, giving Vincent full rein. "You tried to kill Clarissa King?" Vincent snarled.

The man's eyes were glazed, and he twitched back and forth, murmuring incoherently about the voices in his head. "She was crying, cried for the dead. She wanted to be with them. They're her friends."

"She didn't want to be buried alive," Vincent growled.

"Yes, put her out of her misery, that's what the voice said." Crane jammed his hands on his ears and rocked himself back and forth. "No control. No control. He made me do it. The voice told me to."

"What voice?"

"The voice in my head. It tells me to do bad things." He lapsed into a crazed litany about different monsters invading his mind, then jumped up and paced across the room, pounding his head with his fists.

"Make them stop. Can't make them stop." He turned to Vincent, a cackle erupting. "Tell me to kill. Like the blood, to watch them die. Bugs eat the flesh. You know that. Bugs eat the flesh. It rots off the bone and turns to dust."

Vincent tossed the crime-scene photos on the table. "You killed Tracy Canton, Billie Jo Rivers, Daisy Wilson, Jamie Lackey. Cary Gimmerson."

Crane paused long enough to stare at them. "Put them in the ground, covered them with dirt. That's what I do."

"Tell me how you killed them," Vincent demanded. "How did you know their fears?"

"Pretty little girls," Crane cried. "So pretty. So pretty to watch them die." Another crazed laugh. "I dug their graves. Hear them scream when I cover them up, just like Clarissa does."

Vincent drilled him with more questions, but Crane was obviously insane. He continued to rant about the voices, beating his head, then laughing hysterically, and ranting again, all lucidity gone.

Scrubbing a hand over his neck, Vincent stepped outside and met Waller in the hall. "He's incoherent. Needs to be locked up."

Waller nodded. "I called his doctor to come in and examine him. He'll probably wind up in the sanitarium."

Waller's phone rang, and he answered it, a scowl on his face. "All right, Trina, we'll check around."

"What?" Vincent asked when Waller hung up.

"That was Petey LaCoy's babysitter. Trina claims she saw Sadie Sue shaking the baby, thought she was going to kill him." He pulled at his pants. "Said her eyes looked funny, that she was out of her mind. Sitter thinks she's on drugs." He glanced back over his shoulder. "I need to wait here on the state psychiatrist. Do you mind driving around town and looking for Sadie Sue?"

Vincent's chest suddenly tightened, the air barely making it past his lungs as he tried to breathe. He'd assumed all along that the killer was a man. But Sadie Sue had made a deal with the devil, and she hated Clarissa.

What if she'd gone after her now?

CHAPTER TWENTY-FIVE

Vincent phoned the hospital to alert security in case Sadie Sue showed up and attacked Clarissa. Then he phoned the Bare-It-All, but she hadn't shown up for work. Frantic, he called the babysitter.

"I've never seen Sadie act like that or lose her patience with the baby. Her eyes were so wild, as if she didn't have control." Trina's breath rushed out. "I think she scared herself, 'cause she handed me the baby and ran out like a bat out of hell."

He frowned. If she'd scared herself and really loved the baby, maybe she was fighting the demon's control. "Think hard, Trina. If she was upset, where would she go?"

A long silence followed, the sound of the baby's cooing echoing in the background. "I don't know, maybe the river."

"The river?"

"Yeah, at that little church where she was baptized. When she's upset, she goes there to think."

"Thanks, I'll check there now." He climbed in the SUV and spun from the parking lot, spewing gravel.

The night seemed black, inky, silent, so tense that he could hear his own breathing in the silence of the car as he raced toward the river. Headlights of an oncoming truck nearly blinded him, and he swerved, his SUV skimming the guardrail and sending sparks flying. But he managed to correct himself and stayed on the road.

Sadie Sue had enthralled him at one point—did she have the power to do so again?

He wouldn't let her.

His tires churned on the asphalt, gears grinding as he braked and slowed around the curve, then turned onto the dirt road leading to the church.

The area looked deserted, weeds dotting the ground, ancient trees framing the wooden church. The river water glimmered beneath the faint moonlight, and he spotted Sadie Sue's rusted Chevy parked in the empty lot.

But a quick glance indicated Sadie Sue wasn't inside the car.

Bracing himself for her seductive powers, he screeched to a stop, threw the SUV into park, and jumped out.

He checked for his weapon, hoping he didn't have to use it, then flexed his hands, thinking that he also held power there.

Pulse hammering, he stepped into the tepid air, caution slowing his movements as he walked toward the river. The water lapped against the rocky embankment, the sound of crickets chirping and frogs croaking resounding in the silence.

But a shrill, pitiful keening rent the air.

He hesitated, skimming the darkness for the source, then realized it was Sadie Sue. Moving slowly, he inched toward the river until he spotted her head bobbing in the water. Sobs wrenched the air, her pleas for death to take her reverberating against the heavens.

"Please, God, save me, take me now so Petey will be safe."

He wasn't sure he heard her correctly. Or maybe this was a twisted ploy to trap him.

Then lightning flashed from the heavens, the sound of thunder rumbled, and her head dipped below the water.

Vincent dropped his gun to the ground, then raced into the river to save her. Sadie Sue flailed and fought him, trying to drown herself, but he lifted her as if she weighed nothing, then carried her to the shore.

"Why didn't you let me die?" she sobbed, beating her fists against him. "I have to die to protect Petey."

Another boom of thunder sounded, and lightning lit around Sadie Sue in a circle.

He froze, shocked, wondering what had happened.

"I love my baby," Sadie Sue wailed. "I begged for forgiveness."

Vincent laid her on the grass, then looked into her eyes. They were normal, soft, loving.

She had been released of the demon. "You're free now, Sadie Sue. You don't owe the devil anymore."

She hugged her arms around herself and sobbed, whispering her thanks to the heavens.

In her unselfishness, she'd found a way to break the deal she'd made.

Maybe he could find a way to defeat the demon inside himself.

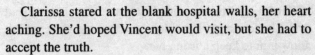

Clarissa stared at the blank hospital walls, her heart aching. She'd hoped Vincent would visit, but she had to accept the truth.

He didn't love her. Didn't want her. Was going to leave her alone again.

She couldn't stand in his way. He had demons to battle, a much more important destiny than being with her.

The door screeched open, and he walked in. All six feet four of muscle, brawn, and brooding darkness. He was so sexy that he literally took her breath away.

He paused in the doorway and met her gaze. She read the pain and turmoil, yet hurt still gripped her.

"Are you all right?" he asked in a gruff voice.

"A few stitches," she said, avoiding his gaze. "But I'll be fine." Except for a broken heart, and the fact that she still hadn't seen the spirits cross into the light.

"Do you think Hadley killed all those girls?"

He nodded. "It appears that way. He claims he's heard voices ordering him to do evil things."

"What about Sadie Sue?"

He explained about the babysitter's phone call. "I found her at the river where she'd first been saved. She tried to drown herself."

"Oh, my God." Clarissa frowned. "Is she okay? What about the hold the evil had over her?"

"I guess she broke the spell when she tried to sacrifice her life to save her child."

"That's what a mother would do," Clarissa said, her voice choking.

His expression contorted in pain, and she realized he must be thinking of his own mother.

She bit her lip, wanted to beg him to stay, but realized it was better he go. He didn't love her, and she couldn't allow him to keep hurting her.

He stared at her for a long moment, emotions warring in his eyes. Pain. Regret. Acceptance that he had to leave. That he hadn't made any promises. He'd told her his rules.

Yet he'd broken them for her.

His eyes flickered with emotions, then he cupped her face between his hands and fused his mouth with hers. The kiss was tender, erotic, hungry, except not nearly long enough. Her heart ached, words of love lodging in her throat—he was everything she'd ever wanted in a man.

But she bit back the words as he abruptly pulled away. She looked into his eyes. The coldness had softened, but the pain was back, even more intense than before.

Then without another word, he turned and walked out the door. He didn't look back, and she didn't call out for him.

Instead she rolled to her side and let the tears fall.

Saying good-bye to Clarissa was the hardest damn thing Vincent had ever done.

As much as he didn't want to care about her, he did.

But love—no, he didn't know what love was.

If his destiny was to fight demons the rest of his life, he'd do it. But he wouldn't bring her into the fight.

Regardless of his rationale, her trusting, loving eyes

haunted Vincent as he drove back to his cabin and let himself inside.

He stripped and lay down on the bed, then fell into an exhausted but fitful sleep. His dreams were filled with fighting demons, with bloodbaths and sadistic murders that no human should see firsthand.

By dawn he woke and dressed in running clothes, then jogged into the woods. The forest seemed unusually quiet this morning, almost too quiet, but maybe the creatures inside could rest because the demon haunting the land had been caught.

A ten-mile run, then a shower, and he had breakfast in the lodge. He checked his watch. Time to get the hell out of town.

He headed outside, yet the ground rumbled slightly and a vile scent rose from the woods beyond.

Feeling uneasy but not certain why, he checked over his shoulder and scanned the road as he drove toward the highway leading out of town.

⟶

One day until the rising

Tormented cries from the dead girls drove Clarissa from her hospital bed. She struggled to get dressed. She had to leave. Talk to her grandmother. Find out if the danger was over.

And if so, why the girls couldn't move on.

They should have crossed over by now.

The fact that they hadn't, that she'd seen their terrorized, skeletal faces all night, warned her that the danger might not be over.

She punched the call button and asked for the nurse, then relayed that she wanted to be released.

A few minutes later, the doctor appeared and examined her. "Your vital signs are good," the doctor said. "I'll get the paperwork for you."

"Thank you."

A knock sounded at the door, and Tim Bluster poked his head in. "Hey, Clarissa, how are you feeling?"

Clarissa sighed. "All right, but I'm ready to go home. Vincent came by and explained about Hadley and Sadie Sue. He's probably already left town."

Tim smiled. "Yeah, no reason for him to stay now."

Right.

The doctor rolled in with her release papers, and she hurriedly signed them.

"I thought you might need a ride home," Tim said.

She nodded. "Thanks, that would be great."

He jangled the keys and went to retrieve the car while the nurse wheeled her down to the exit.

She settled in his car, aware of his smile as he helped her with the seat belt. She didn't want to give him false hope, not when her heart ached from loving Vincent. "What happened with Hadley?"

"The psychiatrist said Crane is schizophrenic and needs to be hospitalized." Tim cursed. "He'll probably plead insanity."

So had the voices he'd heard been due to his mental condition, or the evil source's possession?

Silence stretched between them as she contemplated the question.

He parked in front of her house, rushed around, and helped her from the car and up the walkway to her house.

"Thanks, Tim," Clarissa said as she unlocked the door.

"Do you want me to come in?"

She shook her head. "Not now. I'm still pretty tired."

Disappointment lined his face, but he nodded. He lingered for a moment as if he wanted to say more, but refrained. "All right, call me if you need anything."

She thanked him again, then let herself inside. Wulf raced to her and she bent to hug him. "It's you and me again, buddy." He nuzzled her and followed her up the stairs to the attic. The curtain flapped beneath the flow of the ceiling fan, and she set the candles in a circle and lit them. Hands trembling, she knelt.

But before she could summon her grandmother, the air in the room changed and the candles flickered out. A chill of foreboding washed over her, then a massive black darkness swept through the room.

A sinister orange light blinded her eyes, and she fought to drag her eyes away. But it was too late.

The evil creature's hands clutched her, lifting her, carrying her through time into an ominous darkness until she could no longer see anything but a mass of black souls and orange eyes.

Until she heard nothing except the voices of death beckoning her.

~

Vincent's palms began to sweat as he neared the county line. He'd come here to find a killer, and he'd found him.

He'd also discovered the truth about his past, a past he'd run from years ago. One that had traumatized him as a child but shaped his destiny.

He had to be alone.

He should feel relieved to get out of town. So why did he feel as if he needed to turn back around?

A sharp pain shot through his chest, and he pressed a hand over it, gasping for a breath. The tires squealed on his SUV as he careened sideways and screeched to a stop on the embankment. Heaving for air, he unfastened his seat belt and clutched his chest as another pain ripped through him.

Clarissa's face flashed into his mind, the past coming in rapid snippets. Her eyes, too big for her face as the kids had taunted her.

The day she'd stuck up for him when those bullies had taunted him. The day she'd sneaked up to his house, looked into the window, and seen him and his father arguing over the amulet.

The beating he'd taken to keep his father from going after her and doing God knows what.

And since he'd returned . . .

He'd been terrified of the feelings she'd evoked in him. Not just lust, but she made him want more. More of her. More of a normal life.

Someone to care about.

So he'd pushed her away, just as he had time and time again since he'd come to Eerie. Even at the pool in the sacred place when she'd confessed her love.

How could she love a man like him? A man who was part demon?

The pull to go back to her was just as intense as the pull of evil.

He straightened, sweat pouring down his body, and turned the keys, firing up the engine again.

He'd been a coward not to admit the truth, that he did care about her.

Just as he'd been a coward to run from his past.

He refused to be a coward anymore. He loved Clarissa and had to tell her.

His pulse pounding, he spun the SUV around and headed back to Eerie. Yet as he drew closer to the town, his senses jumped to alert. The heat was oppressive, the stench of death vile, the rustle of a demon's breath swirling in the air warned him that there were still demons in Eerie.

A burning sensation seared his chest, the amulet pulsing against his heart. Alarmed, he removed the angel medallion and twisted it between his fingers, stunned at the way the bloodstone suddenly glowed against the darkness.

He had never seen it light up before, except as he'd pulled it from the fire where his mother had died, but now it was hot, burning his fingers, pulsing and glowing.

What was happening? Was it magical? Trying to tell him that Clarissa was in trouble? Or that he should have left it with her for protection?

His pulse racing, he punched information, got the number for the hospital, and called to check on Clarissa.

"Miss King was released," the nurse said. "Deputy Bluster picked her up and drove her home."

Bluster.

Dammit. The man wanted Clarissa. And now that Vincent had left her, he would move in.

Again the air stirred outside in the woods. A vile scent filtered through his closed windows. Was there still a demon in town? Had Crane simply been crazy and not the one the demon possessed?

If the demon wanted Vincent, if he'd killed these girls to draw Vincent back, was he still here now?

Would he give up without getting Clarissa?

Fear strangled him, and he gripped the steering wheel tighter, speeding up.

Something niggled at the back of his mind. Bluster had dated one of the vics. The women in town would trust him.

Vincent hadn't heard back from McLaughlin on the background check on the deputy, so he punched his number while he steered the car toward Clarissa's.

The phone rang three times before McLaughlin picked up. "It's Valtrez. Listen, did you find out anything on that deputy I asked you to check on?"

"Yeah, as a matter of fact I was getting ready to call you. It took a while, because he went by his middle name, Gordon, in Nashville."

"He changed it when he came to Eerie?"

"Guess he didn't want his past following him."

Vincent scrubbed a hand over his head, his heart hammering.

"He was questioned regarding a serial-killer case back in Nashville," McLaughlin continued. "Seems he dated a couple of the vics."

Vincent's blood ran cold. He'd also dated at least one vic here. "They find any proof?"

"No, finally collared a mentally challenged guy in the town. He's in jail now."

Vincent scowled. Sounded similar to what had happened in Eerie. What if Bluster had framed that man and

Crane? Bluster was a young guy, appealing to women. They'd trust him if he approached them.

He flew around the curve, adrenaline pumping. He had to get to Clarissa.

Bluster had been interested in her all along. What if his interest was because he was the killer?

CHAPTER TWENTY-SIX

Clarissa slowly regained consciousness as if she'd fallen into a deep sleep. Her attacker hadn't been Hadley.

But he was a demon in a human body. One she'd trusted.

Pain and betrayal knifed through her, along with cold terror.

The screams of the dead surged to life again, more shrill and demanding.

Desperately working to block them out, she opened her eyes, but darkness cloaked her surroundings, a black so void of light that she couldn't discern her location.

The scent of death, blood, woods suffused her.

She tried to move, but her wrists and ankles were tied to a wooden stake. Where was her abductor?

Was he going to kill her now?

Her lungs ached for air, and she tried to yell for help, but her throat was too parched and dry to scream.

A vile breath suddenly broke the eerie silence around her.

She wasn't alone. The monster who'd trapped her was

here now, skulking in the dark, watching her. Enjoying her fear while he waited to kill her.

～

Vincent's heart pounded as he drove up the winding drive to Clarissa's.

The house was dark, empty, eerily silent as he let himself in. Wulf met him at the front door, then barked. Concerned, Vincent followed the dog, checking the house thoroughly, but there was no Clarissa.

Wulf pawed the floor and trotted up to the attic, and Vincent followed. He stopped in the doorway and stared at the candles on the floor in a circle—she'd been communing with the dead.

Where was she now?

He called her name, but Wulf pawed at the floor as if trying to tell him something.

Sheer terror froze Vincent to the spot.

A piece of black rock lay in the center.

Rage bolted through him. God, no. He'd left Clarissa last night thinking she was safe. Had left her to *keep* her safe.

But now she was gone . . .

Emotions crowded his chest, so painful that he nearly doubled over. Then the rock began to move.

His eyes widened in shock.

Hands fisted, he watched as the rock scrawled the words "Black Forest" onto the wood floor.

Swallowing back fear, the truth hit him, the truth he'd feared all along.

The demon had come for him and had taken Clarissa.

He intended to use her to destroy Vincent and force him to join his father's side.

Dammit. He didn't care about himself or his damned soul.

But he had to save her.

Downstairs, the floor creaked, and he froze, senses alert as he reached for his weapon. Slowly, he moved into the hall and down the steps, checking the shadows and corners.

Just as he made it down to the second floor, he spotted the silhouette of a man in the hall.

He inched closer, weapon poised. "Stop, or I'll shoot."

"Valtrez?"

Bluster's voice. The son of a bitch.

He lurched from behind the corner, aiming his gun at the deputy's chest. "Where's Clarissa?"

Bluster's eyes widened. "That's what I came to find out. I called and she didn't answer."

"You took her, didn't you?" Vincent inched closer, fury in his voice. "What did you do, Bluster? Trade your soul to the devil?"

"What in the hell are you talking about?"

"I know about Nashville," Vincent ground out. "And the black rock, that it came from the cave in the Black Forest, that that cave was built as Satan's palace on earth."

Bluster shifted, blew a breath between his teeth, then held up his hand in surrender. "It's not what you think," he said. "You have to hear me out."

"Just tell me where Clarissa is, dammit!"

"I don't know," Bluster said. "I'm not the enemy here, Valtrez. I thought you were. That you'd come to hurt Clarissa."

For a long minute, the two men engaged in a standoff, distrust and suspicion hanging between them.

Then Bluster slowly lowered his gun. "It's the truth. I came here because of what happened in Nashville, but not because I'm the killer. Because I thought something weird, something supernatural happened there."

Vincent narrowed his eyes. "What do you mean?"

"Back in Nashville. I wasn't convinced the mentally challenged guy committed those crimes of his own accord. The crimes were too sophisticated. And the things he said . . . they made me think he might be possessed. I heard about this town, about Clarissa being a medium. So I came here to get to know her because I thought she might be able to help."

Vincent's heart pounded. Bluster sounded convincing. But so could the devil.

"How do I know you're telling the truth?"

Bluster dug in his pocket and removed several sheets of folded paper. "Look at those. It's a profile of her, and of you. I checked you both out." He huffed. "There's also notes on all the legends here in town and of other supernatural sightings across the States."

Vincent examined them, saw the research Bluster had done. Other crimes in various areas that he'd suspected might be paranormal-related. Bluster might be on to something. "Why didn't you tell me this before?" Vincent asked.

Bluster's eyes narrowed to slits. "Because I didn't know if you might be one of them."

A demon?

He was. But he refrained from sharing that detail.

Instead, he turned back to his main focus. Finding Clarissa. "I think he has her," Vincent said instead.

Bluster jerked his head up toward the attic. "How do you know?"

Vincent explained about the candles and the black rock. Bluster insisted on seeing them for himself. Vincent didn't quite trust him yet, but he followed him, scrutinizing his every movement.

Bluster studied the candles. "She was communing with the dead."

Vincent nodded. He just hoped she hadn't joined them.

Then something shiny and metallic glinted in the dim light. He strode over and picked it up. A badge.

He glanced at the deputy, and recognition dawned, as well as the truth.

The badge didn't belong to Bluster.

It was Waller's.

Clarissa swallowed, struggling to keep her voice from cracking and feeding his pleasure by crying. "I know you're not the sheriff, not the man I've trusted all my life. So why don't you leave his body and show yourself?"

A sinister laugh reverberated through the darkness, and then a strange, throaty and sinister voice rumbled from Waller. "I am Pan, the god of fear."

"Why take over the sheriff? He was a decent man."

"He's old, and his heart was weak," the demon voice said. "When it failed, he chose his path."

Clarissa had to do something. "Fight him, Sheriff. Make him release you."

"I can't," Waller's voice rumbled out weak and strained. "It's too late for me."

"Yes, you can, Sheriff. You've protected the town all these years."

"But I let him use me for evil because I was afraid to die. And now all those girls' deaths are on my hands."

"Death is not the end," Clarissa said. "You can pray for redemption."

Waller's shadow moved, but the sinister laugh reverberated again, and a black aura totally engulfed Waller, obliterating his face. The demon was too strong, had totally possessed the sheriff.

Her chest ached. "Where am I?"

"The cave of black rock, Satan's palace." The demon's voice again, as cold as ice.

She choked back tears, didn't want him to see her fears. "Why here?" she asked.

"Because this is where it began, where my power is the strongest. Where Valtrez will reunite with his father."

"Vincent is coming here?"

"You sound shocked?" Another grating laugh. "You didn't think he would come for you?"

She refused to answer, but her mind spun with the truth. This demon intended to use her to bait Vincent.

"Your plan is flawed."

"Flawed. How, Clarissa?"

"Using me to get to Vincent. He doesn't care about me."

A flash of jagged teeth and reddish-orange eyes lit the inky darkness. "Oh, he will come, Clarissa. He has to. It is his destiny."

Clarissa closed her eyes, willing herself to be strong. If Vincent came, maybe they could destroy this demon together.

She had no idea how to fight him, though, so she prayed to the spirits to help her.

"Stay strong, Clarissa."

The soft voice broke through the barrier of the spirits' screams, silently entering her thoughts.

"Mother?"

"I'm here, baby."

Tears filled Clarissa's eyes. She thought she'd never hear her mother's voice again.

"Pan is now the god of fear, Clarissa. Another god of fear destroyed me years ago. You must fight him with every ounce of your being."

"I don't know how," she whispered silently.

"Yes, you do. You're strong—don't let your fears defeat you."

Other voices screamed in her head, though, the cries of the lost souls. A hundred all at once. Her head throbbed, and her vision blurred as helplessness set in.

"He's summoning the dead to torture you," her mother said softly. "Close your mind to the cries. Defeating this demon is the only way to save the dead and the living."

"I can't," she whispered. "I'm not strong enough."

"Yes, you are. Do not succumb, and you can vanquish him."

The demon's voice intruded, breaking the connection with her mother. "Trade your soul to me and I will let you live."

"No," Clarissa said between clenched teeth. "I'll never give you my soul. Never."

"Then you will burn at the stake, and your precious Vincent will watch just as he watched his mother die."

Bastard.

"You can kill me, but even in death, I'll fight you,"

she shouted. "I'll help the lost ones cross into the light, and you won't be able to stop me, because I'm not afraid of you. And I'm not afraid of dying."

The demon's laughter pinged off the dark black walls, sending fear zinging through her veins.

But she felt her mother's presence, and the vile sound of his laughter only intensified her resolve to destroy him.

~

Pan tasted the heady flavor of victory on his inhuman tongue. Clarissa was ready to break. Her head resounded with anguished spirits. Summoning them to torment her had been simple.

Their pleas would push her over the edge.

Burying her alive, beneath the ground with the bones of others who'd passed, where she would forever lie in the midst of the dead who screamed for her help, seemed like justice.

But he had another plan.

He was, after all, the god of fear. Watching her suffer gave him great pleasure.

And Valtrez would come for her. He knew it.

Just as he'd used the girls' greatest fears to kill them, he would use Valtrez's to destroy him.

For Vincent's greatest fear was that he would be like his father.

Now Pan would wait for Vincent to come to the cave of black rock.

The place where it all began.

The place where it would end, and he would win.

CHAPTER TWENTY-SEVEN

Vincent shuddered.

Black Forest, a place so dark that no light existed. A place his father had called the land of the dead because it was even more desolate and filled with misery and loss than Hell's Hollow. A place where flowers couldn't grow, where there was no color. Where strange, inhuman creatures existed, where poisonous plants and venomous snakes sucked the life from any human who passed through.

Except he and his father had survived it unscathed.

Because they weren't human . . .

The truth struck him so swiftly that his legs buckled. He didn't know who had sent him the message, the demon or one of the spirits, but he understood the meaning. He would find Clarissa in the Black Forest in the hands of the demon.

And he'd used Waller as his vessel.

His heart stalled in his chest. Bits and pieces of the last few days snapped into place. Waller had called and specifically asked for him because he knew the Black

Forest. Waller had known about Vincent's past and his family.

He had suffered a heart attack the week before.

That must have been when the demon took over his body.

Holy hell . . . everyone in town trusted him, especially Clarissa.

But Vincent had been running in circles, dodging his past, and hadn't seen it.

Sweat beaded on his brow as he turned to Bluster. "I have to go into the Black Forest. That's where he's taken Clarissa."

"I'll go with you."

"No, it's too dangerous." Vincent hurried toward the door. "You need to stay here and protect the town in case I fail."

Although failure was not an option.

Bluster nodded, and Vincent ran toward the door, jogged downstairs and outside to his car, and jumped inside. He reached inside the SUV's glove compartment and retrieved the maps he'd bought of the area, spread them out, and searched the mountains. His mouth tightened into a flat line when he located the forest, and he switched on the engine, barreled down the drive, and spun onto the road through the mountains.

The Black Forest lay northeast of Hell's Hollow. Tension knotted his shoulders as he maneuvered the curvy roads and raced around the slower traffic. He took a curve too fast, his tires screeched, and the SUV skidded toward the guardrail. Dammit. He tried to compensate but sent the SUV into a spin.

Inhaling sharply, he righted the vehicle and barely managed to avoid going over the ridge, then continued deeper into the mountains. The sharp ridges and jagged peaks taunted him as he neared the Black Forest, and the scent of death and evil permeated the air when he parked and climbed out at the overhang. Void of a path, he had to hike in on foot.

Although his gun would probably be worthless against the monster he faced, he tucked it in the waistband of his jeans anyway and entered the dark recesses of the wooded land of horrors.

Immediately, the sounds of life so familiar in the mountains died, and an overwhelming sense of death and doom engulfed him. Flickering patches of red and orange that looked suspiciously like floating eyes followed him as he traveled deeper into the bowels of the blackness.

Screeching sounds grated through the eerie silence, echoing around him. Inhuman noises, cackling and chomping, teeth gnashing, filled the air, air that was so hot it felt like the devil's breath burning his skin. Maybe this was a wasteland for the lost souls who worked for Satan.

The thick, tangled vines clawed at him, trying to strangle him, and he removed his pocketknife and hacked at them, ripping them from his legs. As if the vines were alive, a shrill cry of anguish splintered the air, but he plowed on, slashing them viciously.

Snakes hissed and slithered around his feet, snapping at his legs, but he kicked them away, then used his hands as a weapon, literally sending them flying, popping, and exploding. Snakeskin floated like dust in the air, lighting on his hair and shoulders, but he forged on. Yet the floating eyes followed him, glowing like monsters waiting to attack.

His lungs begged for air, but the vile taste of death filled each breath. Some kind of large creature suddenly snarled and hissed, its body an apelike animal, its head human.

Cursing violently, he swung his hands out and the creature suddenly exploded. Hair, blood, and inhuman organs burst and spewed, and he swiped the sticky substance from his hands onto his jeans.

A mile deeper and another mile; the smell of death grew stronger until he finally spotted the cave.

For a brief moment, fear totally paralyzed him. But through the darkness, Clarissa's soft cry for help floated to him.

He closed his eyes, saw her as she'd offered herself to him the first time he'd taken her, then remembered the tender way she'd given herself to him by the sacred pool, the way she'd looked into his eyes with total trust and love when she had no reason to trust or love him.

Emotions he never wanted to feel again clenched his heart. He didn't want a heart. Having a heart meant hurting, sorrow, excruciating anguish.

But his own pain didn't matter. Only Clarissa's did.

Hardening himself against the emotions, he forced himself to enter the cave.

He didn't care if he died. As long as he saved Clarissa.

～

Pan watched as Vincent entered, taking immense joy at the tortured expression on his face. He had been here years ago when Vincent had killed his father, Zion.

But Zion had earned a second chance and would rise

as the leader of evil at midnight. Pan wanted his sacrifice to be ready.

He would win Vincent tonight. The medium was the key.

Pitting the lovers' greatest fears against each other would ensure his win.

Time for the fun to begin.

～

As Vincent stepped into the cave of black rock, visions of ancient demons assaulted him, as if he could see demonic wars and shattered alliances from times past. Centuries of evil bred from Satan had congregated here for strength, forming coalitions and planning strategies to overtake the world and obliterate good.

The Black Forest. Satan's palace. A place where life no longer existed, where souls had been bartered to the evil source and the screams of the tormented creatures who'd succumbed to the darkness boomeranged off the walls.

His gaze found Clarissa, and his stomach clenched. She was tied to a stake in the middle of a circle of stones and flaming torches, just as his mother had been.

"Where's Waller?" he growled.

She gestured behind her with a jerk of her head, and suddenly Waller moved in front of him, only a black shadow shrouded his body. And his eyes were bright red and orange, the voice that emerged foreign, sinister, and raspy.

"You've lost, Valtrez."

"No." He raised his gun and fired, and Waller's body dropped to the ground with a groan. He frowned, thinking that was too easy, then realized it was.

Slowly, a misty black ominous shadow floated from Waller's corpse, a mass of suffocating evil and a vile stench that clouded the cave.

"You are mine now, Valtrez," the demon said. "Your father rises tonight at midnight. He needs his son by his side to help him lead the minions. You must follow your destiny."

Vincent felt his own dark side emerging, heat and fire seeping through his blood. *Bad blood, bad blood, bad blood . . .*

He was just like his father. He couldn't control it.

No . . . He wouldn't give in to it. He loved Clarissa.

If she died, he'd die with her.

CHAPTER TWENTY-EIGHT

The amulet burned against Vincent's chest in his shirt pocket, the bloodstone pulsing with life and energy. He had to save her and put it back around her neck.

Pan raised his ugly black hand, his voice a command. "Kill her now, Vincent. It is as it was meant to be."

Never.

The amulet throbbed again, and another memory rose to the surface. The angel floating above his mother's burning body, her wings lifting him and carrying him out of the Black Forest, to a safe place where he'd been found.

Even in death she had protected him.

"Let her go, and you can have me." His words bounced off the stone walls, echoing harshly in the silent chamber.

"No, Vincent," Clarissa whispered. "You can't give in to him, or he'll win."

If Clarissa died, he'd win anyway.

He flexed his hands, determination roaring. "He won't win, Clarissa. I won't let him."

He was stronger than his father. He would show them now.

Pan raised his arms, the shadows of his demonic body creating a hawklike wingspan that shrouded the light, encircling them as if to draw them into his demonic world. "You will join the dark forces. Zion is waiting!" He swept toward Vincent, and his inhuman roar rocked the cave walls and sent black rock crumbling and raining down upon them. With a flick of one hand, he knocked one of the torches over, sending the flames toward Clarissa.

"I will never join my father!" Vincent raised his hands and flung them out, concentrating all his energy and rage on destroying the demon. Rocks crumbled and shattered, the earth shook, the cave walls trembled. Pan dodged the first blow, and sent another torch falling.

"Give me your soul and you can save her."

"No!" Clarissa cried.

Vincent raced toward him, using his hands as lethal weapons.

Pan roared in protest, a horrendous sound that vibrated through the tense silence, and then his black mass exploded, splattering particles across the walls of black rock. The particles glowed momentarily, then disappeared into the rock as if the stone had absorbed the demon.

A terrible stench filled the air as the last remnants of the demon slowly disappeared, and outside in the forest, screams and cheers resounded as if the creatures there were celebrating a new one joining their realm.

Vincent turned and walked through the fire toward Clarissa. Heat scalded his feet and legs, flames nipped at his clothing. The raging fire was about to consume her. She cried out as the flames ate at her dress, kicking wildly.

He ripped apart the ropes with his bare hands, beating at the flames, then scooped her into his arms and ran through the heat. The floor vibrated and shook, the cave resounding with the force of Zion's protest as Vincent raced toward the cave exit.

Remembering the dangers in the Black Forest, he pressed Clarissa's head against his chest, tucking her tightly in his arms as he raced outside. Adrenaline gave him superhuman speed and strength as he raced through the woods, fending off the inhuman creatures. Snakes and plants sucked at his feet, the screeching sounds of the monsters trying to snatch them brutal and relentless. But he didn't pause until they'd cleared the forest.

As soon as they entered the clearing, fresh cool air brushed his skin and a gentle rain began to fall, washing away the stench of the dead demon and the horrors of the forest, cooling the fire that the devil had cast upon the land.

Moonlight fought through the ominous clouds and shone down to illuminate Clarissa's beautiful face. A face streaked with soot and tears, one that had held terror. Pain clenched his chest.

Still he couldn't release her. He'd almost lost her . . . had almost lost himself to the darkness, but she had saved him.

"I'm sorry," he groaned as he clutched her to him. "I told you I was dangerous." He dropped his head against hers, his breathing ragged. "I love you, Clarissa. God, I'm so sorry—"

Clarissa pressed a hand to his cheek. "You saved us, Vincent. I knew you would." She kissed him on the cheek, then the lips. "I love you. I love you with all of my heart."

He nuzzled her cheek with his, then his gaze met hers, emotions clouding the troubled depths. "How can you? You know I was born part demon?"

"And I talk to ghosts," she whispered against his neck. "Besides, you're strong and brave and proved how powerful you are."

He still found it hard to accept her love. "But I may lose control again. And this fight . . . it's not over. My father is rising tonight. He'll come after me . . ." He made a low, guttural sound. "He might try to use you to get to me."

"I'm not afraid," she said. "You defeated Pan. You overcame your fear—you can defeat him, too."

"Pan was wrong," Vincent said in a gruff voice. "My greatest fear wasn't that I'd be like my father, but that I'd lose someone I loved again. That's why I tried so hard not to love you."

She pressed her hand against his cheek, tears glistening in her eyes like diamonds. "Then we'll fight him together, Vincent. Maybe our gifts brought us together because that's our destiny."

A smile fought its way onto his mouth. It was the first time he'd smiled in years. She was the perfect woman to challenge him. To be his equal and stand beside him in the war against evil.

His heart, the one he thought he didn't have, burst with new feelings, a happiness unlike anything he'd ever expected or known existed. Then he lowered his mouth and kissed her, pouring that heart into each stroke of his tongue as he claimed her.

His friend, lover, soulmate, the one that he'd never expected to find.

The one he'd never leave again.

~

Clarissa snuggled in Vincent's arms, the voices in her head momentarily quieting. She glanced back at the Black Forest from where they'd emerged and knew it was the miracle of Vincent's birthright and his strength and courage that had allowed them to escape alive.

A bright white light suddenly peeked through the drizzling rain, and Clarissa smiled. Now that the demon was truly gone, the murdered girls could find peace and cross into the light.

Ahead, they raised their hands in thanks, as if to say good-bye, then joined hands and floated into the light.

Vincent hugged her close and carried her to the car and she settled inside. Exhausted, she closed her eyes and offered a silent prayer to her mother for giving her the courage to overcome her fears. Then she squeezed Vincent's hand.

Her heart belonged to him forever.

~

Vincent squeezed Clarissa's hand. "How are we going to explain this to the town?"

Clarissa sighed. "I don't know. Sheriff Waller did a lot of good over the years."

"But he traded his soul and killed four girls," Vincent argued. He tucked a strand of hair behind her ear. "And he almost killed you."

"You're right. He sold his soul, and the families and

friends of the victims need to know that the killer was caught," Clarissa said.

Vincent nodded. "We'll talk to Tim and let him help us."

"Tim?"

He explained about his confrontation with Bluster. Clarissa's eyes widened in surprise. "So he suspected a demon all the time?"

"Yeah, me," Vincent muttered dryly.

Clarissa laughed softly, and Vincent punched in Bluster's number.

"Did you find Clarissa?"

"Yes, she's safe." Vincent hesitated, then explained about Waller being possessed, surprised at Bluster's easy acceptance. "Waller is dead. He tried to kill Clarissa."

"Then you did what you had to do." Bluster huffed as if out of breath. "And I found photos of all the dead girls at Waller's, so the victims' families will have closure."

"Right. And tell everyone that he died in the Black Forest. Everyone around here believes in the legends about that place."

"So what do you think about Crane?" Bluster asked.

"He's schizophrenic and made a good patsy." Vincent cleared his throat. Now that he knew Bluster was investigating paranormal phenomena, things seemed clearer. "They'll need you to take over as sheriff," Vincent added.

"I'd like to do that, watch things, see if anything else strange happens around here."

"Maybe we can create a paranormal investigative unit," Vincent suggested. "You interested?"

Bluster grunted. "Sign me up. When I suggested this in Nashville, they thought I was nuts."

Vincent assured him he wasn't, then told him they'd
talk later and hung up. One day he'd get Bluster's story,
what brought him to believe in the supernatural. But for
now, he wanted to take Clarissa home and make love to
her.

He disconnected but noticed the message light blink-
ing. Dr. Bender from BloodCore had phoned.

His stomach clenched. She was probably returning his call about his blood test. What had she found?
Irregularities?

Demon blood?

A cure for evil?

He was tempted to call her back, but Clarissa leaned
her head on his shoulder, exhausted.

The amulet burned in his pocket, and he removed it,
then slipped it around her neck and fastened it. The angel's wings were back where they belonged—with Clarissa, to protect her.

The call could wait. After all, he had defied his bad
blood tonight.

And he wanted a few hours in bed with Clarissa before he had to face his father's wrath.

EPILOGUE

Midnight

Vincent sat on the floor in the attic and studied the candles as Clarissa lit them one by one.

He'd been terrified years ago when she'd offered to commune with his mother.

Tonight, anticipation zinged through his veins. She'd placed the candles in a circle and cut the lights, then began to chant,

> *"To the present*
> *From the past,*
> *Bring this spirit*
> *To speak at last."*

Suddenly a shimmering light sliced through the darkness. He glanced up, nearly blinded by it, then watched, mesmerized as it slowly faded to a golden glow.

"It's your mother, the Angel of Light," Clarissa said softly.

"Mother?"

"Yes, son, it's me." Her voice was soft, gentle, just as he remembered, and he was starved for it.

"Vincent, you were strong today. I'm proud of you, my son."

"We defeated the demon," he said. "But I've been told that Father has been named the new source of evil, that his coronation is tonight."

"Yes. Listen. I have to tell you about your destiny. You have two brothers, Vincent. Twins. Their names are Quinton and Dante."

Shock bolted through Vincent. "Brothers? Is that true?"

"Yes."

Vincent hesitated, soaking in this revelation. "Do they know about me?"

"No, you are the oldest. You were only two when I got pregnant with them." She hesitated. "By then, your father and I were having problems, and I learned more about the Dark Lords, about the power of having three sons." She hesitated. "Your father was also turning, starting to be cruel to you. I knew the three of you had to be separated for your own sakes."

Pain laced her voice. "Giving my sons up was the hardest thing I've ever done. But I left an amulet with each of them for protection, and to remind them that they carry good in their souls as well as evil."

"But why did you keep me?" Vincent asked, confused.

"I thought I could protect you, but I was wrong, and

I'm sorry." She hesitated. "And the real danger lay in the three of you being together."

"I don't understand."

"Like you, your brothers are Dark Lords, although they know nothing of this destiny. However, they also have special abilities." She hesitated as if to let that sink in, then continued.

"Each of you alone has the power to do great good or great evil. Together your power is magnified by three. But if Zion traps one of your souls, he could use the power he gains to bring all three of you into the darkness. If that happens, you would become the most powerful source of evil of all time." Again she paused. "But if the three of you join to fight him, you can defy him. Then you will be the greatest force of good in the world."

Vincent's head swam with emotions. All these years he'd been alone, had no idea that he had other family. "Where are my brothers now?"

"I don't know," his mother said. "But other demons are looking for them. And when Zion rises, he will send out his minions to solicit them to his side. You have to find them before he does."

For a brief moment, her angel wings glowed, sparkling with a translucent white light that was almost mesmerizing in its beauty.

Then she faded into the distance.

Clarissa slid her hand into his. "You have family, Vincent."

He dragged her into his arms. "Apparently so. I can't believe it."

The earth rumbled beneath them, the house shaking as the clock struck midnight. The clouds moved across the moon, obliterating the light. The eclipse had begun.

Vincent stood.

"That's Zion. I have to find my brothers and get them to help me stop him. There's no way I'll let him win."

THE DISH

Where authors give you the inside scoop!

♥ ♥ ♥ ♥ ♥ ♥ ♥ ♥ ♥ ♥ ♥ ♥ ♥ ♥ ♥ ♥ ♥

From the desk of Amanda Scott

Dear Reader,

An incident during the Lake Tahoe fire of June 2007 proved to me once again that ideas come to a writer from unexpected sources of every imaginable kind.

BORDER LASS (on sale now) was outlined and its teaser chapter written when I decided, because of the way that first chapter brings together the hero and the heroine—Sir Garth Napier (a Scottish knight) and Lady Amalie Murray—that I should add a brief prologue to show readers why Sir Garth acts as he does.

I was sitting on the porch at the cabin where I spend much of each summer, on a lake a thousand feet above Tahoe, trying to decide how I wanted to structure such a prologue, when I looked up to see a yellow-white cloud of smoke billowing above the granite peak that shoots up another thousand feet directly across the lake.

To anyone in a forest, such a sight is terrifying, but with a medium-sized lake and a tall granite mountain to protect me, I felt fairly safe staying put.

The incident that awoke my imagination occurred a few days later when an irate man accosted a firefighter and his wife in a Tahoe supermarket. The firefighter's T-shirt identified him as a member of the South Lake Tahoe Fire Department.

The community had signs out everywhere, thanking the firefighters for all they had done and were doing to save the many, many houses they were able to save. As a result, most folks the firefighters met were friendly and grateful. Many called them heroic.

The man in the supermarket loudly began berating the firefighter about the department's "failure" to bring in "the bombers" (planes dropping retardant) sooner. The firefighter, although exhausted, tried to explain that such planes have to be called in from other areas and asked sympathetically if the man had lost his home.

Admitting that his house was not in danger, the man continued his tirade until the firefighter walked away to avoid losing his temper, only to look back minutes later and see the same irate man approach his wife again in the checkout line and begin poking her in the chest as he shouted at her. Fortunately, a large candy rack stood between the firefighter and the other two, and the store's security people quickly removed the antagonist from the premises, so no blood was spilled.

When I heard about the incident, my always busy gray cells began to turn the incident into a more violent confrontation in fourteenth-century Scotland. Soon I was recalling other firefighter anecdotes I'd heard that likewise suited my hero's character and were irresistibly easy to translate into plausible knightly actions.

My brief comparison of today's firefighters with knights of old gave me a fresh perspective on both. I hope you enjoy the result when you read BORDER LASS.

Until then, *Suas Alba!*

Amanda Scott

http://home.att.net/~amandascott

♥ ♥ ♥ ♥ ♥ ♥ ♥ ♥ ♥ ♥ ♥ ♥ ♥ ♥ ♥ ♥

From the desks of Rita Herron and Diana Holquist

Dear Reader,

Something remarkable happened this month that is too interesting to be a coincidence. In the Deep South, outside Atlanta, Georgia, Rita Herron wrote INSATIABLE DESIRE (on sale now), the first book in her new trilogy *The Demonborn*. Meanwhile, in the deep North, outside of Philadelphia, Pennsylvania, Diana Holquist wrote HUNGRY FOR MORE (also on sale now), the last book in her *One True Love* trilogy. These books couldn't be more different; the authors have never met; and yet, each book is about a being with almost the exact same remarkable talent.

Almost.

The authors discuss:

Diana Holquist: Rita, I can't believe that in your book INSATIABLE DESIRE, the God of Fear touches people, then knows their greatest fear and uses that fear to kill them. In my book HUNGRY FOR MORE, the heroine, Amy, touches people and then knows the name of their soul mate, their greatest love. And guess what—the soul mate almost always turns out to embody the person's greatest fear in some way. Of course, in HUNGRY FOR MORE, no one's trying to kill anyone. . . .

Rita Herron: Yeah, killing demons probably wouldn't work so well in romantic comedy. But seriously, the idea that what people fear most is the very thing they have to face to make them whole is such a visceral, primal theme. It works across genres, from my dark paranormal to your romantic comedy.

Diana Holquist: Which is what makes this month so fascinating: two very different authors treating the same theme. And we really couldn't be more different. HUNGRY FOR MORE is a sexy romantic comedy about a Gypsy con-woman who falls for a sexy chef.

Rita Herron: And INSATIABLE DESIRE is a dark paranormal thriller about a medium who falls for a sexy FBI agent. Only he is part demon, part human, and must battle his inner dark side while fighting demonic crimes.

Diana Holquist: Even the titles of the books are similar. HUNGRY FOR MORE. INSATIABLE DESIRE. Er, do your characters' insatiable desires have to do with sex? Because in HUNGRY FOR MORE, they're not just talking about food. . . .

Rita Herron: Hmm . . . maybe there's another similarity between our books. My hero's insatiable desires are definitely for sex, lots of it. In fact, he needs a woman daily to keep his dark side at bay, and only his soul mate's love can keep him balanced.

Diana Holquist: I love that! It's just like in HUNGRY FOR MORE. Well, the soul-mate-balance part, not the dark-side-at-bay stuff.

Rita Herron: In INSATIABLE DESIRE, the hero also possesses a dark hunger for blood, which enables him to get into the minds of killers and to track them down. And evil has definitely risen from the underworld to test him. . . .

Diana Holquist: OK, so I don't have the blood-lust or evil-from-the-underworld stuff, either. HUNGRY FOR MORE is about really, really yummy food, though. A dark hunger for truffles, maybe—it's about the inner workings of restaurants. Also, it's about how food and sex are linked in mysterious, funny ways.

Rita Herron: Which is why I can't wait to pick up HUNGRY FOR MORE. It sounds really fun.

Diana Holquist: And INSATIABLE DESIRE sounds exciting, scary, and very sexy! I can't wait to read it to see how you treat this material. So let's stop writing and get reading! Enjoy, everyone! Two very different books with a lot in common. Happy reading!

Yours,

Diana Holquist

www.dianaholquist.com

Rita Herron

www.ritaherron.com

Dear Reader,

Look for DARK HUNGER, the next exciting install-
ment in my paranormal romantic suspense series
"The Demonborn," coming in '09 from Grand Central Publishing!

Quinton Valtrez, loner and cold-blooded assassin,
wants nothing from Annabelle Armstrong except
her luscious body. But the sexy reporter from CNN
is determined to unravel his secrets and expose him
as a killer.

Then Quinton receives an unsettling call from a
man who claims not only to be Quinton's brother,
but that they share demon blood. Quinton is skep-
tical, but when a serial bomber strikes, hitting three
targets simultaneously, it soon becomes apparent
that supernatural enemies abound.

When the dark forces target Annabelle to ensnare
Quinton, he must face his destiny by joining
forces with his demonborn brother to save Annabelle and to fight the evil threatening to overtake
the world. . . .

Hope you enjoy DARK HUNGER!

Happy Reading!

Rita Herron

Want to know more about romances at Grand Central Publishing and Forever? Get the scoop online!

GRAND CENTRAL PUBLISHING'S ROMANCE HOMEPAGE

Visit us at www.hachettebookgroupusa.com/romance for all the latest news, reviews, and chapter excerpts!

NEW AND UPCOMING TITLES

Each month we feature our new titles and reader favorites.

CONTESTS AND GIVEAWAYS

We give away galleys, autographed copies, and all kinds of fun stuff.

AUTHOR INFO

You'll find bios, articles, and links to personal websites for all your favorite authors—and so much more!

THE BUZZ

Sign up for our monthly romance newsletter, and be the first to read all about it!

VISIT US ONLINE

@ WWW.HACHETTEBOOKGROUPUSA.COM.

AT THE HACHETTE BOOK GROUP USA WEB SITE YOU'LL FIND:

CHAPTER EXCERPTS FROM SELECTED NEW RELEASES

•

ORIGINAL AUTHOR AND EDITOR ARTICLES

•

AUDIO EXCERPTS

•

BESTSELLER NEWS

•

ELECTRONIC NEWSLETTERS

•

AUTHOR TOUR INFORMATION

•

CONTESTS, QUIZZES, AND POLLS

•

FUN, QUIRKY RECOMMENDATION CENTER

•

PLUS MUCH MORE!

Bookmark Hachette Book Group USA
@ www.HachetteBookGroupUSA.com.